Chapter 1

"Heart's in flame,

heart's on fire,

Lordy, Lordy she's my desire!

Man, I can write better lyrics than half the nerds today.

Hey! Whoa! Watch out where you're going! Idiot! Aaaaaaah!"

I couldn't help but shudder over how clear Scottie's voice sounded to me.

...

"Hey, Germy!" Scott yelled at me over the roar of the mower as he slammed on his brakes and slid up to me on his BMX with his blond hair standing straight up as always—brushed or not. "Why don't you ditch that thing and ride to the store with me? You can always finish it when we get back. Mom wants me to go get chocolate chips and walnuts. She's baking cookies. Says she wants to talk to us. Got big news of some kind."

"No, I can't. You go ahead. Last time I took off with you in the middle of something they lectured me to no end about finishing what I start and all that crap. Don't need to hear it all over again. Besides, I'll be done by the time you get back and then we can take out the gloves and play some catch or go to the skate park or

1

something. We do have to get that throw from the outfield in a straight line so Coach doesn't get a knot in his hemorrhoids, you know."

"Yeah, ok, Germy, be right back."

Scott called me "Germy" when we were tiny little kids because he couldn't pronounce Jeremy. He knew I didn't much like it and preferred "Jeremy," but he never called me that unless he wanted to talk real serious about something.

"Hurry up with those chips. After pushing this damn mower around for an hour, I'll be in dire need."

"Yeah, me too. Later!"

I watch Scott ride off from me shaking his head. I smiled, no matter how irritated I was that I couldn't go with him. My gut screamed at me to say something to stop him from leaving or to jet after him. We were bonded that way, and I was blessed with this ability. It seemed that only moments passed when I sensed a wrenching feeling and a set of flashes forced their way into my mind.

"Nooooooooooooooooo!" I let go of the lawnmower and ran for my bike.

"What's the matter? What are you bellowing about? Where do you think you're going?" Mom asked all concerned.

I didn't have time for all the questions. I had to get to Scott. She stood between our house and the Adam's talking with Sara, Scott's mom.

"Scott's dead!" I roared back at her as I raced down the driveway and into the street.

"Jeremy Wayne Wright, come back here!" She called after me. "What are you talking about?"

I ignored her and pedaled down the street as fast as I could. I could still see it in my mind—Scott singing that stupid song riding his BMX, a red blur whirling towards him, the screaming, the fire hydrant his old dog Mooshy used to pee on with the white strip on it over on Jones Street, and then nothing. Everything went black. "God, I hope he's okay! But, I know he's not! Why, oh why do I get these stupid things popping in my head? I don't want them! Stop! Please!" I yelled out at the top of my lungs as I raced along on my bike.

I knew right where I would find him. I swerved around the corner on Jones and saw a crowd gathered with cars parked all over the place. Sirens wailed in the background.

"Scott!" I screamed leaping off my bike and tossing it aside while fighting my way through the group of people. I could see Scott about ten feet away lying on the ground in a heap covered with blood. Some people were scrunched down on their hands and knees and hovering over the top of him. Before I could get to him, some big dude grabbed me. "Let me go!" I hollered at the top of my lungs. "Let me go! That's Scottie!"

"No!" the man said softly in my ear. "You're not getting any closer. You're not going to look at him that way."

The man probably stood six feet five inches tall and weighed 260 pounds or so. He literally picked me up off the ground and carried me to his car as I kicked and screamed for him to put me down. That bear literally held me off the ground with one hand as he opened the door with the other, turned around and sat down in the seat with me in his lap like I was a two year old or something. He held on tightly.

"Your buddy is very badly hurt. He just might not make it. You can't see him like that. I'm just not going to let you."

"Let me go! Please! That's Scottie! Let go of me!"

"No, calm down," he said to me very softly. "Look, the ambulance is pulling to a stop now. They'll do everything humanly possible to help your friend. You've got to stay back. You'd just be in the way."

They wasted no time loading Scott on the gurney and wheeling him to the ambulance.

"I wanna go with him in the ambulance!" I cried out struggling to get out of his grasp.

"No, the medics have a job to do. They don't have time to fool with you. Now cool it! I'm not letting you go.

My kicking and fighting did me absolutely no good. The guy was strong as an ox.   Right about then, both moms showed up together in our car. Apparently they thought I'd lost it and came looking for me. Fortunately, for Scott's mom anyway, it'd taken a couple extra minutes because she had to go in and turn off the oven and all that while Mom got her purse and keys. One of the neighbors headed them off.

"Scott's hurt! A car hit him and fled from the scene. It looks bad. They've already loaded him into the ambulance," our neighbor told them as she put her arm around Sara and led her to the back door.

My mom stepped away looking for me.

"Mom!" I yelled when I saw her. "Let me go!" I cried and kicked some more at the guy holding me.

The man held on tight with one arm, stood up, and yelled waving his free hand in the air, "Maam! Over here!"

"Oh, God, no!" Mom cried out and grabbed a hold of me. We bawled in each other's arms like a couple of babies. The man positioned himself so he could grab me if I tried to make a break for it to get to Scott. I didn't.

"Mom, he's dead. I know he is!" I cried.

"We don't know that. We just have to hope and pray for the best. Come on, you're going home with me. Throw your bike in the trunk," she told me.

We watched when they finally let Mom Sara climb into the back of the ambulance. Shortly afterwards, it pulled out with the sirens screaming. I know Mom wanted to go with her, but she wouldn't let me anywhere near that ambulance either. I think she knew more than she was letting on.

There were times when I used to think that Mom had some of those flashes of things out there just like me, yet we've never talked about it. I think she knew about my little flashes too even though I've never mentioned them. Anyway, her edginess didn't make me feel any better at all.

When we got home, I finished the lawn and then just waited. "Honey," Mom told me, "I'm sure everything's going to be ok or we would have heard something. He probably had to get a bunch of stitches and maybe a cast or two for some broken bones. Emergency rooms take forever!"

I don't know if she was trying to convince me or herself. It didn't work. Dad suddenly walking into the house three hours early from work didn't help matters either. He never took off work early— ever!

"What have you heard?" he asked.

"Nothing! There's been no word. Jeremy's antsy, I'm antsy. We're driving each other nuts," Mom answered.

"Pacing the floor and staring out the window will just make the time crawl even slower. Haven't you got something to do? Dad asked looking at me.

"Why don't you go down to the family room and play that stupid "Mad Demons" game while we wait. It'll give you something else to think about." Mom said before I could even answer. She had to be desperate to get rid of me. She hated computer games— especially the violent ones. I knew they wanted to talk without me listening.

I finally lost myself in my game and didn't hear it when Scott's parents walked in. None of us ever rang the bell or knocked; we all just walked into each other's houses.

I had lost myself in my game and finally making some serious headway killing the enemy, when Mom called out to me bringing my mind back to the here and now, "Jeremy, would you come into the living room please?"

Her voice sounded very strange so I didn't respond with my normal, "Just a minute! I'm in the middle of my game," routine, I headed that way immediately.

When I walked into the living room, Mom Sara, Jim Dad and my mom and dad were all crying. They didn't even have to tell me. I knew then for sure. Scottie was dead.

"What happened?" I whispered.

Mom Sara spoke first, "Scottie's gone! You know what happened. Someone hit him on his bike. He landed between the fire hydrant and a bush and was cut badly with a broken bottle. He bled to death. The driver never even stopped." She choked up and couldn't go any farther.

Jim Dad, what I always called Scott's dad, continued with the story, "An older gentleman using a cane was walking his dog about a half block down the street and saw it happen. He hurried up to Scott as fast as he could and tried to stop the bleeding, but he couldn't. Scottie had pretty much bled out by the time the man got there. He flagged down the next car coming down the street, and that person called 911 on his cell phone as soon as he saw all the blood, but there was no hope. The police said that if the driver had stopped and applied pressure immediately, maybe—just maybe he or she could have stopped or slowed the bleeding until the ambulance arrived, and he might have lived."

"I don't believe it! He can't be dead! He was just gonna go to the store. I should have been with him. It's my fault," I whispered barely audible.

"What do you mean, Honey?" my mom asked. "How could it have been your fault?"

"He wanted me to ride to the store with him, and I told him I couldn't. He gave me a hard time and said I could finish the lawn when we came back, but I told him no because I didn't want to listen to another lecture about not finishing what I started. If I'd been with him, I could've stopped the blood. I could've called for help. I killed him. I can't live without Scottie. We've always been together. It's like he's part of me and I'm part of him. We're inseparable. I want to die! "

Mom pulled me to her as I sobbed. Everyone told me that I couldn't blame myself, but I wouldn't listen, "It has to be my fault. I should have been with him. I could have saved him. Somehow, some way I'll make it up to him. I don't know how, but I will."

Chapter 2

I don't remember the next few days all that well. They turned into kind of a blur. Our parents talked among themselves constantly planning the funeral, the dinner afterwards, and everything else that I didn't want to hear about.

My thoughts were personal. I reflected on the fact that it seemed like Scott and I had practically spent our sixteen years as twins with four parents– mine and his. We lived next door to each other and grew up as best friends. We always took the same classes in school, went to wrestling camp together in the summer, and were pretty much inseparable. Everyone always knew that if you saw one of us, you probably saw both. That pretty much described our lives, which had been really pretty cool for two kids who just happened to grow up as next door neighbors.

We called both sets of parents 'rents' for short when we talked about them. I called Scott's parents Jim Dad and Mom Sara Adams when I spoke to them. Scott called my parents, Ted Dad and Mom Nancy Wright. If any of the Rents yelled at one of us, they probably yelled at both of us. If they swatted one of our butts when we were little, they more than likely smacked both of us.

Same way with the good stuff, if they gave one of us a treat, we both lucked out. Therefore, it was only natural, I guess, that the four adults planned the funeral together. I wanted no part of it.

I just sat there in a fog. They kept me informed, but I didn't take part in the arrangements. I didn't want to. I only half listened to what they told me. I still hoped that I'd wake up and find out it had all been a bad dream. It didn't happen though. Scottie was gone. He'd abandoned me. The more I thought about it the madder I got.

At one point they sat me down and made me pay attention. Jim Dad asked point blank, "Jeremy, would you like to be a pallbearer for Scott?"

"What's that?" I asked. His question caught me by surprise. I had no clue about what he meant. Other than Grandma's, I had never been to a funeral before. I'd been pretty young at the time and really didn't pay too much attention to the details. Nobody said anything for a few seconds.

Then my dad answered, "During the funeral six people are chosen by the family to help during and after the service. These people sit together in the front row during the ceremony. After the funeral is over, the pallbearers carry the casket with the body in it to the hearse. Then they ride out to the cemetery together in the car behind the hearse and then take the body to the grave site. It's an honor to be asked, and it's an honor to do it, but we are not going to pressure you. If you would prefer not to, just say so. If you would rather sit and be with us, that's okay as well. It's whatever you feel more comfortable doing.

"I don't think I could handle that. I want to be with you."

Two days later any hope of the whole thing being a bad dream came crashing down. My parents made me go to the afternoon visitation the day before the funeral. I wanted no part of it.

"Come on, Jeremy. It's time to go," Mom said as they were getting around while I just sat in front of my computer staring at a blank screen.

"Scott deserted me. Why should I? To hell with him! I'm not going!"

"You don't have a choice. You're going!" Dad said not giving me any alternative

"Dad! I don't want to see him in that box. Please!"

"Sorry, Jeremy, but you have to. No more arguments. Go get in the car!" he said somewhat firmly, but not at all unkindly. They didn't want to do this anymore than I did, but there are some things in life that you just have to do.

After we parked our car at the funeral home and walked up to the door, Mom Sara and Jim Dad met us. They'd been waiting for us. They had all ready been there for about an hour before visitation actually started. They led us up to the casket. Two people took a hold of me—one on each side. I don't even know which of the Rents did it. It could have been any of the four. It didn't make any difference. I stared at the body in the casket. That wasn't Scottie. Not my best friend. That was just some waxy looking mannequin in a box. And there was that smell—flowers, incense? Something sweet. I hated it. I wanted out of there.

I sat down in a chair and just watched and listened. People made all kinds of stupid comments, "Oh, he looks so natural. He looks like he's asleep."

Bull! He looked dead. If they wanted him to look like he was asleep, they would have turned him over on his left side. One leg would stick out straight, and the other would bend at the knee, and he'd have a death grip on his pillow. They'd even slicked his hair down so it wasn't sticking straight up. That wasn't Scott. Finally I just blocked everybody out and let my thoughts go.

I spent the next couple of minutes just yelling at him in my mind. "Scott, you jerk, where are you? Why'd you do this to me? What's Heaven like? Will I see you again when I die? Should I take myself out now so we can be together again? Did it hurt when you died? Were you awake when it happened? What am I going to do? Why'd you leave me? Damn you Scott!"

I really don't even particularly remember the funeral. They held it the next day. I sat there with all four 'rents in my own little world. People talked. People said all kinds of good things about Scottie. The minister looked down at me and asked if I wanted to say anything. I almost panicked. No way! I had things I wanted to tell Scottie, but I wouldn't say them in front of a whole bunch of people. I'd probably start yelling at him again. I just wanted the thing over so I could get out of there. I wanted to go home.

Unfortunately for my frame of mind, it didn't end there. After the service at the funeral home, we all climbed back in that long black car that followed the hearse out to the cemetery. The pallbearers carried that ugly, closed box up a little hill to a stand and placed it there. They said a few prayers and that was it. They planned to put him in that hole—forever. No way would I watch that!

"Mom, Dad, get me out of here! I can't do this anymore," I begged. The whole idea of watching them drop him into that deep opening, throw dirt on him, and fill it up was more than I could handle. I'd had it. If they wouldn't take me home, I'd walk. Enough was enough!

Dad put his arm around my shoulder and led me away, "It's ok, Jeremy. Breathe deeply and slowly. We're going to leave now and head back to the church for the post funeral luncheon and get together. The actual burial takes place after everyone's gone. Come on. Let's walk back to the funeral car." I don't know if I hyperventilated or not, but thank God Dad stayed with me and helped me through it.

After we left the cemetery and drove across town, I couldn't imagine how anyone could even think about eating. When we arrived at the church, the atmosphere turned totally different, and that surprised me. People talked out loud, laughed, told stories, and acted like they were at some big social event. I walked over and sat in a corner all by myself. I didn't want to eat. I didn't want to talk. I didn't want to do anything except go home. Scottie wasn't there, but I gave him hell again under my breath anyway. It still made me mad that he could do such a thing to me. A few of the older ladies came by, patted me on the head like I was some kind of freaking dog, and made stupid comments that I didn't want to hear. Most people just left me alone.

Mom eventually came over and sat down beside me, "Honey," she said as she put her arm around me, "you need to eat something. You'll mess up your system big time if you don't. You haven't eaten a decent meal since the accident."

"I'm not hungry, Mom. I just don't want to eat."

"I know it's horrible for you. It's horrible for all of us, but we have to move on with our lives and make the best of it no matter how hard it is. You know, after all the tragedies suffered by people all over the world, life goes on."

"Mom, Scott has always been my best friend. Why did he do this? It's not fair!"

"You need to get it out of your head that Scottie just up and abandoned you." Then she reached over and took my chin in her hand, turned my head, and looked me in the eye. "He did not do this to you on purpose. He did not kill himself. He did not desert you!"

Just so Mom would quit nagging, I let her lead me over to the table and fix my plate. Grudgingly I ate a little and actually felt better afterwards. However, I still only had one thing in mind. I wanted to go home and get out of those dress-up clothes, and get off by myself where I could think and not be interrupted. Finally, after what seemed like hours and hours, we left and went home.

I sat out on the patio all by myself. Mom Sara and Jim Dad came home an hour or so later. Life already felt different. For as long as I could remember, I'd spent almost as much time at their house as I did ours. They sure wouldn't want me hanging around over there anymore. That would make them just think of Scott. I wondered if they would move.

...

For the next week or so I literally did nothing. I sat on the patio and stared off into space. I played mind numbing computer games. Mom and Dad both tried to motivate me to do something—anything.

One evening after dinner Mom joined my on the patio. "Jeremy, it's time you started the process of healing and letting Scottie go. Go to the pool and swim. Go back to the skate park and practice tricks on your BMX for the August competition. Talk to your baseball coach and see if he'll let you back on the team."

"I don't want back on the team. I don't even particularly like baseball. We just did that for something different to do."

"Well, then maybe you can look for a part time shop," she suggested.

"I don't want a job! I don't want on the team! I don't want to swim or visit friends or go to the park! I want Scottie back!" I semi shouted standing up and stomping into the house. I stormed into my bedroom, and slammed the door. Anger overwhelmed me, and I didn't know why.

Lying on my bed, my mind drifted back to the first week of summer vacation and the stuff Scott and I did. We had a great summer planned—playing baseball, the skate park, getting our driver's licenses. What a trip that would be! It seemed like so long ago, even though it was only a couple of weeks. I spent that first Friday night of summer vacation at Scott's house. Saturday morning started like most Saturdays. Scott sang one of his goofy made up songs at the top of his lungs in the shower while I plugged my ears. When he finally wandered back into our room he started picking on me.

"Germy! Get your head out from under the pillow. You know you love to hear me sing!"

"How can anyone be in such a good mood so early in the morning?" I asked knowing no way I would get a straight answer.

"Just 'cause you're an old grouch in the morning since you want to stay up half the night," he laughed at me as he yanked my pillow out of my hands and smacked me with it.

"At least I don't fall asleep in the chair at nine thirty every night," I growled back at him.

Scott was a morning person and I wasn't. That's all there was to it. We were as different as night and day in that respect.

However, as usual, by the afternoon we were pretty much on the same wave length so Scott and I went out to the back yard and played catch with a baseball. We had joined some summer league just for the heck of it, and our first game had been that morning. Neither one of us played very well, but we had a lot of fun. Sort of like our wrestling—neither one of us did all that well at that sport either, but it was great exercise and we enjoyed it. Who cared? We sure didn't.

Anyway, I played left field and Scott played center so we were close enough to chirp on each other whenever something went wrong—which happened fairly often. That morning was the first actual game of the summer, and we were really kind of excited about it—not that we'd ever admit it, of course.

In the last inning the game was still tied. They had a man on third base with one out. The batter lofted a high fly ball to left and I camped under it. I knew the runner would try to score.

"Go ahead, dick head, run! I'll throw your ass out by five steps," I said kind of like under my breath but loud enough so nobody except maybe Scott could hear me.

I caught the ball cleanly and fired it three-quarters side arm to home plate. I had him by a mile. Half way between third and home the side arm action took over and the ball started curving right and sailed over the fence and into the bleachers.

"Great throw, Germy! You just gave them the game!" Scott howled as he rolled on the ground laughing.

"Get up, you idiot and help me out here. Coach is gonna kill me!" I yelled at him.

Back on the bench, Coach took us aside and strongly suggested, "Between now and practice next week I think it would be a good idea for both of you to learn how to throw overhand so that the ball flies straight and doesn't take off on you.

"Scott, you're cracking up at Jeremy's expense, but you don't throw the ball any better than he does! Both of you get out of here and go on home and learn how to throw OVERHAND! And, oh, one more thing. Jeremy, watch your language out there in the outfield. Swearing's not acceptable!"

"Ooops! Busted!" I thought to myself. I didn't think he'd heard me.

We laughed big time over that one—however, not as much as we did over the driving fiasco that happened later in the day. As soon as we made it home that day, we walked out into the back yard and started tossing the ball back and forth. We worked on our overhand throws for maybe fifteen minutes before Jim Dad stepped out the back door, "Scott, Jeremy, heel!"

We dropped our gloves and the ball right there in the yard and ran up to him. Together we squatted down on our knees with our hands up like puppies begging for treats. "Yes, Dad!" we both said in unison acting like the wise guys we tended to be on occasion.

I have no clue how many times we heard the dads threaten us as we grew up as they held up a thumb and forefinger about a half inch apart while reminding us, "There's about that much difference between being a smart ass and getting one!"

That time he just shook his head, rolled his eyes, and said, "We're going for a ride. Scott is heads and Jeremy is tails!" as he flipped a coin into the air. It landed on tails. "I'll give you two minutes to grab your log books and get into the car. 1001…1002…1003."

We made it with time to spare. The plan was to go on four half hour shifts—two each or until his dad worked up a migraine—whichever came first. Actually he just used the migraine thing as an excuse in case we drove him nuts like he sometimes claimed we did. Can't imagine why he'd ever say that! We climbed into the car with me behind the steering wheel and Scott in the back seat. Right on cue, he gave us the lecture.

"Whoever's not driving sits back in his seat with the seat belt securely fastened and his mouth shut. I don't want to hear one word out of the peanut gallery. Understand?" he asked somewhat sternly.

Having practically lived with each other all our lives, we almost read each other's minds and said things at the same time. "Yes, Dad," we again said in unison with that "smart mouth teenage tone" in our voices.

I backed out of the drive and things went smoothly for me for a change. I drove around town for a half hour making left turns, right turns, and even parallel parked without a hitch. When I finished, I parked at the curb, filled out my log, and Jim Dad initialed it. I had really started to get the hang of this driving thing. However, it was also the last time I drove until the last week of summer.

Scott and I traded places and off we went again. Scott started out his session with a bang. He pulled out of the parking place and headed down the street.

"Turn right at the next corner," his dad told him. "Now slow down and don't take it going too fast."

We made it around the corner ok, but Scott forgot to ease up on his grip on the wheel and let the car straighten itself out. It jumped the curb and stopped on the sidewalk. I turned around in my seat, buried my head in the corner, and practically convulsed laughing so hard.

Jim Dad wheeled around and swatted me half heartedly across the butt, and said, "Jeremy, knock it off. It isn't that funny!"

"Not fair!" I spouted out still laughing. "Abuse! Abuse!"

I don't care what Jim Dad said, it really was funny—at least I thought so. Usually I screwed something up or did something goofy with Scott cracking up. This time the tables were turned. Scott messed up so he swatted and yelled at me—par for the course. Oh well! Scott finally managed to back the car back over the curb, and we went on about our way.

However, Jim Dad told us to pay attention to where we were. "Once we get home, I want the two of you to get on your bikes and come back, knock on that person's door and offer to fix the damage on their lawn."

"Dad!" Scott whined. "There wasn't any damage."

"You don't know that and it's your responsibility to make sure— end of discussion!"

After Scott's half hour was up, Jim Dad figured he'd suffered enough so neither of us had to complete his second planned drive for that day.

When we found our way back to the scene of the crime, we checked it out before knocking on the door. Fortunately for us, Scott had been right. No apparent damage showed on the grass between the curb and the sidewalk. We explained to the man who lived there what had happened, and he acted very good about it. In fact, he seemed to be slightly amused by our embarrassment. He walked out to the curb area and checked it all out, and said not to worry about it. Everything would be fine. When we left, we went over to the skate park and practiced our jumps on the various ramps. There was a big competition scheduled for the last week of August and we wanted to be ready for it.

After reliving that first week of summer break, shedding a tear or two reliving the memories, I finally drifted off to sleep knowing that I had to go out to Scott's grave the next day. Something seemed to be drawing me there.

Chapter 3

The next morning I crawled out of bed, showered, brushed my teeth, and all that stuff. Then I wandered out to the kitchen, filled my cereal bowl, and started eating my breakfast. Mom came out to the table and sat down with me. "What's on the agenda for today, Honey?" she asked.

"I've been thinking. I'm going to ride my bike out to the cemetery and just kind of check things out all by myself. Maybe that way I can get used to the idea that he's really gone and not coming back. Maybe it'll help."

"That's quite a ride. Sure you don't want to put in some of your behind the wheel driving time? You still have a bunch of hours to finish up before you can get your license. I could sit in the car and let you go up to the grave and have your own time with him."

"No, I want to do this myself."

"Do you know how to get there?"

"Yeah, Scott and I used to sneak out there on our bikes just to race on the hilly roads in the cemetery where we could go fast and not worry about cars."

"Ok, but make sure you take your cell phone so you can stay in touch. I'll try not to worry and start calling you every five minutes, so you might want to check in periodically, and wear your helmet," she said with a smile as she stood up and went back to her morning paper. Scottie hadn't worn his helmet that day. That just wasn't cool. I wouldn't wear mine either.

After finishing my breakfast and throwing my bowl and spoon in the dishwasher, I jumped on my BMX and headed to the cemetery. Scott and I had identical bikes except his was red and mine was yellow. The Rents gave them to us a few years back at Christmas. They sure didn't look like much anymore, but were still perfectly functional. They had been through a lot of wear and tear especially at the skate park. There had been many a spill on the ramps. Our parents sure got their money's worth out of those gifts. Wonder what happened to his? I hadn't seen it since the accident. Maybe his mom and dad just threw it away. It was pretty old and probably all banged up from the accident so nobody would ever be able to use it again anyway.

It took about a half hour to ride there. I knew right where to go in the cemetery too. We cruised his area a lot because of the hills. His grave lay up over a little knoll in a section where the road wound around among a lot of big old trees. Getting closer, I knew I only had to go up and over one more little hill, and then I could see it. When I popped up over the top, I saw the mounded pile of fresh dirt with some kid and his dog sitting on top of it. That was total bullshit! Scott had just been buried a couple of weeks ago, and that kid and his dog had taken squatter's rights on top of him with some freaking bike lying on the ground beside him. I started screaming at the top of my lungs, totally ticked and ready to fight.

"What are you doing sitting there? Get out of there. Now!"

"Germy! It's about time you showed up. I've been waiting for you for two weeks," Scott laughed as he jumped to his feet. "Where've you been?"

"Scott?" I asked not believing what I saw.

"Yeah, who'd you think it was?"

"But! But!..." The next thing I knew I lay flat on my back laughing and trying to keep Mooshy's tongue out of my mouth after he attacked me, knocked me down, and slobbered all over my face with that huge tongue of his. Scott stood there laughing his ass off and didn't even call him off.

"Yes, but... Scott, what's going on? Why are you here?" I asked struggling back to my feet, petting Mooshy, and trying to get my breath back. "Why can I see you? Why aren't you in Heaven?"

"I know, I know. I'm dead and you aren't supposed to be able to see me, but you can, can't you? You can see both of us," Scott said.

"I'm freaking out!" I yelled at him knowing I'd just lost my mind or something.

"Now just slow down, Jeremy, before you hyperventilate or have a nervous breakdown or something, and listen. From the time that I died, I've had a guardian out there who's been advising me. It's hard to explain, but he's been telling me all kinds of stuff."

"So what really happened?" I asked finally calming down enough to at least listen.

"You and I both know the basic story line. Some damn car smacked me while I rode to the store on my bike. As the story goes, I cut an artery in my neck on a broken bottle, and bled to death. But that's all I know. I don't know who did it. I think my guardian does, but he's not talking."

"And the driver never stopped?" I kind of whispered.

"No, and not only that, I don't know why the driver suddenly swerved over and hit me. I've got no clue why the person didn't stop. I don't know if he or she did it accidentally or intentionally. I don't know anything for sure, so my guardian said he'd give the two of us the opportunity to find out for ourselves," Scott continued.

"What do you mean he's giving us the chance to find out?" I asked

"You and I get to work on this together just like always. My guardian knows about the bond between us and will give us some time. Once we do, though, I have to move on permanently—more or less. I'll still have the ability to come back ONLY when and if I'm needed."

25

"You're going to be able to come back?" I asked completely confused.

"Yep!" Scott said with that silly grin of his. "He told me that since you're such a screw-up, your life will have a lot of ups and downs so there will be times when you actually need my help. When that happens, I can come back and lend you a hand."

By then I had completely forgotten about being mad at him for getting himself killed. "Scottie, did it hurt? Were you in a lot of pain? Did you know you were dying?" I had so many questions and they just started pouring out.

"No to all. All I remember is that I saw the car swerve and smack into me before I could even react. I remember flying through the air and that's it. I probably knocked myself out when I landed. The first thing I remember is me standing there on the grass looking down at myself thinking, 'Gee, this sucks! There's blood all over the place.' That's when I looked up and this old guy and his dog kind of run—hobble at a fast pace down the street. He used a cane, and couldn't go too fast, but he sure tried. When he got there, he knelt down and felt my neck and swore under his breath. Then he flagged down some guy driving down the street to help him."

"Did he say anything to you?"

"No, and that's when I figured out that I must be dead. I tried to speak to him, but he couldn't see me or hear me. When the emergency crews came, they worked over my body for a couple of minutes before slipping me on the gurney and putting me in the ambulance. That's when I met my guardian right there at the accident site. He showed up with Mooshy and told me that everything was ok, and that I would eventually be ok with what happened."

"Mooshy came too?" I asked.

"Yeah. The first thing I did was play with Mooshy for just a minute then I told the guy that I thought he was nuts. I needed to get to the store and get those chocolate chips and walnuts for Mom. That's when he put his arm around my shoulder and told me I had died in the accident. Then he told me again that I'd be ok with it."

"How'd he figure that?" I asked just seeing in my mind the expression Scott would have on his face when he told a perfect stranger that he thought he was nuts.

"How did he figure that I'd be ok with my dying? I found that really weird too. Then he told me something really strange. That's when he said that after my funeral and everything was over, and everything settled down and kind of got back to normal, that you and I had to work together and discover for ourselves exactly what happened and why. How he knew all about you beats the hell out of me. Anyway, then he said that sometimes things are not as they seem."

"That's really weird. Wonder what he meant by that?" I asked.

"Don't know. Anyway, about that time you came screaming onto the scene and that guy grabbed you and dragged you away from where I was. I came over to the car and tried to talk to you, but you didn't see me or hear me. Then our moms arrived on the scene. I watched my mom go into hysterics and race over to where I had just been put into the ambulance. Some lady officer helped her.

"So what happened then?"

"They took my body to the hospital and laid it on this metal table with a sheet over it. Dad came in and saw me then, and that was a bad scene too. Since then I've kind of tried to stay away from my parents and my body, except I did go to my funeral and that was pretty freaky. Everyone that I love is having a real hard time with this, and nobody realizes that I'm really ok. So the only thing left for us to do is figure out what happened and why, and then you and I can both move on."

"So how are we going to do that?"

"For now you have to go home and act like none of this conversation ever took place. If your parents think that you're on a mission with me, they'll figure you've gone nuts and sick some whacko shrink on you. We don't need that, so this has to be just between the two of us. We both need to spend the rest of today alone thinking about how we are going to do it and make some plans."

"Open to suggestion?"

"Shoot!"

"First off, does that BMX of yours still work? It looks all bent out of shape, and the front tire is flat."

"Doesn't matter. My bike is in the same dimension I am. I guess you'd call it a ghost bike. My guardian told me I would need transportation while we did this so the bike works fine. So what's your idea?"

"I can't be gone too long today or Mom will get all paranoid. Scott, Can you leave the cemetery?"

"I can go anywhere I want. Why?"

Let's meet tomorrow morning at the accident site. There have to be clues there of some kind. There has to be something that the police missed. At least it's a place to start."

"Ok, sounds good to me. Come on. Jump on your bike! Mooshy and I'll race you down to the cemetery gate. Once we get there, you're on your own until tomorrow. And remember. Don't say anything to our moms and dads. They'll think you've lost it."

"Wait, before we race to the gate, tell me about Mooshy."

"Like I said, my guardian brought him with him. I guess he was out there waiting for me. You remember the night he died?"

"I'll never forget it," I told him.

...

Both of our minds went back a year and replayed the scene. We had gone to our high school Valentine's Day dance and planned to spend the night together afterwards. We returned to his house about midnight and accosted his parents who were waiting up for us.

"Mom, what's to eat?" Scott had yelled. "Can we have some of that blueberry pie that's just sitting there doing nothing?"

"No! Eat some cereal and toast and go to bed. Dad and I are headed that way now." Mom Sara had replied.

"Mom!" I whined. "Just a sliver?" I continued with a grin on my face knowing darned well what the answer would be.

"No! That pie is off limits."

We dug out the cereal bowls and attacked the Cap'n Crunch with gusto. "Man, there were some hot looking babes out there tonight. Did you catch that outfit Bethany had on? I thought she was gonna bust right out the front of it when she danced with that dork she's dating," Scottie laughed as he spit out about half a mouth full of cereal.

"Actually I was real tempted to go ask her if she wanted to dance, but I never worked up the nerve. She's so hot!" I said.

"I know! I know! Next time we've both gotta get out there on the dance floor. No way we'd make bigger fools out of ourselves than some of them. You see Bobby Richardson? He can't even walk down the hallway at school without bumping into the wall he's so klutzy, and he danced to practically every song they played."

"Yeah," I answered. "He even went out there a couple of times with Bethany. The way they were going at it, if her top had sprung loose, she'd 'uv knocked him out."

We both laughed at that image as we cleaned up our messes and headed for bed around one in the morning. That settled it. Next time we would actually dance and not just watch the show from the sidelines.

Somewhere late, late into the night Scott yelled, "Mooshy! Damn it! You did it to me again! Now, move over! I don't have any room. And, Germy, quit your whining over there just 'cause I woke you up. Go back to sleep."

Mooshy was a twelve year old, dark brindle Boxer with a pushed in face.

"Scott, just 'cause you couldn't say 'Jeremy' when we were little is no reason why you can't say it now. My name is not Germy!"

"Nag! Nag! Germy – Jeremy what's the difference? The point's the same. Just pipe down and go back to sleep so I can."

"Yeah! Yeah!" I grumbled under my breath. "Maybe you should just shut up and quit yelling at Mooshy just because he outsmarted you again." Mooshy was the funniest dog we'd ever seen. He pulled more crap on both of us than you can imagine.

There were times when we considered the fact that Mooshy just might be smarter than either one of us. Mom Sara's orders were that he had to sleep on the carpet beside Scott. However, what his parents didn't know didn't hurt them. He slept on the bed with Scott most of the time. Most nights he'd sleep on top of the bed spread, but when he cooled off, he wanted to be covered up. What he would usually do is crawl off the bed, mosey around to the other side, and nudge Scott with his nose, Scott automatically lifted the covers, and Mooshy crawled in.

As Mooshy aged, sometimes he couldn't hold it all night and had to go out. That night seemed to be one of those nights. Half asleep, Scott crawled out of bed, stumbled to the door in his pajamas and bare feet, opened it and waited. When Mooshy didn't show up, he knew he had been had—again. There lay Mooshy curled up on Scott's warm pillow and sound asleep with a smile on his face.

That night seemed different than others though. When Scott went back to bed, he noticed that Mooshy was shivering. So he covered him up, tucked him in, and cuddled with him for a minute until he warmed up. Finally things settled down and we all fell back to sleep.

The next morning we crawled out of bed for the day, and Mooshy didn't move. Scott and I didn't think too much of it at first because Mooshy was a little on the lazy side. We went to the bathroom, brushed our teeth, checked our faces for zits and potential whiskers, dressed, and were almost ready to go eat breakfast. Mooshy still hadn't budged.

"Come on Mooshy. Move your ass! I need to make the bed," Scott yelled at him while I made mine on the other side of the room. He didn't stir.

That caught both of our attentions. "Something's wrong!" I said.

I walked over to the bed while Scott gently shook him and tried to wake him up, "Hey! On your feet, little buddy. Jeremy, I don't think he's breathing."

Mooshy didn't budge. Jim Dad and Mom Sara both came in and checked him. "He's gone," Jim Dad announced. "He died in his sleep."

"He fell asleep in the same room with his two favorite humans and never woke up," Mom Sara said wiping tears from her eyes. "That's really pretty special. Let's face it, guys. Twelve years is very old for a Boxer, but kids like you growing up never think of those things. Life just goes on as always."

His death really shook us all up as he was part of the family. Jim Dad called the vet's office when they opened at nine to let them know what had happened.

"We can take him in right now," he had said when he hung up the phone.

"Here's an old blanket to wrap him in," Mom said as she handed it to Jim Dad.

The three of us wrapped him up and carried him to the car. Mom Sara disappeared. We took Mooshy to the vet's office and parked in the lot outside the side door. One of the vet assistants wheeled out a metal cart. Scott and I slid Mooshy out of the back seat and on to the cart.

With tears in our eyes, we both gave him one last hug, and he was gone. The ride home was pretty quiet. Four or five days later Jim Dad called Mom and told us that they had Mooshy's ashes and that they were going to bury them that evening.

"We're going over after dinner for Mooshy's funeral," Mom told me at dinner.

"What do we do?" I asked having never been to a dog's funeral before. In fact, the only funeral I'd ever been to was my grandmother's.

"Not sure what they have in mind," she said. "We'll just kind of follow their lead."

Around seven, Mom, Dad, and I walked next door. Each of us told our favorite Mooshy story. Even though the stories were funny, the night was sad. Other than my grandmother, it was the first time that either Scottie or I had experienced the death of someone or something that we knew and loved. It was a real downer.

One of Mooshy's favorite tricks always happened when Scott and I played games on the computer. Apparently it bored him. He would mosey out through his swinging doggie door and stand in the back yard and bark.

"There's his special bark," Scottie would say grinning. "He wants to play. We don't even have to look to see what he's doing. He's standing in one place with his elbows down on the grass looking straight ahead with his butt up in the air wiggling all over the place and barking his fool head off."

If we ignored him, he wouldn't give up. If we didn't go out to play with him, he barked until one of our parents yelled at us to go out and shut him up.

"Scottie, do you want to have another dog?" I asked him a couple of days later." I can't believe how quiet it is around here without Mooshy."

 He had always been with us as long as either one of us could remember. I knew we couldn't have a dog because of Mom's allergies to most of them. If she spent too much time at their house, her eyes got puffy and watered. I swear Mooshy knew it. He always rubbed up against her and wanted her to pet him every time she went over there.

"I don't know, but I don't think so, not now at least. We talked about that during dinner last night, and I don't think any of us are ready. Maybe someday, but not yet."

"If you were going to get a puppy, what kind would you want next time?"

"I wouldn't have anything but a Boxer. When I think dog, I think Boxer. If I do get one, though, I might want a fawn colored one next time. I wouldn't want him to grow up and look just like Mooshy."

 I couldn't have agreed with him more. I guess that once you've had a Boxer, you measure all dogs by those standards. I also thought that getting a fawn one might be a good idea too. Also, since Mooshy had cropped ears, I would want to leave the next one floppy eared. You would be getting another Boxer, but not replacing the one you had lost.

...

We looked at each other after the flashback and then looked at Mooshy. Both of us smiled as he wagged his stubby tail and grinned at us. It made for a great memory, but it was time to leave.

The race to the gate ended in a three way tie. Big surprise! Just like when they were alive and we raced out here as young kids. Before I left to go home, I had to get all serious for a minute.

"Scottie, I have to tell you something. While I was mowing the lawn, even before I heard the sirens, I knew something bad had happened to you. I saw parts of the accident flash in my head. I raced to the scene as fast as I could, but it was too late. They wouldn't let me anywhere near you. The thing is, that wasn't the first time that something weird like that has happened.

"You remember when we were nine years old, and my grandma died? A few days after the funeral I came to breakfast and saw her rocking in the chair she always sat in. I ran to Mom and told her that Grandma had come back, but she just shook her head and told me that I missed her so much that my imagination was playing tricks on me. She told me not to tell anyone else, not even you, because people would just laugh at me. But, I know it really happened, 'cause Grandma told me she loved me."

"I always thought there might be something a little weird about you," Scott laughed. "Seriously, though. Maybe you have a gift of some kind because you're the only one who has been able to see me and talk to me except for some little kid whose dad's buried close to me. Nobody else has, and I've tried to get the attention of some other people like my mom and dad."

"One more thing! I've been madder 'n hell at you ever since this happened. I know, it's probably stupid, but that's the way I felt. The funny part is, as soon as I discovered that it was really you sitting on your grave, I wasn't mad anymore."

"I know, I know! I've listened to you swear and scream at me ever since the accident. That's another thing my mentor told me. If we could discover what took place and why, it would help you accept what happened and move on with your life. He said you need to do that."

I headed for home knowing that this started something that would be completely new and different in my life. Somehow I had to work with Scottie to discover the details of the accident and keep the whole thing a secret. Oh, boy! Little did I know then what I had managed to get myself into—but I would find out.

Chapter 4

I took my time riding home. Whoa! What a trip that was! Scottie looked and sounded the same as always to me, but he said I was the only one who had been able to see him so far except for some little kid whose dad lay buried close to him. I wondered why nobody else could see him. He said that his parents visited the cemetery a bunch of times since the funeral but hadn't seen or heard him. Said he'd decided to avoid them for now until they can just remember the good times. Right now they felt too much sadness and cried too many tears for him.

When I finally made it home, I parked my bike, looked over at Scott's home which, as usual, seemed awfully quiet. I paused for a second or two and then went into our house. Mom met me practically at the door. "How'd it go, Jeremy? Did you find his grave ok? Were you ok? You didn't call so I started to worry. I almost called you a couple of times."

"Everything worked out fine, Mom. I sat beside his grave for a long time and just kind of let my mind go. It seemed almost like he was squatting there with me. I took a lot of deep breaths but I'm ok."

"That's good. You know that if you ever need to talk, your dad and I are both right here for you any time. Jim and Sara are too. They're lost right now, but they'll always be here for you too. They know what you're going through"

"I know, Mom. Right now, I'm going out on the patio just to sit for a while. Ok?"

"Sure. I'll have lunch around in about an hour. I'll call you when it's ready."

Oh boy, I thought to myself as I flopped down on my chair on the patio. What's going on? Am I a complete lunatic? There is no way that I can see and communicate with a dead person. It just doesn't make sense. And yet, it's happened twice now—first with Grandma and now with Scott. I only saw Grandma once after she died. Is that what it will be with Scott? When I get to the accident scene tomorrow morning, will he be there? Will I see him and be able to talk to him? Will I always be able to see him and talk to him?

...

The next morning I woke up pretty groggy and spaced out—didn't sleep worth a darn. All these questions! No answers. I had no choice. I had to play it out. I'd ride to the accident site around ten o'clock like we planned. Either Scott would be there or he wouldn't. Either way I had to find out.

"So what did you plan to do today?" Mom asked as I cut up a banana for my cereal.

"Thought I'd cruise over to where the hit-and-run took place and check it out," I answered trying to act casual.

"Why?"

"I don't know really. Haven't been there yet, and just kind of need to do it. Then maybe I'll go over to the skate park and work on my jumps."

"There has to be more to it than that. What are you looking for there? It should be completely cleaned up."

"I know, I guess as much as anything I just want to get a feel for what happened. See if I can figure out in my own mind how it happened and why," I said trying to act as laid-back and non-committal as possible. I didn't want Mom getting suspicious because of her reaction when I saw Grandma. I didn't want her to think that I had lost it or anything and end up having to spill my guts to some head doctor. No way would I let that happen! *Oh, yeah, Mr. Shrink, Scott and I have been tracking down his killer...* Right!

"I'm not sure that's a good idea. You know exactly what happened there. You're starting to obsess on this thing a bit too much. Yesterday you went to Scott's grave. Today you want to go to the accident scene. What's it going to be tomorrow?"

"Yeah, whatever Mom, don't nag me! I'm not hurting anyone or anything. I'm just trying to make peace in my own mind. I want to understand everything. Let's not forget that Scott and I practically lived together night and day for sixteen years and now he's gone.

I can't just dust off my hands and say, 'Oh well. Scottie's gone. Time to move on!' It just doesn't work that way and you know it."

"Maybe you should just go out and look for a job and change your whole mind set."

"I don't want a job! I don't need a job! I don't need money! If my twenty dollars a week allowance puts that big a strain on the budget, then just forget it. I can do without it. I am not going to look for a job. Not this summer. Maybe next year," I yelled. I didn't need any more pressure.

"Hey! Calm yourself down. Don't get any more upset than what you all ready are. Go to the accident scene and look it over. It won't do you any good, but maybe it will give you some peace of mind. Then go to the skate park. Ride your bike, practice your tricks, and enjoy yourself for a change. Oh, by the way, another thing. You need to start thinking about wrestling camp. That's coming up shortly."

"Mom, I'm sorry. I didn't mean to yell at you. Just give me some slack this summer. Leave me alone and let me be stupid trying to work this all out in my head. I know you and Dad paid out a bunch of money for wrestling camp, but I'm not going. Not this year. Scottie and I went together for four years and I just can't do it this year. When school starts up again in September, I promise, I'll make new friends, see if I can't find some babe who just can't get by without a handsome dude like me, and move on with my life. Ok?"

"Your decision on wrestling camp isn't going to make your father too happy, but I'll go along with it for this year anyway. I'm willing to give you the rest of the summer to get your head together. However, you have to keep us informed and up-to-date. Your dad and I will try very hard not to interfere. Just remember we love you and will help in any way we can. Also remember that if you become so obsessed that we think you are a danger to yourself mentally or any other way, we will intercede. Got it?"

"Got it! Bye, Mom. Time to run! See you later." I'd had enough of that conversation.

"Love you, Jeremy. Be careful out there."

This could turn into being a royal pain in the butt if Mom started paying too much attention to what I was doing and started micromanaging my summer, I thought to myself. If Scott and I were going to figure out what happened, I didn't need any nosiness or interference from her. If I had to lie through my teeth to her, I would. Sure as hell wouldn't be the first time.

When I skidded to a stop at the scene, I looked around and saw no sign of Scott. Would he actually show up? Could it all have been my imagination? Had I just seen and heard things yesterday? Had I lost it? Mom said she was getting concerned about me. I wondered if I should be.

"Bout time, Germy! You're five minutes late."

"Whoa! You scared the crap out of me! Where were you? I didn't see you."

"Mooshy and I stood right here leaning against this tree. We watched you ride down the street. Wonder why you didn't see us until I spoke?"

"Don't know, but it's all kind of freaky. Maybe you just blended into the tree? Got no clue!"

"Oh well, no big deal. So how we gonna go about this?"

"There won't be any real evidence 'cause they totally cleaned up the place. I thought that maybe you could ride your bike down to here and recreate the accident to see if it jogs anything in your brain, feeble as it is," I said smiling. Had to dig on him a little even if he was dead.

"So just ride up the street, turn around, and ride back to this point and see if I remember anything? Sounds kind of stupid, but it might jar something loose in there worth remembering."

"Yeah. Ride down the street to where you turned the corner and see if you can duplicate your speed, direction, and everything right up to the time the car hit you. Mooshy, you stay here with me."

Scott jumped on his bike and rode down the street doing wheelies and showing off, turned the corner and actually pedaled out of sight. When he came back into view, he just cruised along, not in a hurry but not being pokey either.

"Ok, here goes… I turned the corner right about here and headed your way." He shouted out to me as he rode down the street. "I wasn't really going too fast 'cause I wasn't in any big hurry. Mom said she wouldn't start until after you finished your lawn anyway, so I just enjoyed the ride and sang to the IPod in my pocket."

"You should've hustled!" I yelled back at him. "You were going after chocolate chips. I did my part. I'd been mowing as fast as I could until I saw your accident in my head."

"You and your freaking stomach! I wanted to enjoy myself and listen to some nice and gentle rap."

"Gentle rap? Right!" I said starting to laugh.

"Quit interrupting! I'm trying to remember. I rode to right about here when I heard this car squeal around the corner behind me and race up the street—I only had one ear bud in so I could still hear traffic, rent's orders, you know. I turned around to look, and the car just kind of jumped at me. I was right here." He slammed on his brakes and stopped about five feet from the bush where he had landed.

"When you turned around to look, did you accidentally swerve in front of the car?"

"Hell no! In fact I went the other way towards the curb. It was right here when it suddenly hurtled right at me. It happened so fast I couldn't do anything."

"That sucks! Did you see the person driving? Could you tell if it were a man or a woman? Did you catch the color? Do you remember flying through the air?"

"Nope! Don't remember anything after that until the man I told you about earlier stood over my body."

"Do you know which part of the car hit your bike and where?"

"I'm guessing it must have side swiped me so probably the handle bar hit the side of the car around the door someplace. From the looks of my bike, other parts of it must have hit the car too unless it just got run over."

"Ok. Get your bike out of the road so it doesn't get hit again, and let's look at where you landed."

"Why move the bike? If a car hit the thing now, it would pass right through it like it drove through mist or something."

"Doesn't matter. Let's not take any chances," I said. For some reason I started to get a gut level feeling that Scott left something out of the description of the accident. I couldn't put my finger on it, but I felt like maybe he hadn't told me part of the story. Why would he leave anything out? Didn't make any sense to me. Maybe my imagination was running away with itself again.

We combed the area for close to an hour as Mooshy curled up in the grass and took a nap. Even when he was alive, he always got bored easily when nobody played with him. Anyway, the city workers or someone had totally erased any sign of the accident. We found no sign of the broken bottle, no blood, no skid marks, no spare car or bike parts, nothing.

"So now what do we do?" I asked.

"Let's go back to my place, hang out, and talk about this without being interrupted."

"You mean the house you lived in when you were alive?"

"No, dipstick, back to the cemetery! I don't want to go anywhere near my parent's house right now. They're too bummed, and there's not one damned thing I can do to help them. I avoid them like the plague. Maybe I always will until we're all together again on the other side. I'll have to play that one by ear. Besides, I don't really know what I'll be able to do or where I'll be able to go after we get this all figured out. My guardian hasn't told me everything yet."

So we hopped on our bikes and headed back to the cemetery. It seemed just like old times. We talked and laughed and screwed around all the way. We wouldn't have to get all serious again about this until we arrived, and that would take about a half hour. We enjoyed ourselves.

Chapter 5

Once we rolled into the cemetery, we decided to get down to business and be all serious again – kind of, at least, for us. Our tour of the accident scene hadn't been overly productive. Scott reconstructed the accident somewhat and what happened afterwards but without any real detail or insight. He remembered a lot of movement on the driver's part, but he didn't actually see the person. He sensed it might be a lady but wasn't sure. The driver's head was turned down and to the right like maybe there was another person on the passenger's side that she was paying attention to.

"Ok, that kinda wasted our time. So now what do we do?" Scott asked as we parked our bikes and sat down on the grass beside his grave. Sometimes he'd sit right on top of it, but I couldn't. It didn't bother him one bit, but I felt squeamish about it. Besides, I'd rather be sprawled out on the grass or leaning back against one of the trees.

"Scott! We haven't even looked at that pile of crap bike of yours yet. Maybe there's something on it that will give us a clue."

"How? It's just a bunch of trashed medal now. You thinking about car paint or something?"

"Yeah, that's what I had in mind. Let's check it out."

We scoured his BMX as carefully as we could. We checked all the dented and bent parts. Our bikes were older than dirt so it made it kind of hard to tell which marks were new and which ones were old. The biggest problem was that his bike didn't appear totally clear.

"We could tell better if we could look at my real bike instead of this ghostly thing," Scott said.

"Yeah, this one really isn't all that plain," I said as we stood our two bikes up beside each other and compared them.

"Man, we need to find my real bike and check that out. If there are any paint smudges from the car that hit me on it, we might be able to see them," Scottie said scratching his head.

...

We spent the next couple of weeks drawing a blank when it came to bright ideas about where to look. We had all kinds of dumb thoughts like sliding down the chimney of the police station in the middle of the night so we could literally break in and find the bike on our own. We shelved that idea when I Googled "chimney break-ins" and saw how many people had gotten stuck naked halfway down a chimney or died of suffocation or had to be rescued that way. No way would I do that! It was time to quit screwing around and get some help. Summer would soon be over.

"Mom, what's to eat? I'm starved!" I called out that afternoon after I walked into the house.

"You aren't starved! You just ate your breakfast three hours ago," she replied as she gave me that 'Boys!' look. "Make yourself a shaved ham sandwich or two, but leave me some. I might want one later myself."

"Don't we have any sliced tomatoes? I always put one on my sandwich," I whined standing there with the fridge door wide open. It was the August tomato season and I put tomato slices on everything—especially sandwiches.

"Duh! Take one out of the chiller, use a knife and peel the skin off, and then slice the tomato, Dear. You'll get the hang of it in no time. Be sure not to cut your thumb and bleed on the tomato."

"Mom! Come out here and do it for me, please!"

"Helpless or hopeless?" she muttered under her breath as she came out and took the tomato out of my hand. "You're as bad as your father. How any male child ever matures to the point of being self-sufficient is beyond me? How are you ever going to survive when you grow up and get out on your own if you can't even slice a tomato?"

"Get married," I said ready to duck.

She just shook her head. It took her less than a minute to peel and slice a couple of tomatoes so I was good to go. I had my sandwich all made except for the tomato and spicy mustard. While I finished it up and grabbed the potato chips out of the pantry, I just casually asked, "Mom, where do you suppose Scott's bike is? I don't think his parents ever brought it home, did they?"

"I doubt it. We've never even mentioned his bike. I would assume the police have it impounded someplace for evidence in case they ever find the person's car that hit him."

"You think it would be locked up in an evidence room of some kind at the police station where they keep all the guns and drugs and other stuff they confiscate just like on CSI?"

"I would be very surprised if they had it there. It's probably in some kind of large garage where they could store cars, bikes, snow mobiles, and other large objects like that they are keeping for evidence."

"You suppose the cops would let me see it?" I asked trying to sound all casual.

"Why on earth would you want to do that? Wouldn't you find that a bit gruesome looking at the bike Scott got killed on? I sure would."

"No! It's not just morbid curiosity. I want to see if there's car paint on it. I know the police probably looked the bike over pretty good themselves, but they didn't tell anybody what they found, have they? Besides they probably wouldn't know old paint marks from the new."

"No, and they probably won't let you, and yes, they're probably smart enough to know the new dents and paint marks from the old. These people do have experience at this kind of stuff, you know. It's just that they often times keep details of a crime under wraps until after an arrest is made and the person goes to trial."

"You'd think they would broadcast it on the news and in the paper. They could have everyone looking for a particular color car with a dent in the side and maybe paint on it."

"I just don't know. I'm not in law enforcement so I don't know why they do some of the things they do."

"Uh, would you ask Mom Sara where it is for me? She probably knows."

"No! And I don't want you pestering her about it either. We talk almost every day, but it isn't about stuff like that. They both finally went back to work this week. They decided it was time to move on with their lives, and that's what you should do too now that summer is almost over. By the way, you haven't been over to their house since the accident, young man. What's up with that?"

"I can't. Someday I'll catch one of them in the yard and just wander over and break the ice, but not now. Not yet!"

"The longer you put it off the harder it will be."

"I know. Give me some slack here, Mom."

Rats! I figured Mom would know where I'd be able to find that bike and how I'd get in to see it. No big help on her end. Maybe I needed to find a cop and ask him. I would assume any policeman on the force would know exactly where they had stashed it and how I should go about seeing it. Rain moved in shortly before I could check out that theory, so not having anything better to do, I spent the rest of the afternoon playing 'Mad Demons' on the computer.

...

"Scottie! Where are you?" I yelled out when I arrived at his place the next day. I didn't see him anywhere.

"Ooooooooooooooo!" He moaned as he jabbed me in the ribs with his finger and Mooshy nudged me in the crotch."

"Scott! Don't do that, and Mooshy quit it! That's gross! I almost had a heart attack right on the spot. Where were you two hiding this time?"

"Heart attack nothing. You probably just crapped your pants. I saw you when you came into the cemetery so I hid behind that big tree just to see if I could get your blood flowing this morning. Don't want you getting real lethargic," he said laughing at me as my pulse rate started to drop back to normal.

"You are so funny, dick head! Knock off the comedy routine and let's talk about your bike. Mom says that it's probably been impounded at the police station some place and there's no way they're gonna let us look at it."

"So, we'll break in like we talked about earlier."

"No, we aren't going to do that. We already debated that angle, and I'm not taking a chance of getting stuck naked covered with axle grease like you suggested in some chimney or some other equally stupid idea. Just because you can slide in and out of tight spots like that doesn't mean that I can. Why don't you do your ghost thing and slip into the place unseen and check it out by yourself?"

"No way! My mentor said that you and I should do this together so that's probably the way it has to be be. Besides, it would be kind of funny seeing you all greased up and stuck in the chimney," he laughed again at my expense.

 "Right! You bet! Ok, so I have an idea. It dawned on me yesterday while I played 'Mad Demons.' The cops always hang out at that little restaurant on the main drag where the teachers go in the morning. Let's take a look to see if there's one taking his break now. If not, we can always wait until one wanders in for lunch."

"Beat you to the gate!" Scott yelled as we jumped on our bikes and raced for the entrance just like the old days. At the end of the drive, we slammed on our brakes just to make sure we didn't slide out into the street and run into some car.

Riding into town we behaved ourselves and paid attention to traffic. We didn't need another disaster for our families. When we pulled up in front of the restaurant, it looked like we were in luck. A police car sat out in front.

"Bingo! There's a cop with all kinds of stripes on his sleeve sitting all by himself over in the corner at one of the small round tables reading a paper with a doughnut and coffee sitting in front of him. He might know something," Scott said gaping in the front window as I locked up my bike.

He looked like a relatively young guy. Could have been maybe in his early thirties? Appeared to be in good shape too. Probably didn't live on those doughnuts like a lot of cops did. Man! A couple of them around town were pretty fat and out of shape.

We walked in and headed directly to his table. I asked, "Sir, could I talk to you a minute, please?"

"Sure, sit down and tell me what's on your mind," he answered. He smiled at me as he put down his paper so that put me a little more at ease.

"Are you familiar with that hit and run accident in June where the boy my age was killed?"

"Certainly am. That was terrible. You want to ask me something about that?"

As he picked up his coffee cup and took a sip, Scott reached over and moved his saucer. When he set the cup down, he naturally missed and banged it on the table. He had the strangest look on his face, and Scott cracked up. No way could I say anything to Scott or the cop would think I was mentally deranged. Therefore, I continued on as if nothing had happened.

"Scott was my best friend," I said emphasizing the 'was' as I glared at Scott. "He and I grew up together, and I should have been with him when the accident happened. I probably could have saved him if I had been."

"No! You couldn't. Don't beat yourself up over that idea. One of my friends worked at the scene, and he said that nobody could have saved him. He died within seconds. He severed the main artery in his neck, and bled to death almost instantly. He never knew what hit him, thank goodness."

"See? I told you, Germy. You've gotta get that guilt trip out of your head. Now, in the meantime, watch how I eat his doughnut right in front of him without him catching me. Me and Mooshy will polish it off in no time."

With that he pretended to grab a piece of the policeman's doughnut and eat it and then toss a bite to Mooshy. The cop didn't see him screwing around, but I sure did, and I couldn't say a word out loud. I tried to kick him under the table. He laughed at me.

The policeman's comment did make me feel somewhat better. My parents told me the same thing, but it wasn't like someone in authority saying it. Sometimes parents just say stuff to protect you even if they have no clue as to what really happened. I felt that this guy probably actually knew.

"This probably sounds weird, but I want to see Scott's bike. That's why I came here to talk to you in the first place. How do I go about it?"

"You don't. They don't allow anyone but authorized personnel in the evidence room. That bike is all banged up and still has blood on it. Nobody would have cleaned it up. It needs to be just like it was found for evidence in case they ever find out who hit him. What possible good could come from you looking at it? What are you trying to accomplish?"

"I know the investigators have gone over that bike with a fine toothed comb looking for clues about the car that hit him, but I just have this need to look at it too. All I really want to do is see if there is automobile paint on it and what color it is," I said as I tried to kick Scott under the table again.

He acted like a complete idiot and there was nothing I could do about it. He pretended to take another bite of the policeman's doughnut and then moved the cup and saucer again. When the cop reached down for his coffee cup, it wasn't where he had left it. He kind of scowled and looked at me as if I had done it.

"Well, I know no one will let you in, but I guess you probably need to find out for yourself. What you want to do is go to the main station on Grand River Avenue between nine and five. That's when the offices are all open with an officer at the main desk."

"What do I say?" I asked suddenly feeling a little nervous about the whole thing.

"Explain to him who you are and what you want and why—just like you did to me. If you catch the right person maybe he will let you in the large item evidence room. Just don't hold your breath or be too disappointed if it doesn't work out. If I were on desk duty, I know I wouldn't let you. Rules are made for a reason."

I thanked him, stood up, and backed away from the table so he could see both of my hands. Scott faked again that he was going to grab that last piece of doughnut. Mooshy stood up, stretched and yawned, and headed out with us.

As soon as we walked out of the restaurant, I started yelling at Scott under my breath so no one else could hear me, "You idiot! He thought that was me doing all that crap somehow even though I sat across the table from him. If he had caught you screwing around with his stuff, he would have freaked."

"Yes, Mom!" Scott said very sarcastically as we both laughed. "Besides, so what if he did think you messed with him and his stupid doughnut. What's he gonna do, arrest you? It'll give him something to think about. He could see your hands at all times. Let him try to figure it out," he laughed that evil laugh of his. "Speaking of figuring things out, I can read your mind. You don't have to talk out loud to me. All you have to do is think the words."

"Really!" I said in my head without opening my mouth.

"Really!" Scott repeated. "All the time you were yapping at me about that cop's doughnut in your head, I knew exactly what you were saying. Bully!"

"That's sweet! I really felt foolish standing at the accident scene yelling back and forth at you yesterday. If anyone had looked at me, they would've thought I had completely lost it."

"Well?" Scott said giving me that raised eyebrow look.

He could be such a turd at times. As I couldn't be gone too long at any one time without causing suspicion at home, we decided to meet the next morning at his place as usual, and then go to the police station. The cops couldn't do anymore than say no.

Chapter 6

I clambered out of bed bright and early the next morning. Talked to Mom for a while, gobbled down my breakfast, and headed out to grab my bike in the garage—didn't want to walk all the way to the police station. She thought it was a complete waste of time, but agreed with Dad that it couldn't hurt a thing to at least try. Scott sat out there on his busted up BMX waiting for me. That would save us some time because I didn't have to go way out to the cemetery to meet him.

"Shhhh! Don't say anything. Keep everything telepathic. Your mom's watching out the window. Try to act semi-normal, as difficult as that may be," Scott said as I hopped on my bike and rode out of the driveway ignoring him completely and keeping a straight face.

When we were away from the house, I told Scott, "Listen, Dude, everyone thinks this is absolutely crazy. Mom and Dad both bet that we won't make it to first base. Dad said that the bike is evidence in a major crime, and that there is no way they are going to let some sixteen year old kid go in there snooping around looking at it. However, they didn't really attempt to talk me out of trying. I guess they figure that if trying helps me in any way, why not?"

"So, I guess we aren't hurting anything by giving it a shot," Scott answered kind of non-committal like.

It was a bright, sunny, lazy day so we took our time riding down to the main precinct. We talked and laughed telepathically all the way—mostly about Scott's antics the day before. Amazing how much more daring someone is if he's invisible to the person he's playing tricks on. Of course, in this case, it didn't help me too much because the cop thought I was somehow responsible for his screwing around.

"Scott, yesterday was a bust, but you have to promise me that if by chance we do find ourselves in the evidence room you won't go messing around and goof it up for us."

"Ok, I'll be good—maybe."

"Scott?"

"Ok, ok! What a nag!" he laughed.

When we arrived at the main precinct, I parked my bike on the sidewalk, attached my lock and chain, and leaned it against the building.

"Doof! There's a sign in the street that says no standing or parking in this block," Scott pointed out.

"That doesn't mean us. That's for cars. Besides, we parked on the sidewalk, not the street," I said. Anyway, there's no place else to put the thing.

We walked in and saw all kinds of people milling around. We didn't spot the main desk right away because we were so busy gawking. One policeman led a real scurvy looking dude down the hall in handcuffs. "Probably stole that cop's doughnut," I whispered to Scott.

"Anything I can do to help you?" said a voice from behind a desk that sat practically right in front of us.

"I hope so. Are you the officer in charge who I need to ask about getting to see something?" I asked.

"Kind of a vague question," he smiled, "But try me out. What did you have in mind?"

"We... I need to have someone let me into the large item evidence room. I want to see something in there."

"That's not going to happen, Son. I can tell you that right now. Care to tell me what this is all about? You can start by giving me your name and then going on from there."

So I did in all the gloomy detail that I could. I told him about Scott and me and our relationship growing up, how Scottie had been killed, and how I had this 'need' to see the bike. I promised that I wouldn't touch anything else in the room. I just wanted to look at the bike as a means of my being able to move on with my life.

After I finished my tale, he said he sympathized with me, but the powers that be never allowed any outsiders in there. However, he didn't shoo me off. He said, "Just a minute. Let me talk to someone else about this."

Then he stood up and disappeared behind a closed door leaving us standing there in front of his desk. Scott and I really didn't dare to communicate except telepathically because there were too many people wandering around. I didn't want anyone to think that some kid stood out there talking to himself. If the cops thought I was a can or two short of a six pack, there would be no way I'd ever get in.

"Jeremy, would you come in here for a minute please?" the desk officer asked when he stepped out from behind that closed door. I started to get nervous and paranoid. What was I thinking? There I would be at the police station behind closed doors with a bunch of cops? Were they going to sit me down in an interrogation room and start yelling at me just like on TV?

"Hi, Jeremy. Come in and sit down. My name is Captain Merton and I'm in charge of the building. The desk sergeant explained to me what you wanted to do, but I would like to hear it from you as well. First off, let me get this straight, you were best friends with the boy named Scott who was killed in June by that hit and run driver?"

"Yes, sir!" I answered as respectfully as I could. I tried not to act nervous. Yeah, right!

"Is there anything that you know about the accident that the police don't know? Do you have any suspicions, any ideas, heard any rumors or theories of any kind that were never published in the paper? Were you, by any chance, with him when it happened and maybe fled from the scene?"

"No I went to the accident site and looked around afterwards, and the only thing I could figure out is that the driver must have aimed right at him in order to hit him. Scott and I rode all over this town and both of us always stayed as close to the curb as we could. There is no way he would have been out in the actual line of traffic."

"That's one of the details that the paper never published. Tire marks showed that the car left its normal driving lane and swerved over to hit him."

"So it wasn't an accident. Someone intentionally killed him," I said unable to believe how anyone could hit a person on a bike on purpose. The whole idea ticked me off, and I started spouting a bit out of control. "We've had some of those assholes blow their horns at us, shake their fists, and all that crap, but we've never had anyone actually try to run us off the road or hit us. That's bullshit!"

"Slow down, Son and let's watch our language. I know you're upset, but that's not necessarily how it happened even if it might look like it right now. There are times when something distracts a driver and a car jumps out of its lane for no other reason than someone dropped a cell phone and tried to grab it. I'd like to know how many accidents have been caused by spilled coffee," he said.

I think he thought that I appeared pretty fragile right then, and he should get away from the intentional part of the accident even if it could've been true.

"Yeah, but how could anyone hit someone on a bike and just keep going? That doesn't make sense. It's totally evil," I grumbled measuring my words a little more carefully.

"There could be any number of reasons. One of the most common is pure panic. Probably more often than not, when that happens, the person eventually turns himself or herself in to the authorities after they calm down and realize what they did. Like you, most people couldn't live with themselves."

"But that didn't happen, did it?" I asked knowing the answer to my own question.

"No, it didn't. Not yet anyway. Now, another reason is that sometimes people are already wanted by the law and know that if they stop, they'd get arrested for some other past crime. They tend to be the kind who pretty much doesn't care. They figure that someone else will take care of the victim as they make their getaway."

"And that didn't happen either until it was already too late," I lamented.

"Unfortunately, no. Then there is always the person who honestly is not aware that they hit anyone."

"But, how could you hit someone and not even know about it?" I asked somewhat confused by the likelihood of something like that even being a possibility.

"All kinds of things happen that distract people behind the wheel. Have you taken driver's education yet?" he asked.

"Yes. I'm working on getting all my hours logged so I can get my license."

"Ok, what happened to your friend is one of the reasons that many of us in law enforcement are pushing for laws to ban driver held cell phones, ear phones with music blasting away, texting while driving, and stuff like that. It's way too easy to get dangerously distracted," he said somewhat sternly.

"I know. I hear about that all the time from my parents too," I replied.

"Good! Glad to hear it. However, you aren't here for a lecture on safety. You're here to check out your friend's bike. I'm sorry, Jeremy, but I just can't allow it. As much as I would like to under the circumstances, we don't allow anybody in there except for authorized personnel and with good reason. Everything in there is evidence in some kind of a crime. It either has been or will be tested by forensics. In the case of your buddy's bike, they've already checked it over for car paint, fingerprints, and anything else that might happen to appear on it. That evidence just cannot be tampered with or possibly be destroyed or altered. I'm sure you understand the reasoning here. We're talking about evidence in a criminal trial."

"I guess. I don't like it, but I do see what you're saying. Except, why fingerprints? There probably wouldn't be anyone one's on it except Scott's," I said.

"You never know in a case like this. Just suppose, for instance, that the person who hit him stopped and saw that Scott appeared to be pretty much a goner and probably couldn't be helped, so he picked up the bike out of the street and stashed it next to the body where it was partially hidden between that fire hydrant and bush and then made his escape? The person's finger prints could be all over it. As I said, Jeremy, I would love to be able to let you through that door behind me, but I just can't."

I thanked Captain Merton and walked out the door and into the hall. Scott disappeared for a few seconds while I talked to the captain but had returned.

"The skate park is just two miles from here," he said all kind of excited and breathless. "Get your butt down there and wait for me. I'm gonna get into that evidence room—almost legally. There's a forensics guy out in the lobby waiting for an escort in to look at some evidence from a murder scene. I'm going back to the lobby right now and wait with him. I'm walking in with him when he does. So get out of here! I'll catch up with you at the park."

Instead of heading out right away like he told me to do, I hung back out of sight and watched. It wasn't long before I saw Scott heading for the door behind two people. Only problem was the forensics techie and his escort shut the door practically in Scott's face before he could slip in with them. So what did he do? He flipped the guy the bird and just walked through the wall. That doof could have done that right from the beginning. I didn't know whether to be mad at him or just laugh.

So, anyway, I rode my BMX down to the skate park and worked on a couple of the tricks that I'd been trying to perfect. It turned into pretty much a disaster. My mind wasn't on it at all so I sat down at one of the tables by myself and waited. Maybe a half hour after I sat down Scott showed up.

"Dude! It worked! I went in with them and checked out my bike," Scott yelled out at me as he popped a wheelie just before he slid to a stop in front of me.

"So, tell me. What happened!"

"The lab tech was a young guy. Probably brand new on the job because they didn't seem to know him around there. So after you left, I just sat down with him and waited for our escort. Almost immediately a uniformed lady cop came along and asked if he were Mr. Branson and if he had ID. He told her he was, showed his ID, and away we went. I tagged along a short ways behind them. Hey! I actually behaved myself. Amazing! Not nearly as much fun screwing around unless you're there to appreciate it."

"Yeah, right! And you're also lying through your teeth. I stayed right there and watched when you just walked through the wall after they shut the door in your face," I answered as sarcastically as I could. "Why didn't you do that right from the start?"

Scott continued with a skunk-eating grin on his face, "You weren't supposed to see that. I guess I wanted it to be us getting in there together like my mentor said, but we were getting desperate."

"Yeah, so forget about your mentor's orders. What happened?"

"I stuck with them like glue so I'd know where to go. That lady cop walked us down the steps, through a door and down a hall. At the end she took out a set of keys and unlocked a door and let us in. The room was dark, musty, and huge. She started flipping on lights and then I could see how immense the place is. It looks like an underground parking garage filled with all kinds of vehicles, boats, motorcycles, snow mobiles—you name it."

"Boats?" I asked.

"Yeah. That even surprised the lab tech, Branson. He asked the police lady, 'Surprised to see something like that here. We don't have any big lakes around this neck of the woods. Makes you question how on earth a speedboat could be used in a crime right here in the middle of town?'"

"So, what'd she say?" I asked.

"That's when the cop lady said, 'Believe it or not, the Narcs confiscated that boat as the perps unloaded it into the river down by the dam. They filled it with marijuana and planned to take it about twenty miles downriver to a little marina where they could distribute their goodies from there.'"

"Then Branson asked her, 'How did you ever get wind of that deal? How innocent looking could that be just unloading your boat at the public dock on the river?' She looked at him and kinda shook her head and said, 'Jealous gang member. You wouldn't believe how stupid some of these crooks are. Three guys worked together on this drug deal and two of them decided to cut the third one out. It made him all mad so he stormed into the police station and reported them for stealing from him. We had him cooling his heels in a jail cell waiting for his buddies when they were brought in.'"

"Finally the lady cop showed us the evidence Branson was looking for, 'Ok, here's the baseball bat that she allegedly used on her husband. There's blood, brains, hair and bone all over it. Be careful not to destroy or mess up anything. You can take it into lab number three right over there.' She told him. 'Do you see that little office over by the big ramp door that opens to the street? I have some paper work to take care of so I'll be working on the computer in there. When you're ready to leave, let me know and I'll let you out.'"

"So how did you find your bike?" I asked wanting him to get back to the whole point of his being there.

Scott stared off into space real calm and quiet like for a second or two and then answered, "It sits right out in the open about twenty feet from where we stood. You know, I thought I had prepared myself emotionally, but I guess I hadn't really. The bike's literally covered with my blood, dirt, scratches, and some other crud that doesn't show up on my third dimensional bike—like maybe brain gunk. Really kind of bothered me. Anyway, probably the most important thing as far as we're concerned is the blue paint that I saw. That's new. The car had to be blue that hit me."

As Scott described the bike, I saw the accident flash in my mind again. Only this time it seemed like I stood right there between the hydrant and the bush and watched it happen. When the car hit him, Scott and his bike flew through the air and then skidded across about five feet of pavement, bounced over the curb head first, and both he and the bike landed in a heap in the broken glass with Scott tangled up in it. Nobody had told me the complete story. Yes, he had bled to death wrapped up in his bike, but he also had a crushed skull, broken neck and dislocated shoulder from when his head and upper body hit the curb. If Scott had lived, he would have been a human vegetable.

Suddenly I felt a gentle arm on my shoulder kind of holding me up, "Sorry, Buddy. You just watched the accident as it really happened in a vision, didn't you? I didn't want you to see that. Nobody did. The Rents and authorities decided not to tell you the whole truth. Nobody knew all the details except for me, them, and the police. They wanted to protect you. Why do you have to be so damned sensitive to my spirit anyway? I didn't want you to know about that part either."

I don't know when I'd ever seen Scott as kind, caring and gentle as he acted that day there in the bike park. We'd always loved, protected, and supported each other as best friends and practically brothers, but not quite like that. Neither of us told any jokes, used any cut downs, or made fun of the situation, nothing like that. He acted extremely concerned about me and my feelings, and I appreciated it.

"Scottie, so that's why everyone told me that I would have not been able to save you even if I had been there. You actually died before you and the bike even totally stopped," I said almost in a whisper.

"That's right. That's why you have to let go of the guilt. You couldn't have helped me, and there's always the possibility that you could have been hit right along with me. I just wish you hadn't seen this. However, at least now maybe you'll understand."

"As stupid as it may sound, I actually feel better knowing now that there was no way I could have saved you. It happened. There's no reversing it. I don't feel guilty any more. However, it makes me even more determined to find the bastard that did this to you and why."

Well, that took care of Scott's trip to the evidence garage to check out his bike. We didn't learn a whole lot regarding the vehicle that hit him other that it had blue paint. I could have lived a long time without seeing the really gory part of the accident in my vision, but I did, and maybe it's for the best. So, then the question became, what do we do next?

Chapter 7

Weeks passed and we were no further ahead than when Scott discovered the blue paint on his bike at the evidence garage. He and I sat on the patio trying to decide what to do. It was Wednesday and the last week of summer break. School started up again the following week. Where did the summer go? Scottie's guardian figured he gave us plenty of time to figure it out, and I promised Mom and Dad that I would give up the search when school started. Not having a clue as to our next step, we just sat there and talked until Mom came out the door with her purse in her hand.

"Jeremy, get in the car – driver's side," she commanded.

"Mom! Not now. I'm really busy."

"You aren't doing a thing. You have to log a whole ton of hours behind the wheel before you can get your license. The way we're going, we'll both be old and senile before you finish them."

"Ok," I answered grudgingly sneaking a look at Scott. I sure didn't want to do this especially if he went along for the ride, and I knew darned well there'd be no getting rid of him.

"Yahoo!" Scott yelled. "This is precious. I get to ride along and go crusin' with clutsy boy behind the wheel, and he can't say a bitching thing about it. Awesome!" With that he laughed uproariously as he whacked me on the back like the damn fool thought it was actually funny.

The three of us climbed into the car. Scott managed to do it without opening or closing the back door. He just ended up there somehow. I hooked my seat belt and adjusted the mirrors. Scottie sat right on the edge of the seat dead center in the middle with a huge devilish grin on his face.

"Is everyone sitting back in their seat with their seatbelt fastened?" I asked out loud as I glared at him.

"What are you talking about, Dear? It's just you and me, and both our seatbelts are hooked."

"Nothing, Mom. Don't pay any attention to me. I'm just going through my mental checklist before we start. You know how it is, seat belts, mirrors, seat adjustments, and all that."

"Quit being such a rag," Scott piped up. "I don't have to sit back and wear my seat belt because I'm already dead so it doesn't matter. I'm gonna sit right up here where I can watch you like a hawk. Both hands on the steering wheel, rookie. Let's go! Don't run over the mail box backing out. Look out!"

Would he ever shut up? Some things just never changed. It would have been the same thing if he were alive. He'd sit in the back seat hassling continuously and laughing nonstop. He could be the biggest pain at times—especially when Dad wasn't in the car. Mom tended to ignore his goofing off.

We drove the back streets at first and hadn't been gone too long when we started over an overpass only a few miles from home.

"Germy! Germy! Germy! You didn't look for the ice. It says right there to watch for ice on the overpass."

"It's August, you idiot. You don't see any ice, do you?"

"Jeremy, what are you talking about now?"

"Nothing, Mom. I just saw that sign and thought that it seemed really kind of stupid to have a 'Watch for ice on the overpass' sign out here at the end of August."

"Well, those signs are up there year around. It just wouldn't be practical to change them with the seasons," she replied.

"I suppose," I replied feeling a little stupid.

"Good save, Bro," Scott chirped in my ear. "You almost blew it didn't you?"

I gave Scott another dirty look in the mirror and continued down the road as he laughed hysterically. The next thing I knew Scott had his pants down and mooned a school bus that drove along beside us. "Knock it off!" I said under my breath as I started laughing.

"Jeremy, you're worrying me this afternoon! What's distracting you this time?"

"You see that school bus that drove along beside us until it turned on that last street?"

"Yes, I would imagine it's running through its route getting ready for next week. What about it?"

"I know, but it reminded me of something. Last year when Scott and I went to a basketball game with Brad and Mike, Scott mooned the opposing team's cheerleader's bus. The girls all screamed with their hands over their mouths and eyes glued on his butt."

"That's terrible! I never heard about that stunt," Mom replied not really knowing whether to laugh or get mad.

"And who do you really think would ever tell you?" I asked.

"Probably nobody unless you had been reported to the principal or stopped by the police. And, what were you doing while he pulled this stunt?"

"Rolling in the seat laughing."

"Big mouth! That has to be one of the biggest lies you've ever told about me. I'm crushed! You've probably ruined my reputation with your mother now," Scott whined in the back seat. I just looked at him and smiled my most evil grin.

While I smirked at Scott, he and Mom both started yelling at the same time. I completely ran a stop sign. Never saw it. I was so busy watching Scott's reaction to the mooning fairy-tale, I missed it completely. Fortunately for all of us, no cars came from the other way and collided with us.

"Shit!" I yelled out loud as I slammed on the brake and stopped in the middle of the street. "I told you I didn't want to do this today!" I yelled at Mom as I threw open the door and jumped out. I slammed the door shut hard enough to rock the car, and started walking down the street.

"Jeremy! What are you doing? Where do you think you're going? You can't just stop in the middle of the street, get out of the car, and take off on foot. You're miles from home. Come back here!"

"I'm walking home. Just slide over to the driver's seat and take the car home and leave me alone. I'll get there when I get there."

"Germy! Wait for me," Scott yelled as he ran after me. He laughed so hard his sides ached when he caught up. I'm surprised he didn't piss his pants. "That's priceless! You stopped right in the middle of the street and deserted the car. Your mom thinks you've completely gone off your rocker. I love it! My mentor told me this morning that this would be a good week, but I had no idea how good."

"Your fault, Scott! If you hadn't ridden along and hassled me every second, it never would have happened. I hope you're happy. I'll never get my license now. They'll never let me drive again."

We probably walked a couple miles, and I started getting hot and thirsty. By then I'd stopped being so mad at him, and we both laughed about what happened, the look on Mom's face, and what would probably be said when I walked into the house. We decided right then and there to practice only communicating telepathically from then on so maybe we could avoid people listening to one side of our conversations accidentally like Mom had. Suddenly, we saw a lady watering her flowers in the front yard.

"Ma'am, would you mind terribly if I took a quick drink out of your garden hose? We've, I mean, I've been walking a while and I'm hot and thirsty."

"Of course not," she said as she handed me the hose. "I have some fresh lemonade in the house if you'd prefer that."

"No, the water's fine. Thanks," I said as a little boy about three or four years old came around the corner of the house.

"Hey! It's my little buddy, Bobby," Scott called out.

"Scottie!" Bobby called out as he ran across the yard. Scott knelt down on one knee and they gave each other a big hug.

"Oh, I'm sorry!" The lady said as I slurped another drink. "Bobby has an imaginary friend out at the cemetery that he talks to all the time when I go out to my husband's grave. He doesn't remember his dad. One of those homemade bombs exploded in Iraq and killed him when Bobby was only nine months old. So when I go out to visit, he wanders over to visit the grave of that teenager who died in the hit and run accident in June. I told him that the boy's name was Scott, so he pretends to know him and talk to him. This is the first time he's ever done it outside of the cemetery. I'm terribly embarrassed."

"Don't be. I think it's kind of cool. Scott was my best friend," I told her as I aimed the hose at him and blasted him with water.

"Oh, I'm sorry!" she said. "I probably shouldn't have mentioned that."

"That's ok," I said. "I'm dealing with it a little better now," as I 'accidentally' aimed the hose at Scott again.

"Cute, Germy, but that water has no effect on me. Nothing like it would if I grabbed the hose and squirted you. How would you explain that? Huh? Huh?"

I handed the hose back to the lady, "Oh, that's quite a scar he has on his neck," I commented. "Looks pretty new. What happened?"

"It's really quite a coincidence. His accident happened the same day that your friend Scott died. He wanted a drink of water, and he really loves to drink out of actual glass glasses instead of the plastic ones I always give him. I had been cleaning house and probably not paying as much attention to him as I should have been. He climbed up on the counter and tried to get one out of the cupboard.

"Apparently, when he reached up for a glass, he slipped and fell. The glass broke on the edge of the sink, and Bobby landed in a heap on the floor in the middle of it. He ended up with a jagged cut on his neck and it bled terribly. I'm a nurse, so I knew I didn't have time to wait for an ambulance so I grabbed a wet towel, wrapped it around his neck, picked him up, and ran to the car."

"You must have been scared to death," I replied.

"That's putting it mildly. I couldn't lose him. I lost my husband, and I wasn't going to lose my child. I raced down the side streets as fast as I could. I knew there would be little traffic going that way. I almost made it there when Bobby started having a seizure apparently caused by his loss of blood. I know I swerved all over the road when I grabbed him. The emergency room doctors told me it was a good thing I did what I did because in another two minutes, Bobby would have been gone."

"That's terrible," I said just visualizing what she had gone through.

We talked for a while longer and then I decided that it was time to leave.

 "Well, I need to keep going. Thanks for the drink. And, oh by the way, I sure am glad that Bobby came through the accident ok."

"Me too. I wouldn't have been able to handle it if he hadn't. Eventually everything will be fine. The doctors even said that the scar will fade with time too," she said as I started out towards the street to catch up with Scott who was saying goodbye to Bobby.

"Bobby, next time you come out to the cemetery, I might not be there. I'll probably be gone. Just remember to always be good to your mommy and don't do anything stupid where you will get hurt real bad again,"

"Bye, Scottie! I wuv you." Fortunately, they had walked far enough away so Bobby's mom couldn't hear them talking.

"How creepy does that feel?" Scottie asked as soon as we were alone. "He almost died because of a glass cut to his neck, and I did. Different deal, but, whoa! So close and so related."

"I'll bet that's why he can see and hear you too—it's the bond the two of you share. Face it, the two of you sure do share a lot. How eerie is that?"

It took us a little while to get back to my house. We talked about that and a lot of things mostly unrelated to his accident. We avoided the topic more and more it seemed. When we were just a door or two away, Scott said he was leaving and would meet me in the morning out at his place. The big coward didn't want to go in and hear Mom's rant about my stopping the car in the middle of the road and walking home. Neither did I.

She stood in the kitchen in front of the stove getting dinner around when I walked in. I talked fast and furiously, "Mom, don't say a word. Just listen for a minute," I said before she had a chance to start yelling at me. "I'm sorry! I know I did something really stupid. However, that walk home did me a lot of good. I learned some things about myself, about life, and about priorities. The summer is over so tomorrow morning I'm going to make one last trip out to the cemetery to say goodbye, and that will be it. From then on I'll just go on special occasions like Memorial Day, his birthday, and occasional visits just to say hi to him. If you want to ground me or punish me some other way, that's fine, but you have to understand I need to make that one last visit tomorrow morning."

Mom walked over and took me in her arms and just hugged me with tears running down her face. I think maybe she knew or felt something that she didn't mention out loud. She kissed me on top of the head and told me she loved me and to get cleaned up for dinner.

...

However, summer wasn't over yet, and Scott and I weren't done. I lied. Big deal! We still had the weekend. Saturday morning found Scottie and me at the mall food court killing time wondering if we had finally come to the end of the line trying to piece together what exactly had happened with Scott's accident and why. We spent most of our time together since the funeral looking and all we had really come up with was the fact that he'd been hit by a blue car.

"School starts up again on Monday. When are you leaving, Scott?" I asked feeling pretty down.

"Probably today or tomorrow. I don't know. When my mentor told me this would be a good week I thought he meant we'd find out what happened. Guess that isn't what he meant. I'm kinda bummed out about that."

"Me too, damn it!"

Right about that time we heard this kid crying and carrying on and some woman yell out, "Bobby, in about two seconds I'm going to blister your butt right here in the middle of the mall if you don't straighten up!"

Scott and I looked at each other and grinned as we both jumped up and headed to the rescue.

"Hi Bobby! Remember me? Come here and say hi!" I called clapping my hands together as I squatted down on one knee. He ran and jumped into my arms. I picked him up and whispered into his ear, "Remember Scott's a secret. We can't talk to him out loud. Just talk to him with your head."

Bobby laid his head on my shoulder and zeroed in on Scott who stood behind me and kept Bobby's attention acting goofy while I talked to his mom.

"Looks like it's one of those days," I smiled as I focused my attention on her.

"You have no idea. I dragged Bobby out of bed earlier than normal this morning so I could finish my shopping before noon. It's my dad's birthday, and Mom's throwing him a surprise party this afternoon. I worked every day this week, and I just didn't have time before now. So what happens? Bobby ends up all cranky and out of control at the worst possible moment. Fortunately I finished everything before that happened and only have to go home now and put Bobby down for a nap before we have to leave. Could I possibly impose on you to walk out to my car with us and tend to Bobby while I haul all this stuff?"

"Sure! No problem! I was just hanging out anyway waiting for some of my friends to show up," I lied as we headed for the parking lot.

When we finally made it out to the car, Bobby's head was still on my shoulder and he acted half asleep while he and Scott jabbered at each other telepathically. When Bobby's mom put her packages in the trunk, Scottie said to Bobby, "Ask that guy to look at the 'Boo Boo' on the door that you just showed me."

I had just put Bobby down so he could get into his car seat in the back when he pointed out the car's scratch to Scott while we waited for his mom to get the trunk loaded.

"Hey, Guy!" Bobby yelled out to me. "Look at the 'Boo Boo' on my door!"

His mom and I walked over to see what Bobby was talking about. The blue car door had a major scratch on it with a couple of specks of red paint showing.

"What caused this?" I asked after Scott told me telepathically to find out how that had happened.

"It happened on the day of Bobby's accident," she said. "I never noticed it until the next day when Bobby saw it and showed me the car's 'Boo Boo' as he always calls it just like he did to you just now."

After looking at it, I said, "I know if I had been driving with all that going on with Bobby, I probably could have hit something like a car door opening or a mail box and never realize it. I could have put this scratch in the door and then wondered how it happened," I said trying to fish for information.

"I think the little ding here happened in the emergency room parking lot. I didn't end up real straight in my parking place and I figure somebody with a red car clipped me. There's just a little speck or two of red paint embedded in one of those scratches."

"You call the police?"

"No! What would they have done? I didn't even see it until the next day, and the car that hit me didn't leave a note or anything so it would have been futile. I just haven't had it fixed yet because I have a five-hundred dollar deductable policy, and that's approximately what it's going to cost to fix, so I'm just waiting. No hurry. It isn't hurting anything."

"Dude! Let's get out of here now. We need to talk," Scott hollered over to me.

I helped her get Bobby into his harness in the back seat and all strapped in. I gave him a little hug goodbye which gave me a second to whisper to him. "You and Scott have a good time?" I asked. He gave me that big Bobby grin and nodded his head. Then he told Scott goodbye telepathically. I told him that my name is Jeremy and to have fun at the birthday party.

…

"Oh, boy!" Scottie said as we headed out of the mall parking lot. "Now we know what happened and why. You know this happened just way too easy, don't you? We've always said that we didn't put a whole lot of faith in coincidences. Well, I don't think this was a coincidence either. I know damn well my mentor's behind it somehow. He said I'd have a good week. Well, when you ran that stop sign back there a couple of days ago, I thought that was it, but now I just know that he knew we'd discover the circumstances around my accident this week. I just know he set this up! "

"What the hell are we going to do? Should I notify the damn cops? I could send an anonymous note for them to compare the red paint on her door with your bicycle that's sitting in the impounded lot," I stated not knowing exactly how I felt about it. My head spun out of control. I didn't know what to do.

"Why do anything? She obviously doesn't know that she hit me. If she knew it when it happened, she would have stopped and tried to help, and Bobby would have died too—that's the irony of the whole thing. Then there would have been two deaths instead of one as a result of the accident. If the cops knocked at her door now and did paint tests and found out that it was my bike's paint on her door, what would that accomplish except to fill her full of guilt and remorse for the rest of her life?"

"Yeah, but both of our parents are obsessing over not knowing who or why."

"Do they really need that wound opened up again in their lives with some kind of dumb ass trial that wouldn't solve anything anyway? Does that lady really need it with all she's gone through? And what about Bobby? What would it do to him? He could end up in a foster home or something if she went to jail. Do we want that?"

"No, not at all. Yet everyone needs for it to be over so they can move on. I just don't know about not telling anyone. I need to think about this one. What's more fair for your parents? Knowing all the details once and for all or never knowing and always wondering?"

As we headed for my house, we rehashed a lot of our antics growing up and laughed together comfortably for really the first time since his death. It felt like something huge had lifted off our shoulders. I could finally accept Scott's accident and start to move on with my life. We agreed to meet out at the cemetery on Sunday for one last get-together before he moved on as well.

Chapter 8

The next morning I jumped on my bike and headed for the cemetery. It seemed like a much longer ride than normal. Needless to say I dreaded what we both knew had to happen. Scott would be leaving for good. When I rode up the hill, Scott sat on his new headstone with Mooshy curled up beside it. Workers placed it there the day before while we were gone.

"Check it out, Bro! They etched my handsome face in stone."

Sure enough, not only did the monument have his name with date of birth and death, but also his school picture from last year engraved in color on the black, smooth, marble face of the stone. It looked really impressive as far as tomb stones go.

"Scott, you know that picture flatters the hell out of you. You never looked that good in your life," I had to rip on him. Couldn't let him get a big head.

"Jealousy will get you nowhere, Germy. You know I've always been such a handsome devil!" he laughed as he gave me a little shove for emphasis.

As I stuck my finger down my throat and fake gagged, we both sat down laughing.

"Jeremy, we need to talk serious-like now," Scott started after we settled down a bit.

"Scott, hold it! I think that's the first time you've called me Jeremy since you died. I might be wrong, but I've been kind of thinking about it and paying attention."

"I know, but this is important. You know I have to leave now. I'm not sure how it's supposed to happen, but that's the deal I made with my guardian. He gave us all summer to figure it out, and we did. He hasn't told me a whole lot yet. He said he would tell me more when I joined them for good on the other side. However, this is what I know. Someday every living being that I have ever known and loved will be with me again. So if it takes seventy or eighty years, it won't matter. I won't be aware of the passage of time. You will, but I won't."

"Will you ever come back? Is this the last time that I will see you until I die? I don't think I can handle losing you a second time. The one thing I regret the most is that I never told you how much our almost being twin brothers meant to me," I said sitting there broken-hearted.

"I never told you either, but we both knew it. Remember the other day when I told you that if you really need me to just call. Well, something tells me that I will probably see a lot of you as time goes on since you have this knack for being 'curious' and getting your dumb ass in trouble," he laughed.

We talked a while longer and Scott finally said, "You know, whatever you decide to do about reporting the accident is strictly up to you. I vote for not telling anyone, but you have to do what works best for you."

"Thanks. I don't really know what I'm going to do right now," I answered.

We talked a while longer, and suddenly Scott acted a little distracted. "What's going on, Scott? What are you looking at?"

 "Listen! Jeremy, this is it. Mooshy and I are out of here!"

"Scott, don't go yet! Scott? Scott? I'm not ready."

Scott vanished. Just like that. I didn't know what to do. The whole thing happened so suddenly. We knew that it was coming, but we didn't know when or how. I didn't even get to say goodbye—just like when he died. I sat with my knees up and put my head down on them feeling crushed that I didn't get to tell Scott more.

I don't know how long I sat there with the tears flowing, when suddenly there was a jolt. Mooshy licked me all over my face and washed the tears away. He slobbered all over my eyes, my ears, my face, and even my mouth. I looked up and cried out, "Mooshy!" as he attacked. That's when he stuck his tongue in my mouth. Then he knocked me over on my back and drooled and spit all over my face again—just like he always did any time either Scott or I were upset.

"Germy! Get up!" Scott finally said laughing and calling Mooshy off. "We only have two minutes, and then I'm out of here again.

So, listen up! When Mooshy and I went back just now, the first person I saw was your grandma. She gave me a big hug and said to tell you that she's happy and well—no more arthritis, no more pain. She's the only person I ever knew who died so I guess that's why I didn't see anyone else right away except for my guardian.

"Anyway, Grandma told me to bring you a message so that's why I'm back. She said to tell you that you have a special sensitivity or ability. It runs in your family on your mom's side. It goes way back for generations. Some of your ancestors had it stronger than others. She said that the family thought the sensitivity was dying out because her mother had more sensitivity than she did, and your mom has less sensitivity than she. Anyway, then you come along with the strongest sensitivity of any of the recent generations of your family. That's why you have been able to see your grandma and me after we died. She said that it's up to you to learn how to deal with it and just don't be afraid and don't fight it. Then my guardian also told me a couple of more things so pay attention!"

"I'm listening," I said not knowing really what else to say.

"Like I told you earlier, he reminded me again just now before I came back that I do have to leave now, and I'm not actually supposed to come back unless there is an emergency or something special going on where you really, really need help or just need to deal with some serious problem. He's not talking about you being lonesome or flunking an algebra test and afraid to tell your parents, or flailing on your back when you're about to get your ass pinned on the wrestling mat, I'm talking about some real, bona fide crisis where you need help."

"So tell me. When and how can I get a hold of you?"

"If you ever get into a situation where you have to have me, all you have to do is call and I'll be there. By the way, I can just show up if my mentor or I feel that maybe I need to, and for some reason or the other, I get a feeling that might be fairly often for a while. Now, give me and Mooshy both a hug 'cause it's time for us to leave. Jeremy, like I told you a few minutes ago, some day, seventy or eighty years from now, we'll be together on the other side—not until then. Got it? Don't do anything stupid! Until then keep it in mind—I'll be here if and when you really need me. Remember, ole buddy. We've always been more than just friends, we're damned near twins. We were inseparable in life and I wanna keep it that way!"

I grabbed a hold of him and hugged him as hard as I could—trying to hold on to him and keep him from going, I guess. He and Mooshy started to fade.

"Bye, Scott. Bye Mooshy! Tell Grandma I love her too. Until then..." and they were gone again. I smiled. This has been the damndest experience I've ever had or heard of. I looked over to where Scott had parked his bike. It too had disappeared. He said he wouldn't need it any more, until maybe next time.

So there you have it. I told you at the beginning that I had a story to tell that I'd been keeping bottled up inside of me all summer. I spent the time communicating and working with my best friend who had died. We had to find out what had happened to him, and we did through determination and a lot of good luck and probably a lot of help from his mentor. Whether or not I ever see or talk to Scottie again is pretty much up in the air, I guess.

What is for sure is that Scott will always be there with me in mind and spirit as I move on, and move on I must. There are still some issues that I need to come to grips with, and it won't be easy, but at least now I think I can get my life back to normal. However, school is starting up again next week and that leads to a whole new set of problems to deal with. I'll have to meet new friends and find a different bunch of people to hang with. It's always been me and Scott, and now it's just me and whoever comes into my life next.

Chapter 9

Can you believe it? Mom and Dad plan to go to State's football game this afternoon, and I'm at home lying on my bed staring at the ceiling. Some friends of theirs were given four tickets to the game so they invited the Rents. You know I had to give them a little bit of a hard time. After all, I'm the kid. I'm the one who should be going to the game. When they started taking on a little bit of a guilt trip, I just laughed at them and told them I was joking and to have a good time.

Lying here on my bed with nothing to do, I started thinking. Yesterday Mom Sara came over again to talk to Mom. She was all bummed out and crying when she walked in the door. Sounded like a lot of it had to do with not knowing who killed Scottie and why they would just leave and not try to help. I lay low as usual, kept out of sight, and just listened. She said that everyone kind of ignored the topic of Scott and she wanted to talk about him. She wanted to remember the good times, the funny times, the goofy times when he did the darndest things out of the blue.

She even complained about me a little, "Jeremy has not been over to the house unless he was with you or Ted since Scott died. He would always just walk in and I miss that. He lived there as much as he did here, and now I don't even see him."

"I know," Mom told her. "He's having a hard time. He can't seem to express his feelings. He's keeping it all bottled up inside. I worry about him."

The Rents were obsessing about me again. Maybe the time had come to get my head out of my butt because I missed them too. I always considered Mom Sara and Jim Dad as my parents as much as I did my real ones. They were right. I wasn't being fair.

I slipped around the corner from where I was hiding and listening, "Hi, Mom! Hi, Mom Sara! What's happening?"

They both looked up and greeted me with smiles and "Hi's!"

"I heard your voices and something popped into my head. Remember that time when I got locked in the neighbor's garage and you had the police out looking for me, and the neighbor came home and opened the door to pull his car in and I sat in there bawling?"

"Yes," they both said together giving me their expectant motherly looks.

"Scott did that. We were in that garage snooping around. The neighbors left it open when they went to work so we walked in. There were all kinds of tools and junk to look at. I wandered to the back by the work bench and he played around up by the front by the door. So what'd he do? He upped and started pushing buttons. I don't really think he knew what he was doing, he just did it. The door started coming down so he ran outside leaving me stuck inside. He yelled through the door to push the button, but it was dark in there and I couldn't find it. So what did the maggot do? He went home and left me there. He didn't tell anyone where I was because he didn't want to get into trouble."

"He knew where you were all that time?" Mom asked. "That little brat! He even walked along with me part of the time while I looked for you and called out your name."

"So, while we're playing true confessions here," Mom Sara laughed, "What really happened the night when Scott went out the bedroom window and landed in the snow bank? I don't think we ever heard the full story on that one either."

"Well, you kind of did," I said. "Kinda… We had the window open and pulled up the screen. There was that ledge under the window with good packing snow on it. We leaned out, made snowballs and threw them at our house. We tried to see who could get the closest to hitting my bedroom window without actually doing it."

"My! That was clever!" Mom said.

"I know," I laughed. "Scott actually hit the window with a snowball. That's when I pulled the waist band on his pajama bottoms back and shoved a snowball down there. He screamed and did a half gainer right into the snow bank under the window."

It was funny in the re-telling several years after the fact. Scott could have been seriously injured. However, when you're that young, you don't think of those things. We thought it was funny then, and I guess I still do. Amazingly, neither one of us ever held a grudge. I didn't on the garage caper, and he didn't on the nose dive out of the window.

I guess we sat around for another hour telling "Remember when?" stories and laughing before Mom Sara had to go home to fix dinner for Jim Dad. I think it was a good release for all of us. We needed it.

...

Today with Mom and Dad at the game, it's time to take this thing one step farther, I thought to myself as I jumped off the bed and raced for the door with a smile on my face. My BMX sat on the patio so I hopped on and headed for the store. The Mini Mart was probably a mile away from our house. That's where Scott was going the day he died. I grabbed a large bag of chocolate chips and a bag of unshelled walnuts off the shelf, paid for them, and headed back home. As soon as I parked my BMX, I went next door and walked into Scott's house through the back door just like I had done all my life—except for the past few months. I knew his mom was home all by herself because I saw his dad leave earlier.

"Mom Sara, where are you?" I yelled as I started walking through the house looking for her. I tossed the chips and nuts on the counter in the kitchen on my way through.

"Jeremy, honey, I'm right here," she said as she came around the corner from the living room. She grabbed me and we hugged each other for some time. There might have been a couple of tears too. "I've missed you so much. You have no idea."

"Yes I do. I've missed you and Jim Dad too, but I just didn't know if I would be completely welcome or not."

"You will always be welcome here at any time. There doesn't have to be a reason. Just come on in."

"Well, there is a reason I came over this time. Come on out to the kitchen with me for a minute," I said as she followed me out. "Mom, I'm in terrible need of hot chocolate chip cookies and cold milk. My mom and dad abandoned me today and went to the football game and I'm in dire straits."

"That's kind of right where we left off three months ago, isn't it?"

"Yes it is, and I haven't had any chocolate chip cookies since, and I want some now. Are you going to make them?"

"Of course! Sit down, start shelling those walnuts, and talk to me while I get things started."

We hadn't been gabbing too long when Mom Sara asked, "Jeremy, how could anyone hit a person on their bike and then just keep going like nothing had happened? How could a person even live with himself?"

Oh boy! Now what would I say? I knew what happened, yet Scott was adamant about not telling anyone. All it would do is re-open all those wounds and it wouldn't solve a thing.

"I've been thinking," I told her. "I wonder if there's any possibility that the person who hit him doesn't even know they did it."

"I don't know how that could be. I find that awfully hard to swallow. However, the police said essentially the same thing. Yet, there had to be damage to someone's car. Somebody has unexplained red paint on a fender or door and they have to wonder where it came from," she continued.

"I know. Yet if they've rationalized the damage to their car somehow in their mind, they could be completely clueless as to how it actually happened. Cars get all kinds of dings in parking lots when people carelessly throw open their doors."

Finally we strayed off that topic and talked and laughed just like old times about nothing of any great importance until the first batch of cookies sat in front of me.

As I gnawed on the fourth or fifth one, she turned a little serious on me again.

"Jeremy, have you noticed anything different about the way I look?" she asked.

"No, not a thing," I answered not having a clue what she was getting at. I hadn't really seen her for three months until yesterday.

"I asked Scott to go get the chocolate chips for a reason. I'd planned on the two of you to sit down at the table and stuff your faces while I told you the news," she said with a half smile on her face.

"What news is that?" I asked completely confused by then.

"Jim and I are having a baby," she said. "When the accident happened we had just found out for sure and we wanted to tell the two of you together. We wanted you two to be the first to know. We didn't think we would ever have another baby. We tried for years and nothing happened, so after we gave up and quit trying, Bingo! I'm five months along now and starting to show big time. You thought I was just getting fat, didn't you?" she teased as she pulled the loose blouse tight so I could see the bulge in her belly.

"Honest! I hadn't noticed. That's great. Do you know what the baby is going to be yet?"

"Yes, it's going to be a girl. But to be perfectly truthful with you, I'm scared to death."

"Why? Everything is ok with the baby isn't it?"

"Yes, but with what happened to Scott, I can't help but worry.

When she said that, I faded out for who knows how long. Another one of those visions popped into my head and this time it wasn't something bad. I was sitting on our patio when a car pulled in the driveway next door. A man and woman in their thirties and two little kids jumped out of the car and headed for the door. The man didn't look familiar at all, but the woman almost resembled Scott. She was a little shorter and a bit lighter than Scott, but there seemed to be a family similarity. Mom Sara and Jim Dad stood just outside the door and waited with open arms as the little kids ran toward them, "Grandma! Grandma! Did you make cookies?" one of them cried out as they ran to their grandma and grandpa.

"I sure did, Sweetie. I made chocolate chip cookies just for you guys," she said laughing. Then she looked up and said, "Hi, Emily. Hi Zack! Good to see you too."

"Jeremy! Jeremy! Are you okay?" Mom Sara asked as she shook me awake.

"You seemed to have kind of zoned out there for a few seconds. It's like you were in a trance or something. Is there anything wrong? Are you okay?"

"No, nothing's wrong, nothing at all," I smiled. "Don't ask me how I know, but you're going to be baking chocolate chip cookies for kids and grandkids forever. Emily's gonna be just fine. Trust me."

"For some unknown reason or the other I do, and don't ask me why, but suddenly I feel much better about her now. Another thing I know is that you and your mom don't always tell everything that goes on in those heads of yours either, do you? I never told either one of you the baby's name is Emily, but you both seemed to know."

I just smiled not knowing what to say so I didn't say anything. She was absolutely correct. Right then Jim Dad walked in and saved the day for me. "Hi, Dad!" I said smiling.

He walked over and gave me a big hug and said, "How's my boy? I've missed you."

I guessed we talked for close to an hour and polished off most of the cookies between us when he said, "You know. The way things are going you aren't ever going to that license. I think we should go for a ride. Go get that log of yours and meet me in the car. I'll give you two minutes, 1001...1002...1003"

I bolted out the door laughing and made it back with my log with time to spare. I guess we drove for almost two hours before returning. No incidents, no problems, no Scott in the back seat harassing me to death. Life appeared to be getting back to normal. With all four rents helping, I should be able to accumulate enough hours for my license before my birthday in October. However, a lot of water had to cross over the dam between now and then.

Chapter 10

The first few days back in school were tougher on me than what I had figured they would be. I saw a lot of kids that I hadn't seen since school let out in June. Some of them went to Scott's funeral, but that day remained totally fogged out in my brain.

"What happened?" almost everyone asked. Like how stupid a question is that?

"Some stupid ass driver ran over Scott and killed him and then fled the scene." How else did they expect me to answer that?

What else could I say? I sure wouldn't tell them the gory details of the accident that I saw in my head. Nobody else needed to know that.

"How are you doing, Jeremy?" they would ask.

How was I doing? Absolutely wonderful! My best friend died in an accident, so I spent the entire summer with his ghost looking for the killer. When we found her, we decided not to report it to the authorities. Right! I certainly planned to tell them all about that too. I know! I know! They thought they were being kind and considerate, and they were. It was just me.

Fortunately things calmed down and the questions ended, and I could get on with my school life a bit. Eleventh grade can be a pisser especially when you cram all the really tough classes into your junior year so you can coast a bit as a senior, and that's exactly the way that Scottie and I planned it. We intended to skate through our last year taking such all-time favorites as Underwater Basket Weaving, New and Modern Techniques for Making out with the Babes, and Baking for a High Carb Diet. Ok, ok. So I'm exaggerating just a bit. You get the point.

English class would prove interesting if nothing else. My teacher doubled as my wrestling coach, and I didn't know if I planned to continue on with that or not. Let's face it, my wrestling skills were pretty run of the mill, and it's not like anyone would miss my fifty-fifty record. However, I probably would because Coach was one of these people who wanted everyone to participate, learn, get better, and have fun. He didn't believe in the win at any cost way of doing things we saw with some of the coaches. However, I decided we would deal with that decision in November.

The school year started out with a bang. On day one he assigned the *Odyssey*.

"Oh, boy. I can't wait. NOT!" I whispered to my new table partner.

Either Mr. Andrews decided to try a new teaching technique this year, or the administration stuck him with a bunch of funny little two-three person tables. Anyway, my table partner was a new kid in school who appeared to be just about my size.

"Hi!" I said to him after we both sat down, "My name is Jeremy Wright. What's yours?"

"Marty Johnson—I moved here at the beginning of this summer. I know absolutely nobody here."

Trying to be nice, I continued to whisper to him across the table. "So where you living?" I asked not really caring but trying to be sociable.

"Out on Sherman Road just down from the old abandoned one-room school house."

"Ok, I know where that is," I answered. He lived kind of out in the country away from town. "Your parents get jobs here in town? That why you moved here?"

"Not really. Bruno, my step dad, is kind of a day-laborer and has worked for the same company for a while. We just moved here 'cause it was closer to the job. Before he had to commute about an hour each way. What really sucks is the fact that my mom just up and left right after we moved here in June."

"Really!" I exclaimed. "That's just about the time my best friend Scott was killed by a hit-and-run driver. So what happened to your mom?"

"I don't really know. I came home one day and she wasn't there. I asked Bruno where she went and all he'd say was that she had left and wouldn't be coming back."

"That's all he'd say?" I asked rather dumbfounded.

"He wouldn't talk about it. Even now if I even mention it, he gets all hostile and starts threatening me. He's huge, a bully, and violent so I don't cross him if I can help it. I just kind of stay away from him as much as possible. All he ever told me was that they had a fight and she walked out."

"Why don't you leave? If he's not really your dad, can't you go someplace else like to a grandparent or someone?"

"No, not really," he said with a rather wistful look on his face.

About that time Mr. Andrews yelled at us to pay attention so we did.

We spent just about forever on the *Odyssey*. Trying to keep the names of those people straight proved to be a real picnic. I kept up with the basic story line, but exactly who did what and to whom completely soared over my head and out into space most of the time. Marty acted even more lost than me. I ended up trying to explain what I could to him and that seemed to help me.

I don't think I ever really zeroed in to what happened in the book until suddenly Odysseus visited the Underworld, the land of the dead. Then we learned that the Greek's underworld had different levels of existence. There he met and talked with all kinds of dead people including his mother. Those spirits explained things to him about what had happened in his life and why they had taken place. Whoa! That idea blew me away.

Would you believe I managed an A on the final test? After learning about the various levels of the hereafter they believed in and their ability to communicate with the dead, I totally wrapped my brain up in the book. I even went back to some of the scenes that the dead people talked about to figure out what they meant.

"Jeremy, I never dreamed you would become so engaged in this book. Any idea why?" Mr. Andrews asked as he handed back our final tests.

"Can I come in and talk with you after school tonight?" I have some questions that I don't really want to discuss in class."

"Of course! I don't have any meetings or anything, so come on in. If I'm not right here when you show up, just hang around. I'm probably down to the john or grabbing a cup of coffee out of the teacher's lounge," he said.

The day couldn't end fast enough. When the bell rang after last hour, I dumped off the stuff I didn't need for homework in my locker, and headed for Mr. Andrews's room. He hadn't shown up yet so I just looked at the bulletin board displays for the first time he had of the Odyssey. Some of those battle scenes looked pretty graphic. Chopping someone up with a sword or battle axe would be pretty gory. Yuck!

"Hi, Jeremy," Mr. Andrews said with a smile on his face and coffee cup in his hand when he strolled into the room. He acted like he was glad that the school day had ended too. "You sounded as if something might be bothering you. What's going on?"

"Nothing really serious. With Scottie gone and all that, I just find the concept of multiple levels after death and the idea of communicating with spirits really intriguing. Do you personally think anything like this is even the least bit possible?"

Mr. Andrews just kind of looked at me for a minute before answering, "Jeremy, it really doesn't matter what I believe or don't believe. There's a lot of well known literature out there that deals with spirits in a variety of different ways. I'm sure you're familiar with Dickens' *A Christmas Carol* where he communicates with the Ghosts of Christmas past, present, and future. Next spring we're going to read *Hamlet* by Shakespeare. There's a scene in there dealing with a ghost. There's the play by Henrik Ibsen called *Ghosts*. There's also the *Legend of Sleepy Hollow* by Washington Irving. And that's just off the top of my head. There are all kinds of literature out there on the subject. Why are you so interested?"

"No reason in particular. I just find the whole topic really fascinating," I said.

"I have an idea for you. Look up a person named Edgar Cayce on the Internet. Supposedly he's one of the best known psychics who ever lived. If you're really interested in that kind of stuff, you might enjoy some of the material on him."

"Is he still alive?" I asked.

"No, he died a long time ago, but there's a lot written about him. I think he also wrote a couple of books too."

"Oh, there's something else on my mind. I don't know if I'm going to wrestle this year or not. Scott and I always partnered up, and I just don't know if I want to keep going without him. Besides, even if I don't, it's not like it would be a big loss or anything."

"I really don't give a rip what your record ended up last year or what it turns out to be this year. I want you out there." Mr. Andrews kind of snapped at me. "You are a lot more important to me than your win/loss record. I know what you are going through."

"How could you possibly know what I'm going through with right now? My life is a disaster!" I said not using the most polite tone to my voice. I immediately felt ashamed and apologized.

He smiled and said that it was ok, and then told me a little story. "Most people don't know this, and I would prefer that you don't repeat it, but I lost my twin brother on our fourteenth birthday in a freak hunting accident. Listen to me, Jeremy; I do know what you are going through. You need as much activity in your life right now as you can possibly handle. The busier you keep yourself the faster time will fly and the easier it will be for you. You will never forget Scott and nobody would ever want you to, but the intense pain you're feeling right now will lesson with time. Believe me. I know."

He had told the story very calmly, softly, and gently. When he finished, he reached over and give me a one-handed hug around the shoulder.

"Thanks, Coach. I needed that," I said smiling. "By the way, did you just chew me out or did it just seem like it?"

"Not at all. I just want to help you in any way I can whether it's in class, on the wrestling mat, or just surviving this horrible period in your life."

I found it very intriguing. Coach lost a twin brother at fourteen. That seemed like quite a coincidence. Scott and I were just as close as twins could ever be, and I had lost him. However, life had moved on for both of us. Now what?

Chapter 11

Time did move along pretty fast for the next few weeks. The four rents stuck me behind the wheel of the car almost continuously with the idea of me getting my license before my birthday. Marty and I also started hanging out at school and developing a friendship. We spent quite a lot of time talking in English class, other classes, and lunch while we worked on our projects. He talked about everything except home. He said very little about his personal life. About the only thing I really knew about him was what he told me the first day we met that he lived with his step dad, Bruno Bashore. Also, when his mom left without even a goodbye, it really hurt him because they had always been so close.

I did find out that Marty wrestled at both of his last two schools. He said that he wrestled fairly decently, but nothing special. One day he told me, "My step dad made me go out for wrestling because he wrestled back in his day and won all kinds of medals and awards and that I had better do the same."

"So automatically he expects you to whether you want to or not just 'cause he did," I sympathized.

"Right! Not only that, he brags all the time that he hurt a lot of his opponents and practice partners on purpose just to let them know that he was 'the man' and nobody to fool around with. Which doesn't surprise me the least bit because he likes to hurt people."

"Oh, that's classy! So now you're supposed to intentionally hurt people too?" I asked.

 "That's right! When I told Bruno that I didn't want to hurt anybody, he told me that I better or else."

Marty didn't come right out and say it, but I picked up the vibe that he didn't like his step dad all that well, and that he was also afraid of him. That sucked. I couldn't imagine not liking any of my four parents or being afraid of them.

 That night at dinner I talked to Mom and Dad about him and the fact that he seemed awfully sad. He never smiled, much less laughed.

"Why don't you invite him over some Saturday or Sunday just to hang out? He could spend the day with us and give us a chance to meet him too?" Mom asked. "Maybe all he really needs is a friend and a decent home-cooked meal."

"He told me that he never goes anywhere. After school he always has a ton of chores to do around the house. Since his step dad works or just plain stays gone most of the time, it's his job to do anything and everything that needs to be done at home.

"Don't necessarily want to change the subject, but tomorrow is Friday and I'm taking off work just a little early. I plan to pick you up, and then we'll head to the Secretary of State's office. If you don't screw up your driver's test, you should have your license in time to take my car to the football game tomorrow night," Dad said about the time Mom started cutting the pie.

"Really? I knew I had the hours in, but I didn't know if you trusted me that far to go ahead and get it."

"One condition," Mom piped up with a grin on her face. "You do not panic and park the car in the middle of the road someplace and walk home."

"MOM!"

"Do you want ice cream on your pie?" she asked laughing at my embarrassment.

"You know, I really prefer that you don't have other kids in the car especially at first," Dad said, "but why don't you ask Marty if he'd like to go to the game? You could pick him up. Do you know where he lives?"

"Yeah, he's out there on Sherman Road down from the old school. Thanks, guys!"

Needless to say, I flipped out. Right after dinner I ran over to Scott's house and told his mom and dad. They probably already knew it, but they faked it and pretended to be all excited about it with me. My timing couldn't have been more perfect either. I managed to horn in on the chocolate cake they had for desert too.

Didn't sleep worth a damn that night. Tossed and turned until who knows when. I woke up in the morning as tired as when I went to bed. Oh well, off to the shower I went to drown myself. If I thought I had spent a restless night, it couldn't compare to the day. Fortunately for me there were no tests. That night we celebrated our homecoming game, and everyone pretty much occupied themselves with float making for the football game and decorating the school.

When I walked into English class, I noticed a sign on the chalk board, "Open study period today—try doing something constructive!"

Right! Mr. Andrews actually made a guest appearance about fifteen minutes into the period. Those who were not out on float detail sat around talking. You couldn't find a book open in the place. Didn't seem to either surprise or bother him one bit. He wandered around the room for a few minutes and talked to everyone, and then disappeared. I guess he decided that we weren't going to terrorize the place so he could go back to the teacher's lounge. It was probably full of goodies. That typically happened on special occasion days, and they didn't share. Bummer!

"So, Marty, what are you doing tonight? Are you going to the game?"

"Unfortunately, no. I don't have any way to get there and Bruno probably wouldn't let me go anyway."

"Check this out! My dad's picking me up right after school, and I'm going to take my driver's test for my license. If I pass everything, he told me I could drive our car to the game. He also said I could come out and pick you up if you wanted to go. Bruno doesn't have to worry. We can't be out late. I have to be off the streets by midnight on the weekends—state law. You'll be home by eleven thirty at the latest."

"Awesome! You're really getting your license today? Wow! Bruno won't even let me take driver's ed. He says we can't afford to let me drive. The insurance is too high."

"So you want me to pick you up?"

"I'd love to go, but I know he won't let me. He's such an asshole! However, if you just showed up..."

"How about if I just appear at your door right around six-thirty unannounced since the game starts at seven – that is provided I do get my license. If I don't, I can call you."

"We don't have a phone, so if you don't show up, I'll know you didn't get it. This could prove interesting! Wonder how dear Bruno will stumble through this one?" Marty said with an actual smile on his face as he thought about it.

After what seemed like an eternity, the two fifty-five bell finally rang. I raced to my locker, dumped my books, and ran out to the parking lot. "Slow down!" Dad laughed at me. "You're going to have a coronary the way you're going."

He sat in the passenger seat so I jumped in behind the wheel. Took two deep breaths, and turned to Dad. "This is really going to happen, isn't it?" I said grinning.

"Yeah, but I think we should ride around for a little while and get you settled down before heading to the Secretary of State's office. Let's run down town and find a spot where we can do a parallel park one last time before you have to show off for the cop."

So we did. We drove around for a good forty-five minutes before Dad told me to head for the license bureau. The line was fairly long, but when we made it to the head of it, the person directing people told me I was in luck. None of those people seated in the waiting area were there for a road test. Luckily, I didn't have to take a written test because I took care of that in Driver's Ed. So, I was good to go.

Soon an older gentleman came out with a bunch of papers and looked around, "Jeremy?" he said in my general direction. My heart raced to the beat of 'Wipe Out' and away we went. Dad wished me good luck and exchanged grins with the officer. Show time!

I climbed into the car, put on my seat belt, checked the mirror and went through the rest of my mental check list. I looked over and the officer didn't have his fastened. "Uh, Sir. Your seat belt isn't fastened," I said feeling downright foolish.

He clicked his belt, looked over and smiled, and said, "Well, Jeremy, you just passed step one. When people are with you, don't even start the car until everyone is buckled up. You are responsible for your passengers and their safety. Now, start the car, head out of the parking lot at the far end down there and turn right."

I enjoyed smooth sailing that afternoon. He asked me a bunch of questions about how much experience I had driving and with whom. He questioned me about situations that might show up while driving like what I would do if a car suddenly veered across the medium and headed right at me. That posed a new one for me. I never dealt with that scenario in either Driver's Ed. or with my four rents. I tried to use common sense and he seemed satisfied. Soon, he told me to pull into the parking lot. We were back. I didn't even know how long we'd been gone. Dad said it had been about a half hour.

"So, how'd he do?" Dad asked the officer as we walked back into the building.

"Fine!" he replied. "He seems like he has a good head on his shoulders. I don't think we'll have to worry about this one. He passed with flying colors."

He signed the papers, the clerk took my mug shot, and I was legal. My permanent license would arrive within the next two weeks. I wanted to jump up and down and yell like a little kid with his first bike, but I didn't. I acted cool.

When we finally made it home, Dad dug in his wallet and hauled out a twenty. "Here, you better go put some gas in this thing. Oh, and before you go, check with Mom to see if she has any errands for you to run."

She did. I'm sure they planned it all out in advance. My first solo flight would be running errands and taking care of business, and not just out screwing around. How many times have I heard? "A car is a tool used to accomplish specific goals. It is not a toy." Rents lecture number 401.

We had dinner a little early so I would have plenty of time to go out and pick up Marty by six-thirty. I felt way too excited to eat, but I managed. My parents just laughed at me. "Am I to assume that you're going to skip desert tonight?" Mom asked acting really worried like she would if she thought I had a fever or something.

"No, that's ok Mom. I wouldn't want you to go to all that trouble making it and then not scarf it down," I said well aware she was pulling my chain. She just laughed at me and mussed up my hair. Not cool! I just brushed it before we sat down to eat.

I found Marty's house with no problem. It looked like kind of a beat up shack on a country road with all kinds of broken down cars and other junk around it. I followed the drive around to the back door like Marty had told me. They only used that door. There appeared to be only one other building on the property. A ways back from the house sat a shed covered with weeds and vines and crud like that. Looked like it stood there all kind of dilapidated and unused. I saw no sign of life out and about so I went up and knocked on the door.

A very large man still dressed in his work clothes and not too clean looking came to the door, stood there with his hands on his hips for a few seconds before speaking. "What?" he finally snarled at me.

He looked kind of like a grizzly bear standing on two legs. He had this huge head and red face. I could see why Marty acted afraid of him. He scared me too.

"Good evening, Mr. Johnson, is Marty here," I asked as politely as I could.

"Marty's name is Johnson. My name is Mr. Bashore. Now, who are you?"

Oops! Not off on the right foot here. I knew he was a step dad too. Never dawned on me that his last name would be different than Marty's. Actually, I forgot even though Marty mentioned it once. "My name is Jeremy Wright. Marty and I have English together. Tonight's our school's homecoming football game and we planned to go to the game together so I came out to pick him up."

"He can't go. He has work to do. Besides, he doesn't need to be out prowling around until all hours of the night just because it's the weekend."

"No problem there, sir. I have to have the car home before midnight so Marty will be home by eleven thirty at the latest," I tried to explain.

"Well, he ain't going no place tonight or any other night, so you might as well turn right around and get the hell out of here and don't come back," he snarled slamming the door in my face leaving me standing on their porch all by myself. I never did see Marty. Had no idea where he might be. Probably hiding and horribly embarrassed. I know I would be. When I left, I told myself that I would blow it off Monday in class. Hopefully, he didn't hide in there close enough to the door so he could hear his dad.

With nothing else to do, I headed back to town to the game. Man! The game rocked! We finally won in overtime by a field goal. Afterwards, I went down to the burger joint near the school where everyone hung out and chowed down on a burger and fries and had fun celebrating the win with my friends. The night turned out great—except for Marty. I made it home at quarter to twelve and had to tell the Rents all about it. About twelve-thirty I crawled into bed as happy as if I were in my right mind. Yet, I had this nagging concern about Marty. Would there be anything I could do to help him?

Chapter 12

I didn't happen to see Marty around school Monday until he walked into English class. He normally ate his lunch at our table so I would see him then anyway, but not that day. He showed up right at the bell, slipped into his seat, and tried to act like he was being really attentive as Mr. Andrews took roll.

I tried the light hearted approach pretending that absolutely nothing had happened, "Hi, Marty. You have a good weekend? I spent entirely too much time on home work. At least I finished Andrews's report, and it isn't even due until tomorrow. Must have set a record on that one."

"I'm sorry," Marty said very softly as he hung his head. "Bruno is such an ass!"

"Don't apologize. It's not your fault. Are you okay?" I asked.

"I'm fine. I just can't stand him. No reason for him to treat you that way Friday night. He could have just said that I couldn't go and left it at that, or he could have let me do it. But no, he had to be a compete jerk!"

"I hoped you didn't hear him. I thought he acted kind of scary?"

"I did, and that's exactly what he wants. He likes it when I and other people are afraid of him,"

Right about then Mr. Andrews started class so we said no more about it. I figured it was much better if I didn't mention it again. I would just find a way that I could get him out of there once in a while for some fun anyway. He had to be miserable.

One thing I noticed, Marty never called him "Dad" He always referred to him as Bruno or his old man. I hadn't worked up the nerve to ask him about that one yet, but I would eventually. He acted totally different than I did when I talked about my dad or Jim Dad. Where I obviously loved both of my dads, he just as obviously did not even like his step dad and feared him big time. What a bummer! I couldn't imagine living like that.

Marty and I kind of ignored his home life situation for the next couple of weeks. Towards the end of the season we decided to try another game—sometime in early November. He didn't have a whole lot of hope for any different outcome, but at least it was worth a try.

***

"Hey! You know your birthday is Saturday. The five of us are going to go out for brunch about noon to celebrate. Should be fun," Mom told me on Wednesday when I came home from school. "Where you want to go?"

"I don't care. What do you think?"

"We thought maybe someplace like The Flamingo unless you had another place you'd rather go. It is one of the nicer restaurants around here and not far from the house."

"That's fine with me," I said. "Kind of expensive though, isn't it?"

"Well, it sure isn't fast food, if that's what you mean, but it's not that bad. It'll be nice."

The three of us arrived before Scott's mom and dad showed up. We grabbed a big table and ordered our drinks before they came in. Mom Sara's belly stuck out big as a barn. Wouldn't be too much longer before baby Emily arrived. Hope they didn't plan on my doing much in the baby sitting area until she was at least house broken. Don't know if I could handle a messy diaper or not. Yuck! I knew darned well that I didn't really want to find out either.

She waddled on over to the table exaggerating it big time, and we all laughed at her. Fortunately, she had remained awfully good natured throughout her whole pregnancy and liked making fun of herself. It made it easier for us to pick on her.

"I think I need a piano bench instead of a chair," Sara laughed as she sat down kind of gingerly on the chair that Jim Dad held out for her.

"I asked, but they said no way," Dad said pretending to be serious. "Something about it not being built to hold a whole passel of people at the same time or some such excuse."

With everybody horribly excited about the arrival of the new baby, it stayed pretty much the major topic of discussion for brunch.

"Jeremy, you have to come over and see the nursery," Mom Sara told me. "You'll never recognize it. Besides, I need to show you where we have that big supply of diapers stashed so you'll be able to find them when you have to change her."

"I can't believe that you actually said that with a straight face," I told her absolutely grossed out with everyone laughing at me.

They had totally redecorated Scott's old room into a nursery. Probably a good thing. After he died, they closed the door and pretended the room didn't exist for a long time. Then, out of the blue, they decided to turn it into the baby's room. Worked for me.

During lunch nobody said anything about it being my birthday. No cards. No, "Happy Birthday!" Nothing! They pretty much ignored me most of the time. Maybe the Rents just couldn't handle my having a birthday and all because of Scott. I tried to understand. I only semi felt sorry for myself.

Two hours later with lunch long over and the table cleared, everyone finally stood up to leave. We walked out into the parking lot, and headed towards our car. We all talked and laughed and had a good time as we plodded across the huge parking lot making fun of Sara—somebody even mentioned plopping her belly in a wheelbarrow. Just before we reached our car, everyone stopped. Jim Dad stuck his hand in his pocket and pulled out a set of keys and slapped them into my hand. "Oh, by the way," he said. "Happy birthday!"

With that came all the hugs, "Happy birthdays," and cards. It totally confused the hell out of me. We stood right there in the middle of the restaurant parking lot while I opened and gawked at both of my cards. Each had a fifty dollar bill with a note attached. The one from Mom and Dad said "Fill up number 1 plus change." The one from Scott's mom and dad said, "Fill up number 2 plus change." Obviously, a part of some master plan, and I had absolutely no clue.

So I asked, with what I'm sure was a completely stupid expression on my face, "What's going on?"

Everybody started laughing at me. They could tell I was completely baffled, and they found it hilariously funny—especially when my face turned all red. This all happened as we stood right beside this sharp looking black car that didn't appear to be more than five years old. Dad put his arm around my shoulders, and said, "Why don't you take those keys that Jim handed you and try the door on this thing?"

When I did, Mom said, "Get in and try the engine and see if it runs."

Duh! The bright lights flashed in my head. The Rents went together and bought me a car for my birthday. It was gorgeous! Shaking like a leaf, I started the engine. It sounded great. I turned off the ignition and climbed out. "Is it really mine?" I asked still not sure if I believed it or not.

"Yes, it is," Dad said. "This is from all of us. Jim drove it over from where we had it hidden while Sara drove their car. That's why they showed up later than us. Are you surprised?"

"And here I thought everybody was just ignoring my birthday?"

"We were. Now how about a hug before you head out?" Dad said to me as everyone laughed at me again. This time I laughed along with them.

I passed out hugs and 'thank yous' all around before I climbed back into my brand new car. I listened to all of the, "Drive careful, pay attention to what you're doing, and obey all traffic laws," lectures from all of them. They all gave me instructions at the same time. I laughed.

While I went through the check list—seat belt, rear view mirror, side mirrors, seat position, and everything else I could think of, two cameras flashed into action. Dad and Jim Dad both snapped away.

When I started to pull out, Mom told me, "Be sure to be home by seven o'clock for a late dinner. We'll have your birthday cake then."

Mom Sara then piped up, "Oh, Jeremy, by the way, you will learn how to change a poopy diaper." Everybody enjoyed that one including me that time.

I pulled out of the parking place feeling as excited and happy as I could ever remember feeling. I had wheels!

I had my new car, a full tank of gas, and two fifty dollar bills in my pocket. I was in hog heaven. I spent the first half hour just trying it out and getting used to it. Then I decided to go for a little ride. I would drive past Marty's house just to see if he happened to be out and about, and then I would just cruise for awhile.

Fortunately, the car had a GPS unit that the Rents made me program in before I left. I never did the greatest when it came to directions. All of them hassled me to death about the fact that I never knew quite where I was or how to get home. Hey! What kid ever pays any actual attention to where they're going as they grow up with their parents driving?

As I cruised down a country road out in the middle of nowhere, I started really missing Scott. He should have been with me on the maiden voyage of my new car. "Scottie, why aren't you here when I really want you? I know, I can't have you just any old time, but this is huge!"

"If you were a little more observant and a little less dense, you'd know that Mooshy and I came on board right when you pulled out of that restaurant parking lot. I wouldn't miss this for anything. If you run any stop signs, I'm telling your mom."

"Mooshy's here too? Where?"

"Of course, you know we're always together. Now don't look around, we don't need you to run off the road, but 'Mooshy, give Germy a kiss.'"

And he did. It felt so good and so natural, I couldn't believe it.

"How come you didn't say anything?"

"We've been enjoying the ride wondering if you have any idea where you are, where you been, or where you're going," he said yanking my chain as always.

We bantered back and forth just like we always did. I'd want to go one way; he'd want to go the other. I had no idea where we were. He asked about school and what was going on there. I told him about Marty and how I thought maybe things were not exactly right out there.

"You wouldn't believe the jerk he has for a father," I told him. "When I went out to pick him up, his old man yelled at me and basically kicked me out and told me not to come back."

"Sounds like a real winner," Scott answered.

"Yeah, he is. However, we talked about trying it again for the last game of the season," I told him.

"Maybe you better not. It might not be safe. That guy sounds like he's a loose cannon just looking for a place to go off. You can have something come up like engine trouble or whatever where you can't make it that night. You can go to the game without your car if you have to. Scott talked and acted much more seriously than normal so I didn't just blow him off.

Trying to move the conversation back to a lighter mood, I asked, "By the way, Scott, did you know that you're going to have a baby sister soon? Her name is Emily"

"Yeah, and I expect you to look after her and keep her safe and out of trouble."

"But that doesn't include changing crappy diapers, right?"

"Whatever it takes, Bro, whatever it takes!"

"Thanks a lot! I can just see it now with you hanging over my shoulder laughing your ass off."

"That's for damn sure, and don't you forget it! Seriously, though, this is good for Mom and Dad. They always wanted another kid and it just didn't happen. Under the circumstances this is perfect timing. Have you seen my old room? That sure looks different with all that frilly baby girl stuff in there. But that's okay too."

"So you finally went back and checked out your old home," I stated wondering how he felt now. At first he wouldn't go anywhere near the place. His parents were too sad and it hurt him because there was nothing he could do about it.

"Yeah, everything's cool now. Mom and Dad are coping well especially with Emily coming along. That really helped them move on."

Time kind of raced away from us, and before we knew it, it was almost seven o'clock. I had to get back. Having no clue where we were, I set the GPS unit for home and away we went. Somewhere in route, not exactly sure when or where, Scott and Mooshy disappeared on me, and I was back on my own. I pulled in the drive right at seven and just in time for dinner. What a day!

While we ate, I told Mom and Dad all about my first ride, where I thought I had gone, and using the GPS unit to find my way home. Obviously I didn't mention Scott or Mooshy. I did say that it seemed strange driving all that way all by myself. When I did, Mom gave me the funniest look, smiled, and said, "Uh huh."

About eight o'clock Jim Dad and Mom Sara came over, and we had cake and ice cream. Everyone sang happy birthday to me, and then I had to tell Jim and Sara all about my first outing with my new car. The next birthday we celebrated wouldn't be so happy.

Chapter 13

On Sunday morning, November 11th, I slipped out of the house early and headed for the cemetery before anyone else even stirred. I hadn't slept very well so I managed to crawl out of bed bright and early for a Sunday.

After I parked, I walked up the little knoll to his grave. It was a beautiful morning. The sun shown brightly and the temperature hovered in the high twenties, and everything seemed very quiet and peaceful. "Happy birthday, Scott. Just wanted to get out here before anyone else. I'm sure all the Rents will be here at some point, I just wanted to be first. Don't ask me why, I just did. I bought you three chocolate covered doughnuts and a large Coke—your favorite snack. You don't even have to steal them from some cop this morning.

"Wrestling practice starts tomorrow. Gonna really seem weird without you, Dude. Marty is going out this year too so maybe we can help him out a little somehow. He's just about my size and weight so I will probably work out with him most of the time.

"Not gonna to be a whole lot longer before Emily arrives on the scene. I think she's due around the first of January. That'll be weird having a baby in the family."

I gabbed at Scottie for close to an hour before I headed back home. He never showed his face or acknowledged my presence, but that was okay. Probably not a great day for him either. Besides, I couldn't expect to have him show up every time I happened to want to talk to him. I felt in my own mind that he'd know I was there, but he probably had other things to do.

When I walked into the house, nobody asked anything about where I'd been. They knew. Dad read the Sunday paper while Mom cooked breakfast and everyone more or less ignored me. Good! I didn't want to talk right then.

Later in the day Mom and Dad rode out to the cemetery themselves. They asked if I wanted to go along, but I said no because I had already been. I didn't think I could handle another trip out there on that particular day. When they came home, nobody said anything about it at first. Later that afternoon while I played the mind numbing "Mad Demons" game on the computer, Mom stopped beside me. "Scottie hasn't eaten his snack yet," and that's all she said. I wanted Scott's birthday to be over.

...

Oh, the excitement and drama on Monday morning in English class became almost overwhelming. Mr. Andrews passed out our new book, "*A Tale of Two Cities*." From the looks of it, Marty and I guessed that it had to be at least a thousand pages. While he handed it out, Mr. Andrews really hyped it up by telling us how much the blood thirsty boys in the class would absolutely love it.

"He has absolutely lost it!" I whispered to Marty. "Look at the size of that freaking thing! We'll never finish it. Ever!"

"I hate to read! I've always hated to read! Why am I in this stupid class? I should be in something cool like Truck Driver's school learning about reading road maps and filling out travel logs. I could care less if I ever learned about the French Revolution," Marty whined.

"I know, and what makes it even worse is the fact that wrestling practice starts tonight so you know he'll have his thumb on us making sure we keep our grades up."

"That reminds me. There's something I wanted to tell you about tonight."

"What's that," I asked?

"Bruno's gonna show up at practice. He'll come to every practice. He won't say a word, but he'll scowl and stare a hole through both of us when we work together."

"That'll be spooky. Parents don't ever come to practice. Does Mr. Andrews know he's gonna be there?"

"He does. I had to tell him and get his permission before Bruno would let me come out this year. Coach said it will be fine as long as he doesn't interfere."

"How's that going to make you feel?" I asked.

"Like a total idiot! What do you think? Here I am the new kid in school, and my old man shows up at practice. And it won't be just tonight, he'll be there for every practice."

"Doesn't he have to work?" I asked.

"This is their slow period so he only works mornings. I think he could probably work full time if he wanted to, he just doesn't want to. He wants to come hassle me and make my life miserable. It's not that we couldn't use the money, you know. He had to go to the Salvation Army and mooch my 'New' winter coat off of them. It doesn't even fit right."

"That sucks! So why does he go, really? Does he try to help teach you the moves or something?"

"No! He does it to see if I will ever get any meaner or tougher. He thinks I should try to hurt people in order to intimidate them and make everyone afraid of me. You know, the really smooth way to make friends and influence people?"

"But why? Why would he want you to intentionally hurt someone?"

"Because he's a total jerk! That's what he did as a kid wrestling in high school and that's the way he is today. He loves it when people are afraid of him. That's why he acted the way he did that night you came out to the house. He doesn't want friends, and he doesn't want me to have any either."

Oh, boy! That guy's a total loser. No wonder Marty always acts so unhappy. I wonder what Scott would think of him. I'm sure he'd have plenty to say, I thought to myself smiling.

Sure enough, that afternoon Marty's dad stood right there leaning against the wall. He never said a word. He just scowled and stared. I couldn't help but notice the way Marty acted. The whole scene cowered Marty big time. He never spoke or smiled. Nothing. We went through the drills, and we practiced some moves on each other, but Marty never said a word. I tried to start a little conversation going every now and then, but he just kind of grunted and didn't really answer.

After practice when we went to the locker room, I said, "I see what you mean. He never cracked a smile all practice."

"He hasn't cracked a smile in his entire freaking life."

I'm sure that was a slight exaggeration; however, from what little I'd seen, maybe not. "So what will he have to say on the way home? Will he talk about the moves or what?"

"Well, the first thing he'll rag on me about is not throwing an elbow in your face trying to break your nose so you'll be afraid of me. Then he'll grumble that Coach's not nearly tough enough on us. He'll decide that we're all a bunch of pussies and probably will never win anything all year. Then he'll rant on and on about what he'd do to toughen everybody up."

"Sounds like a real joy, Marty," I said as I threw my towel into my gym bag. "I'm out of here. See you tomorrow."

"Yeah, later!" Marty answered as we separated at the outside door to the locker room. Right then he turned around with the saddest look on his face, "Jeremy, I'm sorry," he said and then hustled off to where his dad sat in their old beater pickup.

The rest of the week stayed pretty much the same. Marty acted as friendly as could be in class, lunch, and around school, but when practice started he morphed into a different person. He almost looked like a mini version of Bruno. He scowled, he grunted, he never cracked a smile, and on Wednesday he even semi-tried to throw an elbow in the general direction of my face.

"Hey! Knock that crap off. You try that again and I'll deck you right on the spot!" I snapped clenching my fists and thrusting my chest out at him.

We glared at each other and then worked a move. We dropped down on the mat with our heads turned away from his dad when he smiled and said, "Thanks."

"No problem!" I whispered. "I thought we put on a good show."

By Friday, practice smoothed out and fell into a routine. After going to the locker room, showering, and getting dressed following practice, I asked Marty, "What are you doing tonight? The weather stinks out there with that cold steady rain we've had all day and I'm bored out of my mind. I want to do something different."

"Oh, I'll sit at home and watch mindless TV like I do every night. Bruno's scared to death that I might actually go out and have some fun some time."

"That sucks! I thought I might run over to Hannah's house tonight. She's throwing one of her wild parties. From what I hear they're a blast. A bunch of real characters show up and make it interesting."

"Jeremy, are you sure you want to mix yourself up in something like that? From what I hear, those are strictly booze and pot parties. If the thing's raided, it could mean big trouble for you. Even if it doesn't, you sure wouldn't want word to get back to Andrews."

"I won't do any drinking or smoking that's for sure. That would be crazy especially during our season. I just want to go out and do something different for a change and watch all the idiots make fools of themselves. Seems like a good way to let down, get away from everything for a while, and have a few laughs at someone else's expense."

Right! Sounded like a plan. However, things didn't quite turn out that way.

Chapter 14

I rationalized going to the party the best I could in my own mind. I didn't plan on staying long. I'd see a bunch of people, dance with some of the babes, chow down on some of their food, and then get out of there before the cops raided the thing. From what I had always heard, if you left before midnight, you were safe. Our local cops never bothered any parties before midnight. That's when the rookies took over the late shift and tried to prove what studs they were. The old timers on the force didn't seem to care all that much as long as nobody caused any trouble.

I waited for the right time during dinner to bring up the subject of staying out late—like during dessert. "Dad, can I have a little extra money for gas tonight? I know, I get my allowance tomorrow, but I'm a bit on the short side."

"Why? What's going on?"

"Since there isn't a dance tonight, there's going to be an open gym night where we can go and shoot hoops and run the halls. There's a bunch of the guys supposedly going. Afterwards some of us just might go to the 'Y' to lift weights and swim. That's great exercise and a good break from just running constantly to keep in shape."

"You know you can't just pile a whole flock of kids in your car and go ramming around," he said somewhat sternly.

"I won't. You don't have to worry about that. There probably won't be more than one or two besides myself."

"What about afterwards? You planning on coming right home after that?"

"I don't intend to. After all, it is Friday night, and I would kind of like to go hang with my friends for a while afterwards and get something to eat if it's okay with you."

"I suppose, but you still can't be late. Your license doesn't allow you to drive past midnight," Dad said as he pulled a ten out of his wallet and handed it to me.

I didn't ask if he would deduct that from my normal twenty dollars a week allowance. Sometimes he did, and sometimes he didn't. I'd find out the next night. I felt guilty enough about lying about my plans without worrying about anything else.

"Don't worry. I'll be home in plenty of time unless some fine young lady grabs me by the ear and drags me off into the bushes," I joked.

"You just make sure that's the only thing she grabs and drags you away with," he said as he turned away from Mom and winked at me.

"Theodore Robert Wright! Both of you should be ashamed of yourselves!" Mom yelled as Dad and I both laughed at her. Dad normally goes by Ted except when he's catching it from Mom. However, she's never serious when she yells out his full name. She's just giving him a hard time. However, when she yells out, "Jeremy Wayne Wright," that's an entirely different matter. Then it's time to duck. Mom's name is Nancy, but you don't hear that too often. Even Dad calls her Mom when he's talking to me about her.

"Okay, you go and have a good time, but behave yourself," Dad said smiling.

"Both at the same time?" I asked grinning. "I'll see you guys in the morning. Don't wait up for me."

When I'd almost reached the door, Dad yelled out, "Hey! Pull up your pants. You don't need to be out and about with six inches of your 'cute' yellow and orange checkered boxers showing."

"Yes , Dad!" I said grinning with only a slight rolling of the eyes as I pulled them up. They'd slide down again as soon as I slipped through the door, and we both knew it. Let's face it. Everybody wore their pants that way out of their parent's sight.

About seven-thirty I pulled into Hannah's drive. It curled about two hundred yards into a little wood lot off the main road meandering far enough in to be very secluded so a whole ton of kids could park back there and not be seen from the main road.

Some other kid walked up to the house at the same time that I didn't know. "Man!" he said. "This place is huge. I've heard her old man's income matches it too. By the way, I haven't seen you here before. This your first time?"

"Yeah, not yours I take it. Didn't know for sure if I would come 'til I actually got here. I hear it's a little different in there."

"Kind of a strange situation according to rumor," he said. "Apparently her parents leave her at home alone for the weekend almost every week. Supposedly they own a log cabin on some lake in the north woods and spend most weekends there."

"So that's why Hannah throws a party almost every Friday night?" I asked. "From what I hear somehow she manages to get a keg or two every weekend."

"That's why everyone who comes to her parties chips in a few bucks to help pay for the snacks and booze. The druggies bring their own crap," he said.

"Seems like with all these people there'd be an awful mess," I mentioned.

"She has plenty of time over the rest of the weekend to get everything cleaned up before her parents came home on Sunday night. They never seem to catch on to what's going on. At least that's how the story goes around our school. Maybe they just don't care as long as everything's cleaned up and back to normal when they show up. You know the old saying, out of sight—out of mind."

"So what school do you go to? I don't think I've ever seen you at mine," I asked.

"I go to Holter! When you look around inside, you'll notice there are as many kids from there as there are from yours," he told me as we walked into the house.

He immediately spotted some friends and we separated. I never saw the kid again. I didn't even learn his name. Just as well probably. He didn't hear mine either.

Feeling a bit uncomfortable, I shuffled through the house knowing darn well that I shouldn't be there. Rap music blared in the back ground. I walked around a bit and took in the sights. You could cut the blue, smoky, pungent, and thick air with a knife. You could almost get a headache just walking through the house. I knew my clothes would reek when I left.

I wandered around a bit more, said hi to everyone I knew, and picked up a lot of strange looks from classmates who couldn't believe they were seeing me there. Fifty or more kids stood around talking, shouting, drinking, and smoking. You couldn't buy most of the stuff being smoked locally in a store. I found the whole scene really weird—with people attempting to out-yell each other telling stupid jokes that weren't even funny, and then everyone trying to laugh louder than everybody else. I seriously thought about turning around and heading right back out the door. I didn't find it one bit cool.

Right then someone slapped me on the back, shouted something in my ear, and shoved a beer in my hand. "No, thanks!" I yelled in order to be heard. "I'm the designated driver."

We both laughed as I set the beer down and grabbed a can of Coke out of the ice bucket. I leaned back against the wall and took a really good look around. I knew about half the people there. The other half apparently went to Holter. There were some real surprises there for me too. I saw kids drinking and doping from my school that I would never have suspected—I mean, like, kids with really good reputations. Anyway, I decided to just people watch for a little while and then scram out of there. Everyone acted so stupidly, I didn't find it much fun being totally sober and alone in a place like that. I felt very out-of-place.

I wandered around checking out who else might be around that I knew. With the Coke running through me, I walked down a hallway looking for a bathroom. That's when I heard an angry argument spilling out of one of the bedrooms—Hannah and her boyfriend, Moose, were screaming at each other at the top of their lungs.

"You two timing pig!" Hannah screeched. "Get out of my life! I don't ever want to see your stinking face again!"

"I'm out of here all right, Bitch! Good luck getting your kegs next weekend without me!" he bellowed as I slipped into the bathroom and shut the door—drowning out most of the noise. I didn't really need to hear all of that. I took my time.

Moose's parents had the cunning foresight to name him Mortimer after some long, lost relative. No kid in his right mind, even a basketball player, would ever allow himself to grow up being called Mortimer. So, since he was huge from day one, he grew up known as Moose. Rumor has it that his grandmother gave him the nickname. The majority of the kids at schools didn't even know Moose's real name.

About the time I wandered out of the bathroom, Moose and Hannah stormed out of the bedroom and practically ran over me. He looked all red-faced and pissed, and her face was smeared with tears. Moose grabbed his coat out of the closet and burst out the door slamming it behind him. Everything just kind of stopped as everyone listened to Moose slam his car door, race the motor of his car, and squeal out of the driveway and into the street. The street was almost an eighth of a mile away, but everyone could distinctly hear it as he burned rubber when his tires hit the dry pavement.

"I hope he doesn't kill himself," someone said rather softly to nervous giggles.

"Come on, everybody, back to the dancing and drinking." Hannah called out with a pasted smile on her face. "Don't worry about Moose. He's just a big hot-headed fool. Anyway, I want it known here and now, Moose and I are through! So, all you unattached guys out there look out! Hannah's on the prowl!" She said very dramatically.

Everyone cheered and laughed and the party continued. Maybe five minutes later I stood in the kitchen thinking I'd had enough when Hannah sidled up to me and said, "Hi, Jeremy. You here all by yourself?"

"Yeah, I am. I tried to talk that new kid Marty into coming, but his dad's a control freak and won't let him out of the house. His dad and Moose would make a good pair," I joked. "I couldn't find a date at the last minute when I finally decided to come, so I came by myself. That's okay, isn't it?"

"Sure, that's fine anytime. In fact, it's great tonight. Would you be a dear friend and just help me make it through this party? I'm so depressed! I need to talk seriously to someone levelheaded like you."

"Okay, but this is hardly the place to have a normal, serious conversation, if that's what you want. Why don't we go for a walk or something? The party can run by itself for a while without you here, can't it?"

"Sounds great to me," Hannah said. Tell you what; Mom's Lexus is parked right outside the door. Let's go for a ride to the gravel pit. I'll go grab us something to drink. Meet you out by the car. You drive."

"Hannah, I'm drinking Coke!" I told her wanting her to know right up front that I wasn't boozing.

"Whatever! Be right back."

According to the rumors around school, Hannah's dad's company leased two luxury cars a year for him as part of his compensation package. Both cars were loaded with every conceivable gadget imaginable. Choosing between taking the Lexus and my car? That's a no-brainer. Of course I would drive her mom's car. I crawled in behind the wheel and subconsciously drooled as my imagination got the best of me while I waited for Hannah.

"Here's your Coke. I grabbed myself a giant mixed drink at the bar made with vodka so nothing would smell on my breath. I bought you a six pack of Coke. Who knows how long we'll be gone,"

Hannah laughed as she jumped into the passenger seat and hooked her seat belt.

If nothing else, I thought, Hannah knew how to throw a wild party. "You must be serious about wanting to get away for a while and unloading." I said as I started the car and headed down the driveway.

The old abandoned gravel pit was a local teen hangout. A dirt road wound for about a quarter of a mile through the trees before it opened up into a large, open area that made it easy to spot police cars well in advance when and if they happened to show up. Gave you lots of time to dump and hide anything that you might have so they'd think that all you were doing was making out.

When we found our parking spot, neither one of us said a word until I backed the car in and turned the lights out. "This is weird," I finally said. "We're the only ones here. Everyone else must be at your house."

"Yeah, but it's early. There will be a lot more people around here later."

We sat there for a long time and just talked. She said she wanted to know all about Scott's accident. She had been at their log cabin for almost the entire summer and didn't know the details. However, for some reason or the other, the conversation kept going back to Moose.

"He's such a louse! Such a dirty rotten scum bag!" she kept saying. Then she'd take another sip of her drink.

"You know, Hannah. You still haven't told me exactly what he said or did in there to piss you off so bad."

"It's just too personal. You wouldn't understand unless you were there. Here, have another Coke," she said as I opened my third or fourth of the night.

After another hour of that, I had to go. Sometimes liquids do that to me. Seems like the stuff flows in one end and right out the other. "I'm going to go run behind the tree line and get rid of some of this. Be right back."

"Well, hand me your drink. You don't need to take that with you out in the woods. That'd be gross," Hannah said as I passed it over to her while I slipped out the door.

When I returned to the car, I finished my drink and started another. All of a sudden my eyes started getting really heavy. I could barely stay awake. It didn't feel like a normal sleepiness either. I felt like I should get out of the car and walk around a bit, but I just couldn't muster up the energy. Hannah talked nonstop about who knows what. Soon her voice started fading into the background and then it totally disappeared.

The next thing I remembered was Hannah shaking me, "Wake up, Jeremy. Wake up!"

I jerked up in my seat kind of semi-alert, "Where are we? What time is it?"

"It's four o'clock in the morning, and we're just down the street from your house. Now, what are you going to do about this fender?"

That really woke me up. "What fender? What are you talking about?"

"The front fender you smashed on my mom's car when you insisted on driving. You were drunk out of your mind. You passed out in the lane coming out of the pit. The car went off the road and hit a tree. That's what! Don't pretend you don't remember. What are you going to do? How are we going to fix it?"

"Drunk? Come on, Hannah! I didn't have one drink tonight. All I drank at your party was Coke, and you know it."

"Yeah, whatever! If that's the case, then you must have been drinking before you showed up. You acted weird as hell all night. I don't know why I didn't just grab the keys when you demanded to drive Mom's car. I'm going to be in so much trouble. What are you going to do about it?" she said as she started to cry.

"I have no clue especially at four in the morning. Now quit crying! I'll call you in the morning when I get up, and we'll figure something out."

The only thing I knew for sure right then was that I'd better get out of that car before I threw up all over it. Puking all over her mom's new car would really wow Hannah especially with everything else that had just happened.

As soon as I stepped out of the car, Hannah pulled away from the curb, and I puked. Classy! I wiped my face with my shirtsleeve, and then yelled out, "Crap!" loud enough to wake the neighbors. I just remembered that I'd parked my car out at her house three miles away. I started walking. If nothing else good came of it, I figured that I should at least be able to clear my head before I had to drive home. I retched my guts out twice more along the way and that seemed to help. I just couldn't understand what made me so sick. I'd put nothing on my stomach since dinner except for a total of four or five Cokes and a handful of nuts at Hannah's house. I wondered if maybe I had come down with the flu or something. By the time I pulled into my own driveway, my watch screamed five am at me. Not cool! I sneaked into the house and crawled up to my bedroom unheard by the rest of the family. I didn't even take off my clothes. I flopped on the bed and went out like a light.

About noon I finally woke up and stirred around a little. I held out my hand and watched it shake. That kind of scared me. I'd never had anything like that happen before. I peeled off my clothes and stumbled into the shower. The hot water felt so good I drained the tank on the heater. Then I dressed and kind of staggered, stumbled down the steps to the living room. Neither Mom nor Dad said a word. Mom gave me a weird look, gathered up her pencil and Sudoku book, and left the room.

Dad put his paper down on the stool, "That must have been quite a party last night."

My mind bounded to full alert, "How did you hear about that already?"

"Well, it seems like the Spanglers drove home a day early from up north because Mrs. Spangler didn't feel well. The house looked like a disaster area, and her car had a big dent in the right front fender. They rousted Hannah out of bed and found out what had happened. Then after hearing her story, he called to let me know all about your part in the mess. He said that they have a five-hundred dollar deductable policy, and that the insurance company would probably collect it—and he expected us to pay for it on principle. He said he'd be calling them the first thing Monday morning and that he'd let me know for sure."

"Dad, something is totally screwed here. From the time I left our house until I came back, I had nothing but a bunch of Cokes all night. Yes, I did get sick and pass out, but it's got to be the flu or something. I did not drink and you've got to believe me. All I know is that Hannah and I talked in the woods for quite a while. She acted all depressed about Moose and wanted to get away from her party for a while. She asked about Scott, but most of the time we talked about her love life with Moose and how rotten he is. After who knows how many Cokes, I had to pee so I stepped out of the car and went into the woods and took care of things. She held my pop can when I went out there. After I came back and finished that one, I started feeling woozy. I remember hearing her voice fade out on me. The next thing I knew she'd stopped a couple of blocks away from here and Hannah was shaking me. I don't remember a thing in between."

"I'm not too surprised that you don't' remember anything. According to Hannah's version, you were out of your head. She said you were drunk, obnoxious, and insisted on taking her mom's Lexus for a ride. She said that when you saw the electronic

147

ignition device on the seat, you jumped in and decided to just take off with it. Fortunately she managed to scramble into the car with you."

"That's not true!" I insisted.

"Maybe it is, maybe it's not. Right now it's your word against hers. Anyway, she said that you wanted to go back into the pit because you said you wanted to make out with her. She claimed to be scared and didn't want to just jump out leaving you alone with her mom's car. She didn't know what to do. She then said that you passed out in the lane going back into the pit, veered off the path, and hit a tree. That's where she shoved you over and drove you home."

"Bull! Dad, that's a lie. That isn't what happened at all. I didn't do anything wrong. I didn't drink anything. I didn't take any drugs. I didn't wreck that car. I didn't do anything! The only thing I did wrong was to go to that freaking party in the first place. My life's totally boring so I just wanted to do something exciting and different for a change."

"Okay, Jeremy. Calm down. I want you to go back to the very beginning and tell me everything, and I mean everything. Leave nothing out. No lies. No exaggerations. I want every single detail from the time you left the house last night until you staggered back in at who knows when. You have nothing further to lose because as of right now you're grounded until you finish med school."

So I did. Mom came in and sat down as well. I spent a long excruciating time that afternoon telling them every single detail one at a time as I remembered them. I left nothing out.

Dad paused for a second and then said, "I think I agree with you that there is something horribly fishy going on. I want to believe that you're telling us the truth, but let's be realistic, like I said before, at this point it's your word against hers and you're the one who ended up all screwed up and passed out."

"But, Dad! I didn't do anything wrong!" I insisted again for the umpteenth time.

"Maybe so, but unless something happens and somebody comes forward with a different story, I don't see any way out of this mess for us. Mr. Spangler is going to call his insurance company Monday, and we're going to be liable for five hundred dollars that we don't have. In the meantime, you are still going to be grounded forever. After wrestling practice you're to march yourself straight home. No friends hanging around, no car, no phone calls, no computer except for homework. While we are setting the ground rules, give me your cell phone, car keys, and driver's license."

For once in my life I had enough sense to keep my big mouth shut and just do what he said. Dad said he thought he believed me, but he sure didn't cut me any slack. Mom just listened and didn't really say anything. Being cooped up in the house and not being able to go anywhere would turn this into a long, long winter. At least I still had wrestling for a diversion. With nothing else to do, I went to my room, lay down on my bed, and stared at the ceiling.

"Scottie, I need you! Where are you when I want you?" I said more in a whisper than anything. I was in deep trouble and I needed help.

"You have done some really idiotic things in your life, but that stunt last night has to be your ultimate accomplishment in pure stupidity," Scott lectured. He squatted Indian style at the foot of my bed and scowled at me. Curled up beside him and sound asleep lay Mooshy.

"Thanks, Scott. I really need to have someone else on my butt. You know, I could use a friend and a little help about now. I didn't do anything."

"You did! You went to that freaking party at Hannah's in the middle of wrestling season. You ought to have your head examined."

"If all you're going to do is bitch at me, go back to wherever it is you go when you leave. I feel bad enough as it is that nobody believes me. I at least thought I could depend on you!"

Mooshy saw that I was all upset and came up and started licking my face all over. At least I had one friend left.

"Just cool it!" Scott said using a little different tone. "I believe you. We've just got to figure out a way to get to the bottom of this. Now, tell me exactly what happened. I wasn't there, you know, so I really don't have all the details."

So I went over the whole ridiculous story again just like I had with Dad. Scott just sat there with his chin resting on his folded up hands with his elbows propped on his knees. Every once in a while he would ask a question or make a comment, but mostly he just listened.

When I finished, Scott looked up again and said, "One thing that seems kind of odd here is that Hannah wanted to hold your can of pop when you went out to pee. How many times have we done that in the past when we were out camping in the woods? Let's face it. It only takes one hand."

"I know, she just said that she found it gross."

"How would she know? She's not a boy. Oh, by the way, before I forget it, thanks for the goodies on my birthday. I didn't eat the stuff until after everyone left that night. I spent most of the day sitting on my grave marker enjoying all the company. All the Rents came along and also a bunch of kids from school showed up. When your mom and dad came, she saw the doughnuts and pop, looked me straight in the eye, nodded her head, and winked. I smiled back and told her I loved her, but I don't know if it registered or not. I'm not always sure just exactly what your mom sees or senses."

"Where were you when I went? I didn't see you. I wanted to talk to you."

"I hid when you came. I listened to everything you said, I just didn't want to talk right then. I hope you understand."

"I do," I said. "Probably better that way for both of us."

Scott stayed the night just like he used to. He slept in his old bed, curled up on his left side, and shared his pillow with Mooshy who actually snored louder than he did. When he crawled out of bed in the morning, there wasn't one wrinkle in it. He didn't even have to make the bed. That sucked.

Monday morning finally arrived. Scott hung around all weekend, so we spent most of the time hidden out in my room trying to figure out what we were going to do. We knew that it wouldn't be easy or happen all by itself. We had to have a plan. My school morning routine was usually a little sluggish. My alarm would go off, and I would hit the snooze button. The second time it rang, I would get up and head to the bathroom, brush my teeth, check for whiskers, and then dress for school.

By the time I finally made my way downstairs, I was running late, like always, so I had to fight with Mom over breakfast. She wanted me to sit down and eat cereal, toast, juice, and all that. Usually I only had time to grab a banana and head out the door. When I did have time to eat, the Rents were usually pretty chatty. Not that morning, however. Nobody said any more than they had to.

Scott decided that he would walk to school with me that day and then disappear. He said he had some things he had to tend do. After we left the house, Scott gave a big sigh, "Whew! Things are still pretty icy around here this morning. You are definitely on a short leash right now."

When we approached the door at school, Scott disappeared and I headed in. When I showed up at English, Marty wanted all the details of the party. He sympathized with me and acted very relieved that he hadn't gone Friday night.

"If that happened to me, Bruno would kill me. Literally! I have no doubt about it. Sounds like your parents at least handled it ok," Marty said with kind of a far off look in his eye.

There were times when we talked that I had the impression that Marty truly feared for his life around his step dad. Like maybe he would literally kill him? I asked him about it one time, and he denied it. He just said that Bruno treated him really strict and cut him no slack. However, he didn't go into any detail.

When lunch time came, I felt starved as usual. One lousy banana in the morning doesn't have a whole lot of staying power. Marty and I sat down with our lunches, and who should wander through the cafeteria but Hannah and Moose hand in hand and lovey-dovey as ever.

"Hey, Dude!" Moose bellowed at the top of his lungs. "That little escapade Friday night is going to cost you five-hundred big ones. That's what the deductible is on the Lexus so you'd better cough up some big bucks and fast. Old man Spangler is getting a little antsy for his money."

"What the hell's that all about?" I asked Marty. "The accident only happened Friday night. There's no way that Mr. Spangler could have notified the insurance company all ready—much less told them about it."

"Wonder how is it that Moose knows all the details all ready? Why's he so worried about the money getting paid?" Marty asked as we looked at each other totally puzzled.

"Not only that, but it looks like the big love affair that ended 'forever' Friday night sure patched itself up in a hurry," I commented to Marty as we headed to the pizza line.

"Yeah," Marty answered. "I wonder what those two are up to. Something smells like rotten fish."

That night Mr. Spangler called Dad again. Sure enough, we had to pay that huge deductable of five hundred big ones. He mentioned again that it wasn't the money, but the principle of the thing. He felt I should be responsible. Have no clue where he ever got the idea that I'd have five hundred dollars stashed some place.

What he also probably didn't realize, because Dad sure as hell wouldn't tell him, was that Dad would have to make a trip to the bank, take a half day off work, and try to come up with the money. He sure didn't have five-hundred dollars lying around for something like that either with work being as slow as it was. If somebody didn't come up with a bright idea of some kind quick, I would quit wrestling and go find a part time job. No way would I let Dad take that load on his shoulders all by himself. I just couldn't!

Chapter 15

That afternoon Scott waited outside of the locker room door for me after practice. When I came out, we started the long walk home. We decided that he would meet me every day at the same time until we somehow worked out the problem. If nothing else, Scott made a good sounding board for me, and he actually did give pretty good advice.

"Scott, what am I going to do? I can't stick Dad with that five-hundred dollar deductable. Maybe I'll just have to drop out of wrestling and find a job. Right now I don't see any other way."

"Before you do anything else stupid, why don't you go and talk to Coach. I know he's helped other guys who worked themselves into jams. I also know he's very good at keeping his mouth shut. It's at least worth a try. You know he always treated us fairly even when we weren't the world's greatest wrestlers."

"You might just have an idea there, Scott. I hate to do it because you know he's going to drill me good for going to that party. However, if he can help me out of this mess, it's well worth it. I'll just tell him the truth and let the chips fall where they fall."

"Why don't you catch him right after school tomorrow before either of his assistants show up? They're so damned nosy, they'd have to hang around and listen, and it's none of their business. Besides, the fewer people who know about it, the better."

I agreed big time, so the next morning I raced down to class trying to be the first one there. When I went in, Mr. Andrews was sitting behind his desk looking over some papers from the quiz the hour before. I slipped in and waited for him to look up.

When he did, I started, "Coach, I'm in big trouble. I really, really need to talk to you privately. Is there a time and place that we can without getting interrupted?"

"Sounds serious. What do you have fifth hour?"

"Computer applications, and I'm ahead on my project."

"Ok, that's my planning period. How about if I write you a pass to come here to this room fifth hour? We can shut the door and talk without interruptions."

"That'd be great. You have no idea how much I appreciate it," I told him.

The day dragged by. I didn't think fifth hour would ever get there. When the bell finally rang, I raced down to computer applications and caught Mrs. Lange outside of the door. She gave me a hard time, as usual, just in fun of course, signed the pass, and away I went.

When I showed up at the door to Mr. Andrews's room, he waved me in and said, "Hi, Jeremy. Come on in, shut the door, push the lock, and have a seat. You sounded pretty upset this morning. Hope it isn't anything too serious. What's going on?"

"Well, it is serious. In fact, it's so serious I think I just might have to quit wrestling."

"Ok, take a deep breath and calm down. Most problems aren't as bad as they seem on the surface. Start at the beginning and tell me everything. The door is closed. It's just you and me. Don't leave anything out."

I told him everything from start to finish. I even told him the bit about Moose and Hannah walking hand in hand on Monday after the huge break up scene Friday night. My telling Coach how I'd made a complete fool out of myself hurt. Realizing that I'd had a little outside help doing it made it all the worse. I had to be the laughing stock of all of Moose and Hannah's friends. Coach just sat there and listened. Once in a while he would want something clarified a bit, but for the most part I did all the talking.

After I finished the entire dismal story, Coach leaned back in his chair with his hands folded behind his head thinking without uttering a word for a minute. I didn't know whether to say anything or not, so I kept my mouth shut and waited.

Finally he just kind of gave off a deep sigh, looked me in the eye, and started, "Well, let me do a little snooping around and see what I can come up with. I do believe you, but I think you realize that I also have to do something because you went to that party knowing that drinking and smoking would be going on even if you didn't do anything. You implicated yourself just by being there, and who knows what kind of stories they'll spread. There were certainly enough people there and some of them probably don't like you and would love to mire you in deeper than you already are."

"I know. I really screwed up," I said pretty quietly almost to myself.

"Obviously, you've made wiser choices in your life. So, as far as the team's concerned, you're suspended from competition for the next two weeks. However, I still expect you to be at practice early every day and working your tail off."

"I will, Coach, I promise," I told him.

"I don't know what I'm going to tell the team yet, but I'll think of something. I don't think it would be smart to tell them the whole story right yet, if ever. There'll be plenty of rumors floating around to keep everyone's curiosity occupied for the time being. I just hope you realize that you not only screwed things up for yourself, but your team as well. This is not just all about you."

"Coach, you have no idea how sorry I am, not only for myself, but the team, you, and particularly my parents. Dad went to the credit union yesterday and came home in a sour mood. I don't know what happened, but he wouldn't talk to me about it. What I do know is that work has been real shaky for him lately, and they are behind paying the bills without all of this."

When I walked into the house from practice that night and sat down for dinner, things were still pretty gloomy around there. I told them about my talk with Coach and that he had suspended me from meets for two weeks. Dad appeared to be in a foul mood and not horribly interested, and Mom more or less ignored my dilemma as well. I didn't say anything more about it. We ate in silence.

Finally, Dad blurted out, "Jeremy, I have no idea if I can get a loan or not. It's not all that much money, but we're behind on almost all of our bills and the credit union knows it. They didn't sound all that encouraging. They just said that the loan committee meets on Friday and there'd be no answer before then. If the credit union doesn't come through, I don't know what we're going to do."

After dinner I helped Mom clean up the kitchen and then went upstairs to do my homework. I didn't have all that much to do so I finished rather quickly and just stood there staring out the back window wondering how we would manage. Under normal circumstances they probably could have borrowed the money from Scott's mom and dad, but with the baby coming, they'd spent everything they had on getting the nursery finished.

As I stood there staring out into space, Dad came to the steps and called up to me. "Jeremy, would you come down here for a minute? Coach Andrews is here and wants to talk to us."

"Sure, Dad. Be right down."

Now what? What on earth would Mr. Andrews want this time of night? I sure didn't want to create any more problems for Dad than I all ready had. Hopefully, Coach just wanted to make sure they knew the details about my suspension. Fortunately, I'd already told them. It would've gone over like a lead balloon to hear about it from Coach first.

I walked into the living room. Dad and Coach both had a cup of coffee and were laughing about something. So far, so good, I thought. This was one of those times when it would be better to be seen and not heard so I just kind of waited there with my mouth shut.

"Evening, Jeremy," Mr. Andrews said with a wry smile on his face.

"Hi, Coach," I answered as low keyed and politely as I could. Something seemed to be up, but I had no clue what.

"Ted, I don't know if Jeremy told you and Nancy that he came to see me today or not. Anyway, he did, and I believe he confided in me honestly the whole story. He also indicated that with your partial layoff, and this horrible economy right now, that coming up with five-hundred dollars would be pretty tough. He even suggested that maybe he needed to drop out of wrestling to go find a job so he could pay the deductable."

"That's putting it mildly," Dad said half thinking out loud to himself. "Right now I have no idea when work will pick up again, and what I'm making and partial unemployment sure doesn't pay all the bills much less an additional five-hundred."

Mr. Andrews paused for a few seconds like he was putting something together in his head before he started, "For Jeremy's sake, as well as the team's, the last thing I want to see right now is for him to drop out of wrestling and go out looking for a job to pay for the insurance claim. Let's face it, in this economy there aren't any jobs out there for kids anyway. Out of work adults are grabbing up all those jobs the kids used to take.

"Anyway, I have a proposition. I think you know that I manage the golf course during the spring and summer as the club pro. I also do all the hiring and firing of the greens keepers and other people who work on the course. So, here's what I'd like to propose. I want to lend Jeremy the five-hundred dollars out of my own personal money to pay the insurance deductable."

He pulled five one-hundred dollar bills out of his pocket and laid them on the coffee table. I don't know whose eyes popped larger, mine or Dad's.

"Next spring," he continued, "I expect Jeremy to work for me at the golf course and turn over one-half of his weekly net pay until he repays five-hundred and fifty dollars. That will more than cover the interest I lose at the bank, make him responsible for his own debt, give him a little bit of spending money, and allow him to stay on the team. The only stipulation that I ask of any of you is that this remains strictly among the four of us. I don't want Marty or anyone else to know about it."

Coach saved my life! He solved our problem, and I could continue wrestling after I completed my two week suspension.

As soon as Coach left, you wouldn't believe the atmosphere change. As I headed up to take my shower and get ready for bed, I even heard Mom and Dad laughing about something. Things were back to normal. With the water pouring on my head, I looked up and said under my breath, "Scottie, Mooshy where the hell are you? We need to talk."

"Why are you calling me while you're in the shower? That's disgusting! Don't you have any pride? I don't want to talk to you now. You're all wet, covered with soap, look like a drowned rat, and Mooshy's getting all wet trying to drink out of the tub."

"Oh, just shut up and listen! This is important. Coach saved my ass! I went in and talked to him this afternoon like you told me to, and he came over to the house tonight. He loaned me the five-hundred dollars so all is square with Spangler. I have to work it off next spring at the golf course. In the mean time I'm suspended from competition for two weeks. I'm still on the team and have to practice, but I just can't wrestle in a meet."

"Awesome!" Scott said as Mooshy started licking my ankles. "Now, hurry up and get out of there and get dressed so we can talk about how we're going to break down Hannah and make her tell the truth. Believe it or not, I do have a plan." With that he grabbed my towel and tried to snap me with it.

He actually had a plan, and it sounded totally sweet! It started with isolating Hannah in the drama class room during lunch where she and Moose met every day to make out. Then we could set Scott's plan into action.

"Scott, how do we separate her from Moose? They're practically attached at the hip during lunch."

"Don't sweat the small stuff. I'll take care of it," Scott assured me.

And fortunately for me, Scott came through again. Where he came up with his ideas at times blew my mind. I think his mentor fed him a lot of stuff on the sly. Whatever! The plan worked like a charm.

Chapter 16

Scott and Mooshy spent the night again last night while we finished making our plans. While I raced through breakfast, Scott sat across the table and made faces at me like a two-year old. I had a horrible time keeping a straight face. When I put my jacket on and gathered up my books, Mom came over and gave me a little hug and told me that she just had a feeling that today would be a good day.

When you walk into the main entrance of our school, the office lies immediately to the right and straight ahead there's a large commons area. That's where we eat lunch and hang out in the morning before going to our first hour classes. That morning Moose and Hannah sat in the corner doing what they always did as they gazed into each other's eyes and salivated like a couple of dogs in heat. Moose started each day with a giant Dr. Pepper with tons of ice that he brought in from Mini Mart down town.

Scott immediately walked over to where they sat and pulled something out of his pocket. He unscrewed the cap off, poured the ingredients into Moose's cup and walked away. "There, that will get Moose out of our hair by the time lunch rolls around."

"What did you just pour into his drink?" I asked.

"A pint of magnesium citrate," he answered smiling.

"What's that?" I asked having no clue.

"When you turn fifty or so and are like really old, and you have to have one of those colonoscopy things, that's what they'll give you to flush you out. In about a half hour from now the cramps will start, and Moose will spend the rest of the morning in the john. I would guess that by the time lunch comes, he'll be home wondering what the hell happened."

"How'd you ever know about that trick, and where'd you get it?" I asked wondering if it would really work.

"My mentor, who else? I sure don't get any useful ideas out of you."

Before I could respond, Marty showed up. "What are you snorting about? You look like the village idiot sitting here all by yourself laughing. Are you having your own personal mental breakdown this morning?"

"No, I just thought of something that Scott and I did a long time ago when we were little kids. I spent the night at his house one time during a blizzard. The snow piled up really deep all over the place, and the swirling wind blew a lot of it against the house by the driveway. Anyway, we opened his bedroom window and started making snow balls with the snow that had built up on the ledge. We started horse playing and Scott ended up taking a nose dive out the window and landing in the snow bank that had piled up under his window.

"He didn't have anything on but his pajamas so he about froze to death before they yanked him back into the house and warmed him up. The Rents didn't find it one bit amusing. After their panic attacks settled down and they put Scott back into dry pajamas, his dad gave us both a swat across the butt and sent us to bed. It wasn't really hard, but he did get our attention." Fortunately, I had that story readily available after just telling it to the Moms a few weeks back. I probably did look like a complete doofus sitting there all by myself laughing.

Marty laughed. I'm sure he would have loved memories like I had instead of the ones he had. He never mentioned anything funny that had ever happened to him. The only things he ever mentioned were stories showing how close he and his mom were. He acted like they had a conspiracy against Mr. Bashore. That's why it confused him so much to think that she just walked out and left him with that man.

Just about then the five-minute bell rang and everyone stirred around and headed for class. Marty walked on my left while Scott and Mooshy trudged along on my right. "Nice save!" Scott said laughing at me. "You're getting pretty good at that. Personally, I kind of like the idea of you having your own personal mental breakdown."

So there I was walking down the hall headed to my first hour class and practically biting my lip trying to keep a straight face while Scott harped on me all the way. Ever try to throw an elbow at absolutely nothing? Not easy. I'm sure it looked real clever too if anyone noticed—some kid walking down the hall throwing an elbow at thin air.

Morning dragged like you wouldn't believe. My classes all pretty much turned into a blur. My mind wandered elsewhere. Lunch period finally arrived, so I headed for the room where they held the drama class. Sure enough Hannah stood outside waiting for Moose.

"Hi!" I said as I walked up to her. "Moose running late?"

"Don't know if he's coming or not. He felt pretty crappy when I saw him after second hour. Said he had all kinds of cramps. Normally he would be here by now."

"Maybe he started puking or something and went home and didn't have time to tell you," I suggested.

"Could be."

"Hannah, while you're waiting, let's go inside and talk. You know, I would really like to let bygones be bygones so we could be friends. I don't know what happened out there that night, and I really don't care anymore. I guess it's just impossible for me to carry a grudge. Is that even possible?" I asked as we walked in and closed the door.

"Sure! Why not? Maybe after your season is over, you can come back out to one of my parties again?"

"I just might do that? Maybe if I drink enough, I'll show everyone my secret talent. I normally never let anyone see me do it. It's pretty much hush-hush."

"What's that?"

"Promise you won't tell anybody?"

"Yeah, whatever! What's your big secret talent?"

"I can do anything with my mind that I can do in the flesh. For instance, see that pop machine over there? Let's say we drink a Coke while we talk and I can show you?"

"Okay," she said as she started to head for the machine.

"Hold on! Let's sit right here at this table while I get them mentally," I told her as I dug into my pocket and pulled out a couple of dollar bills and set them on the table. On cue, Scott, who waited right beside us, picked them up and walked over to the machine. She could see the bills floating through the air but that's all she could see. We watched as he put them in the machine one at a time and listened as the cans klunked into the tray. Scott picked them up and brought them over to the table. He set one in front of Hannah and popped the top while she sat there staring at the can.

"That's freaky. How'd you do that?" she asked with a hint of panic in her voice.

"I told you. I can do all kinds of crap with my mind. Now watch this!" I said as I waited for Scott to go into action again.

Suddenly a rubberized cape that they put around the actors when they apply makeup for plays came floating through the air and wrapped around Hannah's shoulders.

She freaked, "Get that thing off of me!" she screamed as she jumped out of her seat and threw it on the floor.

"Wait! Wait! It won't hurt you any more than I would. Remember, it's all coming from my head so maybe it's not really happening? Just relax and play along for a minute."

She sat back down nervously as Scott adjusted it around her shoulders. As she stared at me, Scott snapped a pair of stage handcuffs around the leg of the table and her ankle all in practically one motion.

"What are you doing to me? What do you want?"

"The truth," I told her very calmly.

"The truth about what?" she croaked hardly able to speak.

"The accident and what all happened at your party that night," I told her.

"I told the truth. You know what happened!"

"I don't think so. Guess it's time to show you why you're wearing a cape," I told her staring a hole through her with my eyes wide open so I'd maybe look a little crazy to her.

Scott bought in the large bowl of warm soapy water. Then he bought in a vial of something and poured it into the water. The water started bubbling and gave off the most god awful stench you've ever smelled. I laughed.

"What is that? What do you think you're doing?"

I pulled a pair of latex gloves out of my pocket and started to put them on, "Why, Hannah, I'm going to give you a shampoo. You're going to love the results!" I laughed.

"Screw you! You aren't touching me! What would that do to my hair anyway?" she asked in a near panic.

"Not sure which vial I grabbed, but I think this is the one that will make all your hair fall out from the looks and smell of the solution. You don't have to worry though, it's not permanent. It'll start coming back in after about six months. The only problem is you never know what it's going to look like when it comes back. Sometimes it's straight, sometimes kinky, almost always a different color. Oh well, we'll just have to see what happens down the road." I stared at her with wide open eyes and a slight grin trying my best to look just a tad deranged.

"Jeremy, you little bastard, I told you that you aren't touching me. You come anywhere near me and I'll knock you on your ass. Now give me the key to those freaking handcuffs," she all but screamed at me.

"I won't touch you, but maybe someone or something else will. You're gonna tell Mr. Andrews the truth one way or the other."

With that Scott put his hand on the back on her neck and gently pushed her head down towards the bowl. She reefed back and threw off the cape.

"No!" she screamed. "Don't touch me!"

"The truth, Hannah, the truth! Now, if you don't want the cape on, you should probably take off your sweater so you don't ruin it with the shampoo," I said wide-eyed and calmly before I started laughing again.

After that Scott, who stood right behind her, started slowly lifting her sweater from the bottom just like he intended to pull it off.

Hannah shrieked and threw her arms down pulling her sweater down with it. "What do you want? Why are you doing this to me?" she said as she started crying hysterically.

"I want the truth. I want you to walk down to Mr. Andrews's room with me and tell both of us the truth as to what really happened that night to your car."

"Ok, I will. Only stop all this freaky stuff that you are doing. You're scaring the hell out of me.

"One more thing before we go," I told her. "I think you need to keep in mind that if you ever tell anyone about this little demonstration of my mental abilities, I will totally deny it and everyone will think that maybe you have gone off the deep end. Could you imagine what Moose would say if you told him this yarn?"

"Whatever you say! Just let me out of here. I don't want to be alone with you. You scare me. I'll tell Mr. Andrews, the principal, my dad, whoever. Just leave me alone."

With that Scott unlocked the handcuffs, and I opened the door for her. We headed down the hall to Mr. Bruner's room just as he started his planning period. Scott stayed behind and cleaned up the mess before following us. Would the truth finally come out?

Chapter 17

We walked into Mr. Andrews's room just as he sat down with his coffee in front of a stack of papers he planned to correct. Hannah was still sniffling and looked a mess. He slipped a box of tissue across the desk to her and asked, "What's going on, guys? Looks serious."

"Hannah?" I said as I spread out my arms and gave her my wide eyed creepy look.

"I told Jeremy that I would tell you what happened that night at my party if that freak would just promise to never speak to me again," she blurted out. "Moose and I set Jeremy up. He didn't wreck my mom's car, Moose did."

"Hold it. Don't say any more. We need to have Mr. Bishop come down here and listen to this." With that he picked up the phone on his desk and called the principal. He told him what Hannah had said and that he wanted him in the room.

Seemed like it took forever, but after about ten minutes, Mr. Bishop finally walked through the door. He closed it, and moseyed up to the desk, "We are all going down to the conference room. I called both of your parents and your dads are on the way. I couldn't reach Moose's parents right away so I'll have to bring them in on this after the fact. My secretary will keep trying to get a hold of them during our meeting."

Nobody really said anything except Hannah who mumbled, "Crap!" while giving me another dirty look. We stood up from our chairs and the four of us headed to the conference room. When we arrived, Mr. Bishop asked Hannah to sit on one end of the long conference table and me at the other so we faced each other. It looked to me like we should maybe forget about classes for the rest of the day.

My dad showed up first. He came in and the principal asked him to sit in the seat to my right. Then we waited for Mr. Spangler to show up. He appeared maybe five minutes later.

After all the introductions, Mr. Bishop looked up at Hannah and said, "Hannah, some really serious allegations have been made against Jeremy resulting from the party you had at your home. You accused him of practically stealing your mom's car and then wrecking it because he was intoxicated. That resulted in him having to pay the five-hundred dollar insurance deductable on the car, lose his wrestling privileges for a while, plus other penalties his parents have enforced—to say nothing about what has happened to his reputation.

"Now, this morning you and Jeremy walk into Mr. Andrews's classroom and tell him that you and Moose set Jeremy up, and that Moose was really the one responsible for the damage to your mom's car. I guess we need to clear the air and get to the bottom

174

of what happened. Would you please start at the beginning and tell the whole story, please? Also, keep in mind that the wall camera is taping everything that is said."

Hannah's eyes misted up again. I noticed that she never once looked at her dad after she started telling her story. She stared a hole through me most of the time. "I have a lot of weekend parties at our house because my parents are never there, and I'm home alone and totally bored to death. I hate that log cabin because it's so out in the middle of nowhere so I don't go. Anyway, Moose took the car and went out for supplies for the party. I guess he started drinking a little earlier than usual and probably shouldn't have been driving. Anyway, he managed to swerve around a corner too tight, bounce over a curb, and clip a telephone pole," she said and then paused.

"Go on," Mr. Bishop told her.

"When he showed up back at our house with the dent, we figured we had to find some patsy to take the blame. So who should show up but Jeremy. He's never been to one of my parties before or anyone else's for all I know. He's one of those nerdy jocks who never do anything exciting and fun. Anyway, Moose and I faked this big fight in the bedroom and he stormed out. I came out of the bedroom pretending to be in tears and all that. That's when I moved on Jeremy.

"I talked him into going for a ride. He had his own car, but that wouldn't work. I suckered him into driving the Lexus. I stood in front of the dent and hid it from view as he admired the car. He was more than happy to drive Mom's car.

She told all about going to the gravel pit and all of the preliminary stuff and then she kind of slowed down, like she didn't want to go on. She was right to the point where I took a pee break in the bushes. Scott, who had been standing by silently all this time, noticed Hannah faltering. She wanted to chicken out. He whispered in my ear, "Nobody's looking at you but Hannah so point at your zipper on your sweat shirt and then put your hands behind your head."

So while she kind of mumbled and stalled while trying to figure out how she would get herself out of this mess without telling the rest of the story, I caught her eye and pointed at my zipper. Then I leaned back in my chair with my hands behind my head and let Scott take over. As I stared straight at her and didn't move, my zipper started going up and down kind of slow like. I couldn't help but smile.

"Okay! Okay! Jeremy, knock it off! I'll tell everything, just leave me alone!" she yelled across the table at me.

Everyone looked my way so I acted totally confused and just shrugged my shoulders with a really puzzled look on my face like I had no idea what made her babble on like that.

"Please continue with your story, Hannah," Mr. Bishop told her.

"Jeremy drank probably six cokes and had to get out of the car and go take a leak. He started to take his drink with him so I told him to let me hold it. It would be gross to go in the woods while you had your pop can in your hands. So he gave it to me to hold. While he went in the woods, I poured some of it out, filled the can up with vodka, and slipped a Roofie in it. I knew he would never taste it."

Right then my dad piped up, "Excuse me, but what is a Roofie and what does it do?"

Mr. Bishop answered, "Roofie is the street name for a common date rape drug. Roofies and vodka can kill you. Fortunately, Jeremy drank nothing but Coke all night or he might have been in real trouble. More than likely he just became sick as a dog and didn't remember a thing. Sounds to me like the object was to get him so he didn't know which end was up. With absolutely no memory of the evening, they could pin the accident on him and he'd never know the difference. So, Hannah, is that pretty much how it went?"

"Yes! That was the idea. It didn't take very long at all and Jeremy passed out. I started to get a little nervous after awhile because he wouldn't wake up. I thought he'd just go into some kind of stupor. I had no idea that he could have died from it. Moose didn't tell me that."

"So, then what happened?" Mr. Bishop asked.

"I jumped out of the car, went around, and literally pushed him over in the seat so he leaned against the passenger seat door. Then I drove out of the pit and cruised around town with his window rolled down for hours. It must have been close to four in the morning before he started to wake up. When he did, the first thing he said was that he wanted to throw up. I stopped the car and let him out. No way would I let him puke all over Mom's car. We ended up close to his house so I told him he could walk home from there. I didn't even think about his car being parked in our driveway or I might have taken him back to get it."

"If you had thought of it you would have taken him back and let him drive home in that condition?" her dad asked in total amazement.

"Whatever!"

"Did you ever stop to consider that you could have killed him with that combination of drugs and vodka?" her dad asked.

She looked me right straight in the eye and said, "Maybe it's too bad it didn't happen that way. The world would have one less freak, he would have been blamed for the accident, nobody would have ever become the wiser, and I wouldn't be sitting here right now going through all this crap!"

The meeting came to an abrupt end. Mr. Spangler apologized to me and Dad for Hannah, the false accusations, and a lot of other unnecessary stuff. I just wanted out of there. Dad put his arm around me as we walked out, and Scott hooted in my ear continuously about the 'freak' comment. Trying to block him out and pay attention to Dad at the same time wasn't exactly the easiest thing in the world to do.

That night Coach Andrews called and talked to Dad for quite a while. When he hung up the phone, he told me what happened after our meeting. "After we left school, it seems that the secretary finally contacted Moose's parents at home so the others went over to his house to meet with him and his parents. They took the recorded session with them. Moose and Hannah ended up accusing each other of everything from buying beer and pot illegally, to hosting the parties, to setting you up, and everything else. To make a long story short, Moose and Hannah will split the five-hundred dollar deductable so Mr. Andrews can get his money back."

"I wonder if that means that I don't have a job this summer after all," I asked somewhat wistfully.

"As a matter of fact, Coach said to tell you that he looked forward to having you work for him this summer. He said he always knew you were a good kid, but he never realized how good."

So there's Dad passing on all of these compliments from Coach making me feel really good about myself for a change, and there stood Scott leaning on the wall by the fireplace sticking his finger down his throat fake gagging. There were times....

That night when I started getting ready to go up to bed, Dad looked up from the book he was reading, "You know I'm really curious about something."

"What's that, Dad?" I asked.

"You were under the influence of a date rape drug and out of it for over four hours in a car alone with a young lady who demonstrated to all of us that she has no morals or scruples. I wonder if she took advantage of you."

...

The next day when I came down the stairs about ready to go to school, my keys, cell phone, IPod and everything sat by my place at the breakfast table. I was un-grounded, and I hadn't even finished med school yet. I could hardly wait to tell Marty what all happened. Naturally, he was very happy for me. Two other very strange things were obvious that morning at school. Neither Hannah nor Moose were anywhere to be seen.

It took a few days for the rumors to filter through the school, but they all made me smile. Hannah and Moose enrolled in private high school military academies several hundred miles apart. From what I heard, both of their days started at six in the morning with a ten mile run before breakfast. Apparently the rest of their days went downhill from there. They were allowed none of the items that had been taken away from me—cell phone, computer, IPod, etc. for the rest of the school year. I couldn't keep the smile off my face for the rest of the day. Life was good again. Would it stay that way?

Chapter 18

Back on the wrestling team, participating in the meets, enjoying school, and my reputation seemed to be back in tact—life was pretty good once again. Marty and I grew to be pretty close friends, and Scott and Mooshy managed to disappear again. Marty still couldn't leave his house at night or on the weekends, but he was a lot of fun in school, and he needed a friend. We agreed to make our relationship appear to be all business during practice and pretend that we really didn't like each other all that much because his dad showed up every day, leaned against the wall with his arms folded, and glared at us. That's what he wanted, and that's the way it would look.

The season started to wind down and it wouldn't be long before tournaments started. First there would be our league meet, next districts, then regionals, and finally states. Once districts started you had to keep winning or your season ended. Marty and I both had winning records. They weren't anything to get excited about, but they were okay.

On the Monday practice before our league meet, everyone acted in a really good mood. We had unexpectedly won our own school's invitational the previous Saturday. Everyone wrestled exceptionally well that day. Everything jelled as people competed better than they ever had. I placed fourth and Marty placed third in our respective weights. That surprised most everyone because of the fierce competition. It had just been one of those days.

Practices averaged two hours a night as the season wound down. Coach put it to us big time. About a half hour into practice, Marty and I worked a move and he slipped. I automatically rolled him over on his back and pinned him. It happened so fast and unexpectedly that we both started laughing as I pinned his arms down with my knees and thumped him on the chest with my knuckles.

We were still laughing when this big booming voice right above us bellowed out, "Get on your feet!"

Mr. Bashore, Marty's step dad, seethed above us. We both jumped to our feet and Marty looked scared to death. Before Coach could get over to where we were, Mr. Bashore yelled at Marty, "Get your loser ass to the car! Now!"

Marty shot out of there on a dead run as Coach came up and very quietly said, "Mr. Bashore, let's you and me step outside for just a minute."

They left as one of the assistant coaches took over practice. I hooked up with two other kids about my size and we practiced as a threesome. Coach came back in a little while and nothing more was said about it.

I felt really sorry for Marty about then. His dad didn't like what happened. Okay, I understand that, but he could have waited until after we finished to yell at him. Instead he jerked him out of practice early and made a federal case out of it. I wondered if yelling would be the only thing Marty faced when he went home.

The fun, positive atmosphere that practice started with after our Saturday victory disappeared. Nobody laughed, smiled, or anything else. Everyone acted much like me. They just wanted to finish what we had to do and leave.

Practice finally ended, and I headed for the showers. Like always I took my time, relaxed, and kind of used that time to contemplate what had happened that day. Typically, I would be one of the last ones to leave. That afternoon turned out to be no exception. In fact, I managed to be the last kid out of the door. I stopped to talk to Coach for a few minutes so that made me even later. He wouldn't tell me a thing about Mr. Bashore or Marty. He just said that some things are privileged information and the least talked about the better.

That morning I had parked my car almost to the end of the parking lot which was around the corner and pretty much hidden from view. As I stood there with my hand in my pocket digging out my keys, something hit me right in the back of the head. I fell like a rock to the ground as someone jumped on top of me and pounded my face and head.

Before I blacked out I heard this muffled voice yell at me. It sounded like the person had covered his face with something, "Really funny wasn't it? See how funny you think this is!"

The next thing I remember was waking up in the hospital. Mom had my hand and kept repeating over and over, "Jeremy, honey can you hear me? Jeremy, wake up."

I forced my eyes open and looked up. Mom had a death grip on my hand and Dad stood there with a really worried look on his face. I was totally confused and my head hurt like the devil. Mom explained the best she could.

"Somebody attacked you when you left the locker room. The night custodian came out to dump some trash and saw you lying beside your car and heard somebody running away. He called 911 and they bought you here. You're in the emergency room right now."

"How long have I been here?" I asked having no idea the time or anything else.

"It's about 7:30 in the evening. You've been here close to an hour. The custodian found you at roughly 6:30. Thank goodness he came out when he did. Apparently, he scared away the attacker."

About that time Dad started asking questions of another nature, "Who did it, Son? Did you see the person who jumped you? Most of your bruises and stuff are on the back of your head like maybe somebody hit you from behind."

"I didn't see anyone, Dad. I remember hearing a muffled voice asking me if I thought that his beating me on the head was funny, and then I guess I blacked out because the next thing I remember is Mom telling me to wake up."

The doctors and nurses checked on me every so often and finally decided that I should spend the next couple of days at the hospital for observation. They didn't think my injuries were too serious, but I had a concussion, blurry vision, and vomiting so they wanted to keep tabs on that and make sure nothing else was going on like a brain bleed or something. They told me those things can be deadly. They took enough pictures of my brain to fill a photo album. Visiting hours ended at nine so Mom and Dad left and let me rest. My head throbbed, and I felt achy and sore all over, but I surmised that I would live—that is if I could ever stop throwing up.

As I lay there wondering what really happened, I felt a pressure against my legs. I looked down and there lay Mooshy curled up in a ball with his head sprawled over my ankles using me for his pillow. Scott couldn't be too far away. I looked over at the chair in the corner, and there he parked with his legs curled up under him.

"Hi! When did you get here?" I asked him telepathically.

"Rode with you in the ambulance. You mumbled my name under your breath and then I heard the 911 call go out so Mooshy and I decided we'd better check it out and find out what you got yourself into this time."

"Not really sure myself. Somebody sure doesn't like me."

"Any ideas at all?"

"Not really," I answered wondering why anyone would do that. It sure didn't appear to be robbery because my cell phone and car were untouched.

About that time a nurse walked in with a thermometer and stuck it in my mouth and then talked to me like I could really answer her. "How's that head feeling, sweetie? I imagine it's thumping away pretty good behind your eyes right now. That nausea medication working yet?" Fortunately, she couldn't hear or see Scott telling her where she should be jamming that thermometer. With friends like him...

She chatted away as she took my blood pressure, pulse, and all that garbage. When she finished, I asked her, "It's okay if I take a shower isn't it? I took one before I left school, but after rolling around in the dirt out in the parking lot, I feel a little on the grimy side."

"You might not really want to," she said. "Can you wait until morning?"

"Why?"

"Technically within the first hours after a concussion we would have to do it one of two ways. I can bring in a basin of water and give you a sponge bath right here in bed. One of the orderlies will put a rubber sheet under you and I'll bathe you. If that happens, it's a complete bath where I wash everything. If I let you into the shower, I put on a raincoat and rain hat and go in there with you. The third option is to wait until morning, and if everything still looks good like we think it probably will, you can go into the shower by yourself with a nurse standing outside."

"Kinky! Kinky! Go for the shower. That'd be hilarious!" Scott chirped in my ear while I tried to ignore him.

"Uh, that's a no brainer. I'll wait until morning. Why would you have to go in the shower with me? Why couldn't you just stand outside?"

"If you started to pass out, I'd catch you. The last thing we want is for you to fall down and hit your head on the tile wall or floor. Inside the shower stall's not a great place to sleep."

I started laughing. She looked at me somewhat puzzled, like maybe I was cracking up or something. "My shower can wait until tomorrow morning. Now, speaking of sleeping in the shower, I want to tell you a story. About five years ago when I was maybe twelve years old, I stayed overnight with this best friend of mine. We were like brothers until he died in a car-bike accident a few months back. Anyway, our parents changed our bed times from nine to ten during summer vacation. Scottie was a morning person and usually fell asleep in his chair before we had to go to bed.

"Anyway, this one night we were getting ready for bed, and he took his shower first. He had been in there like forever so I checked up on him. There he sat in the corner of the tub with his head against the wall sound asleep with cold water running on his feet. He'd emptied the hot water heater. I slipped out into the hallway and motioned for his mom and dad to come up to look. His dad turned off the water and the three of us stood there laughing at him and he never woke up. He just sat there snoring.

"His mom just shook her head and went back downstairs while his dad and I took care of him. His dad lifted him up on his feet on the shower mat and we both dried him off with a towel. Then his dad sat him down on his knee as I handed him his underwear and

187

pajamas while he dressed him. He ended up carrying him into his room, putting him in bed, and tucking him in just like you would a baby. He rolled Scott over on his side, kissed him good night, and he never woke up.

"That morning we all sat around laughing at him while we told him what happened. He tried to accuse us of lying, but I guess we finally convinced him. From then on he always took his shower in the morning."

"That's quite a story. Bet you couldn't wait to spread that one to all your friends," she said.

"Nah! I didn't tell anyone. It would have embarrassed him too much. We kept that as our own private family joke. Anytime we wanted to see him blush we'd mention it."

When she finally left, I knew I would catch it from Scott, "Thanks a lot, Germy. Nothing like embarrassing me in front of a complete stranger."

"Oh, quit your whining. You know it was funny. Admit it."

"Yeah, yeah! Whatever! Why don't you go to sleep? Mooshy and I are tired. We'll talk more about your so-called attacker in the morning. You probably just fell on the ice and knocked yourself out."

Next morning they brought in breakfast at six o'clock waking me up in the process. Scott and Mooshy were nowhere to be seen. I know they spent the night in the other bed in the room, but they were gone then. I had just finished breakfast when I heard a quick knock on the side of the wall and a policeman walked in. He set his hat and bottle of water on the shelf by the door, and said, "Hi, Jeremy. We meet again. Remember me?"

"Yes! I do, officer. You are the policeman who told me how to get in to see Scott's bike after the accident. I met you at the restaurant down town."

"That's right. So, how are you doing with your buddy's death and all? You doing better?"

"Yeah, it took a while, but I think I'm doing okay now. At least I don't blame myself anymore."

"That's good. Now, the reason that I'm here this morning is I need to pick your brain about what happened last night. You have any idea who might have done this?"

"No, sir. I don't have the vaguest suspicion."

He stayed for about a half hour and asked the same questions over and over in different ways trying to jog something in my memory. It didn't work. When he stood up and started to leave, he paused for a second, and said, "You certainly don't lead a boring life do you?"

"What do you mean?" I asked.

"Well, you lose a friend, you get assaulted and end up in the hospital, and yet you still have this strange way of entertaining yourself."

"I guess I don't understand what you are talking about my entertaining myself," I said confused.

"The magic tricks. At the restaurant you kept messing with my coffee cup and saucer. You sat across the table from me with your hands in plain sight, but I know I saw my doughnut lift off of the plate. Now, come on, Jeremy. Tell me how you did that."

"Sir, I don't really know what you're talking about. All I know is that my headache seems to be coming back real bad. I really need to shut my eyes and rest for a while."

"Yeah, right! Okay, so you won't tell me. Just remember, I know you did it somehow," he said as he headed for the door. "Jeremy!" he suddenly yelled laughing. "When I came in here I set my hat on this shelf bill down with my water bottle beside it. Now it's upside down with my water bottle parked in the middle of it. You are one funny kid!" he laughed as he looked at me waiting for an explanation.

"Oh, my head is pounding!" I said as I rolled over on my belly and pulled the pillow over my head.

"You bet. That line and a buck and a quarter will get you a small cherry slush at the Mini Mart. In the meantime, listen up through your 'pounding' head for just a second. I find you a very, very interesting person, and I would love to sit down and talk man-to-man with you someday strictly unofficially. I won't even wear my uniform. I'll be just plain old Sean O'Connor with no 'Sergeant' tagged to it for the time. Incidentally, I'm a detective sergeant, so I have some leeway regarding on what and where I work."

"Sure! What about? Anything in particular?" I asked wondering why a policeman wanted to talk to me just kind of mano e mano.

"Every once in a while I have these flashes of things in my brain that are totally unexplainable. I've read up on some of this stuff, and I think maybe you have something going on too—I'm just not sure what. I suspect you're doing something with that brain of yours. I'll leave my personal card right here on your night stand. It has my private cell phone number on it. I always carry it. If you ever need help quick, or if you would ever be willing to talk about whatever the weird stuff is that we both have going on, call me. Will you?"

I lifted my face out of the pillow. I couldn't help smiling when I said, "Would you believe it if I told you I could see and talk to dead people?"

"Jeremy, you have my mind so screwed up right now, I just might be willing to believe anything you told me," he said taking a couple of steps back into my room.

Of course my trying to keep a straight face was somewhat compromised by the fact that while we talked, Scott ran over there and switched his hat and water bottle back to its original position.

He turned around and headed for the door where his stuff sat. He took one look and burst right out laughing. I could hear him continue to laugh all the way down the hall.

With him safely out of sight and hearing range, I rolled back over and said, "Scott! You are such a turd!"

"You're just jealous of my superior intellect," Scottie grinned. "Oh, by the way, I hear whispers out there that things aren't going so well with Marty. Maybe you'd better start paying a little closer attention when you get back to school."

With that, he disappeared, and I dozed off.

Chapter 19

They kept me in the hospital until Wednesday morning. I could go back to school on Thursday, but my wrestling season had ended. The concussion didn't end up being all that bad, but they didn't want to take any chances especially at my age. It bummed me out at first, but I really kind of agreed. My season was pretty much over anyway. I might have gotten through districts, but there is no way I would have survived regionals.

In class Marty withdrew and didn't say much. He sneezed and coughed terribly and could hardly breathe.

"Marty, what happened the other night after practice?" I asked when we first walked into class.

"Everything's cool. I really don't want to talk about it," He answered as he struggled to breath.

He showed up at practice Tuesday and worked out with the same two guys that I had after he left Monday. His dad stood there as always and leaned against the wall just like nothing had happened. Marty's two workout partners took it as easy on him as they could because he spent most of the time wheezing and gasping for breath. He belonged in bed, not on the mat.

The next day in English class Marty quizzed me about my attack and sounded like everyone else.

"You have any idea who did it?" he asked. "Did you see the person at all?"

"No, I never saw him," I told him.

"Did the guy say anything?"

"Yeah, he asked me how I liked it, which I thought was a little weird."

"You recognize the voice?" Marty asked.

"Marty, when you get out of school you should go to the police academy or something. You sound just like Sergeant O'Connor. Those are the same exact questions he asked.

"Just wondered," Marty mumbled with a kind of faraway look in his eye. I hoped I hadn't offended him.

Since I couldn't wrestle any more for the rest of the season, I kind of ended up as the team mascot. Coach Andrews treated me great. He told me in class Thursday to come to practice and help out refereeing individual matches, keeping time on the practice sessions, and doing anything else I could to help. He wanted me to stay a part of the team.

The rest of the week went pretty quickly, and we all headed out to the district meet on Saturday. We weren't there too long when I discovered that a couple of our top fans were missing.

I wandered over to where my mom and dad sat in the cafeteria, and asked, "Where's Jim Dad and Mom Sara? They're not here. That's not like them. They come to all the meets."

"Well, Sara's in the hospital. They went during the night."

"Why? What's the matter?" I asked starting to panic.

"Relax! It's okay. Baby Emily decided that it was about time she made her appearance."

"Oh, wow! Is she here yet? I want to see her!" I spurted out all kind of excited.

"Not yet. Jim will call us as soon as it happens. We can't go barging in right now, but tonight after the tournament, maybe we'll go check things out—provided Emily joins us by then."

The rest of the day crawled by. Emily arrived screaming and kicking at four-oh-one, and Jim Dad called to let us know about four-thirty. Mom took the call and could hear Emily crying over the phone. I wanted to leave and go to the hospital right then, but Mom and Dad both said that Jim and Sara needed a little time for just the three of them before we barged in.

Marty lost his second match of the day so that took care of him. He shouldn't have been out on the mat. He felt so weak from whatever it is he had, he could barely function, much less wrestle.

When he came off the mat, he was all red and sweaty and gasping for breath.

I heard what his dad told him and it really ticked me off, "Get your stuff, loser, and get your ass to the car."

That's bull! I mean, like, what did he expect? Marty belonged in bed, not on the mat.

We finally left about seven thirty and headed for the hospital. I sat in the back seat and just concentrated telepathically as hard as I could. "Scottie, come! Scottie, heal! Mooshy, bring Scott!"

When we pulled into the parking lot, I heard Scottie whisper, "All right, already! I'm here. Just shut up and ignore me. I've already been up to see her. She's beautiful."

When we walked into the room, Mom reached out and took the baby from Mom Sara. They had her all wrapped up.

"I wanna see!" Mom said. So what did she do? She stripped Emily. She pealed her down to her diaper, peeked inside to make sure she was a girl, and started counting fingers and toes. She had ten of each. Amazing!

"Oh, she's perfect! Mom squealed.

Big deal! What did she expect? Good God! Both moms giggled like a couple of teenagers. Dad, Jim Dad, and I all kind of looked at each other and shrugged. It embarrassed me. I hope they didn't act like that when Scott and I were born.

Dad took his turn with Emily, and then they had me sit down in the chair. Mom placed her in my arms. I never held a baby before. She seemed so tiny and looked horribly fragile. I worried that she'd break or something. The next thing I knew she grabbed a hold of my finger. I have to admit, that pumped me up. Scott stood right beside my chair and ran his finger up and down her soft little cheek without saying a word. That choked me up. "Why, oh why?" I asked myself.

"So, Jeremy," Mom Sara asked pulling me out of my reverie, "are we ready for our first diaper changing lesson?"

"No! That's gross! If she's wet or something, somebody take her." Everyone laughed at me as Mom took her. I don't think she needed her diaper changed, they just wanted to hassle me. It worked. Besides that way, Mom could hold the baby again.

That night at home my mind swirled on so many things. With the new baby in the family, I had to ask, "Mom, they don't consider her to be Scott's replacement do they?"

"No, of course not. Scott lived for sixteen years. Nobody will ever replace him. Besides, if you remember, she was already pregnant with Emily when Scott died. Emily is her own person. She's new and she's wonderful, but she'll never replace Scott," Mom answered.

That night as I stirred around getting ready for bed my mind still swirled. I sure hoped Mom told the truth about Emily replacing Scott. I also wondered about what had to be going on in Scott's mind? We didn't really ever talk about it. What did he think about having a baby sister? He would never be able to hold her or play with her as she grew up. Would he worry that his parents and my family would just forget about him now that the baby was born as all of us poured our love and attention on her?

"Don't worry, Scottie. It ain't gonna happen that way," I said under my breath.

"I know, and I know what you've been thinking too. I just don't want to talk about it right now. Ok?" Scott said suddenly. I didn't even know he was around.

"Sure! Fine!" I answered and he vanished again.

Then I thought about the deal with Marty. What a crappy life he leads. If I were that sick, I sure wouldn't be on the mat. I would have been at the doctor's office so fast it would have made my head spin. None of the four rents ever took chances with our health. Just like when I had my concussion, the doctor said that it would probably be wise if I didn't wrestle for a while, and Mom just said, "No problem! He's done for the season."

That was it. No big discussion. No argument. Nobody called me a loser because I couldn't go on. My season ended right then and there. Period! Time to move on.

I hoped that Marty would make it to school Monday. We needed to talk. Scott figured that Bruno probably abused him big time. Mom and Mom Sara both warned that I had to be real careful approaching that idea. If there was anything either could do to help, they would. However, one just can't go and accuse someone of something without proof. There was also the potential problem that if they called the authorities, Marty and Mr. Bashore just might disappear down the road, and then there would be no way of helping him.

As I said earlier, my mind just churned for most of Saturday night. Sunday seemed to be a little better. We wandered up to the hospital that afternoon. The doctors scheduled their release for Monday morning so that would be our last visit up there. Scott sat over in the corner watching everything when we walked in. After a few minutes of all of us catching up on the latest baby news, he pointed to the door. I told everyone I was going out into the hall to get a drink and he followed me.

"I rocked Emily to sleep last night," he said grinning.

"Cool! How'd you do it?"

"Mom kept her in the room over night. They gave her a choice of having the baby sleep in the nursery or in a crib in the room. She chose to have Emily in with her. About two a.m. she started fussing so I picked her up and took her over to the rocker and rocked her back to sleep. She zonked right out for about a half hour. Then when I heard a nurse walking down the hall, I hustled Emily back to her crib just in time. The nurse came in and woke Mom up and had her feed the baby."

I laughed, "Next thing you know you'll be changing those crappy diapers."

"Bull!" he half shouted in a nervous sounding voice.

We both laughed at that one. Yet in the back of my mind, another issue lurked on the horizon. Marty was in trouble. Everyone knew it and nobody did anything about it—yet!

Chapter 20

Monday morning arrived and nobody had seen Marty. My curiosity peaked immediately. At lunch I slipped into the office and checked with one of the secretaries. I told her that Marty and I were working on a project for our English class final exam that rapidly approached the next week, and I needed to know when he'd be back.

"I don't know, Jeremy. Nobody called in for him so I have no idea how long he'll be out," she told me.

"How come? I thought parents had to call in."

"Well, they are supposed to. However, Mr. Bashore never does. He doesn't have a phone to call with, and he never bothers to write a note either," She probably told me stuff that she shouldn't, but she had been around forever and everyone knew her as the school gossip. If you ever wanted the scoop on something, you asked her.

Marty didn't show up all week. I assumed he was probably so sick that he couldn't get out of bed and drag himself to school.

Besides, I was busy and didn't have time to check up on him. We had five kids going to the regionals that weekend, and I had to perform my duties as the team mascot—at least, that's what Scott called me. Every night after school I would go to practice and help referee matches, blow the whistle, just like I had done the week before.

Saturday came and they held the regional tournament on the other side of the state. We drove two hours each way just to watch. Dad and Jim Dad went to support the guys, but Mom, Mom Sara, and Emily stayed home. Mom spent a lot of time at their house that week helping out. She cooked, cleaned, and did all the little things around the house while Mom Sara tended to Emily. I wondered at times which one acted the more excited over the baby.

The tournament dragged on for twelve hours meaning that we never made it home Saturday night until midnight. All of our guys lost so nobody would be going to go on to the state tournament the next weekend. Our season had ended. I can't really explain how I felt—glad that it was over, yet sad too. I would not miss the hours and hours of practice, the dieting, the discipline, and all that one bit. I would miss the companionship with the kids, the parents, fans, and the coaches. Of course, I looked forward to the next year. I hoped that I would improve enough to go to the state tournament and with a little luck win a medal.

I slept almost all the way home. Dad drove and Jim Dad kept him company in the front seat. I tuned in my IPod and tuned out the rest of the world. The dads pulled into a drive through for coffee before they hit the highway. They asked me if I wanted anything, but I didn't. I just wanted to crash, and crash I did.

Must have been noon before I woke me up on Sunday. Mom and Dad went to church by themselves and let me sleep in as long as I wanted to—that is until dear Scott started chirping in my ear.

"Hey, sleepy head. You gonna stay in bed all day?"

"Oh, just leave me alone," I grumbled as he grabbed the covers and pulled them off of me.

"Get your lazy butt out of bed before I have to douse you with water or something," he threatened.

"I will literally kill you if you even think of it," I snarled as I crawled out of bed not really considering what I had just said.

He just laughed. "Your mom and dad left a note saying that they were meeting with my mom and dad at the restaurant at one in case you wanted to join them. You can't. We have things to do. Go feed your face so we can start making some plans."

I grabbed a bowl of cereal and a banana and tried to check out the sports page in the paper. It didn't even mention our wrestling team—as usual. Scott snatched it away from me and told me to pay attention.

"Marty's your best friend now so we need to check up on him. I have a strange feeling there's something seriously wrong out there. If he's really all that sick, he could probably stand to see a friendly face—that is, if his dad will let you in to see him. If not, we go to plan B. Finish your cereal and let's get out of here."

When I drove into the drive, Mr. Bashore's car sat parked out by the back door. "Rats! I'd hoped he'd be gone" I told Scott.

"Me too," Scott said. "He's really kind of creepy."

I walked up and knocked on the door. Seemed like it took an awfully long time for anyone to answer, but he finally did. "What!" was his only response when he stuck his head out.

"Is Marty here? I'd like to see him. I know he's been sick, but I thought he'd like a report on the regional meet yesterday," I said trying to be as cheerful and courteous as I could.

"No! He could care less about what happened yesterday, and you don't need to talk to him. Didn't I tell you before to just leave Marty alone? He isn't going to talk to you or go anywhere with you. I told you that I don't want him associating with riffraff like you. So how far did you get in the regional tournament yesterday?"

"I got hurt last week and had a concussion. The doctor wouldn't let me compete."

"Loser!" he said and slammed the door in my face. What a jerk!

Scott and I looked at each other and shrugged our shoulders.

"That guy's something else," I said as we climbed back into the car had headed down the road. About a half a mile to the east sat an old abandoned one-room school.

"Pull in there a minute and check this place out." Scott said. "Looks like a person could park behind it and stay pretty well hidden. If we walked across the road, we could climb the fence and make our way up through the empty fields between here and there and spy on Marty's house."

"Let's double check to make sure there aren't any cows or anything out there. All I need is to get gored by a damn bull or something," I said as Scott laughed. He thought that would be funny.

We spent the rest of the day hanging out at my place playing computer games and sitting on the patio. I even did a little homework. That night just about the time it started getting dark, I told Mom and Dad, "I'm going out and ride around for a little while just to see who's out and about. Have to do my part to keep OPEC in business, you know. I won't be late."

"Be careful!" they both said practically in unison. Some things never changed.

By the time Scott and I made it to the old school, it was pitch black outside.

"There's no moon in sight and not that many stars," I grumbled as I jumped out of the car and tried to get adjust to the darkness.

"Big deal! Get used to it, wimp!" Scott teased. He could see in the dark just fine.

After a few minutes we walked across the street and managed to crawl through the barbed wire fence without me cutting myself or snagging any of my clothes. I shuffled along keeping my feet in contact with the ground all the way as Scott and Mooshy ambled along off to my right. They enjoyed themselves. I didn't. I spent all my time groping along hoping I wouldn't stumble over something and fall.

We trudged along for just a few minutes when my cell phone rang. "Crap!" I exclaimed under my breath. "I forgot all about this thing."

It was a political advertisement. I turned the phone off. "Don't let me forget to turn this thing back on when we leave, Scott. The Rents would scream bloody murder if they tried to get a hold of me and couldn't." Parental orders! I stayed available and in contact at all times. They were stricter about that after Scott's accident.

We made it about half way across the field when I ran smack into another fence. "Ouch!" I kind of yelled out. "Where did that sucker come from? I didn't see it this afternoon when we scoped the place out."

"Where'd it catch you?" Scott asked at least trying to be sympathetic.

"Right across the chest. It stings! One of the barbs bit in just a little. Will not tell Mom and Dad about this! I don't need getting the third degree or a tetanus shot," I whined feeling sorry for myself as Scott tried to keep a straight face.

He and Mooshy stayed a little closer playing Seeing Eye dog in the dark. Finally we got close enough to the house to check things out just a little.

"Doesn't look like there's any activity going on around there," Scott whispered.

"Bashore's car still sits right where it was parked this afternoon," I told Scott. "Apparently he never left the house all day."

While we squatted there out of sight talking about what we were going to do next, Mr. Bashore walked out of the house and headed to his car without a word. My parents always said goodbye when they headed out. I wondered if Marty was even there.

We watched as he turned right out of the driveway and drove down the road right past where my car sat hidden behind the school. His brake lights never flashed so we assumed he didn't see it or it didn't register with him that it belonged to me if he did.

As soon as he disappeared out of sight, Scott said, "Come on. Let's go bang on the door and see if Marty's in there and will answer it."

We hustled up to the house. I knocked on the back door to see if Marty would come out. We didn't hear a sound from inside.

"Come on," Scott whispered. "Follow me."

We crept around the house and tried to look in the windows. It appeared to be totally dark inside. We couldn't see a thing—not even Scott with his night vision. The only thing we accomplished was my tripping over something and falling flat on my face. This wasn't working.

"Let's try one last thing," I said to Scott as I went to the back door, pulled my sleeve over my hand so no finger prints would be left in case anyone ever checked for some reason, and tried the door. Bruno had locked it.

"Let's get out of here," Scott said. "We need to talk about this. We're missing something here."

Feeling totally frustrated we headed out. We walked down the road with our backs to traffic. When cars came down the road from either direction, I ducked behind a tree and hid just in case it happened to be Bashore. Scott didn't bother. Nobody could see him anyway. Fortunately Bruno didn't come back and catch us snooping around.

"I hate to say it, but you're a mess. When we make it to your house, head for the bathroom and clean up. Pretend you have to go pee or something. Just don't let them get a good look before you do," Scott told me as we drove home.

I had no idea what I looked like after I stabbed myself with barbed wire and fell flat on my face in the dirt behind Marty's house, so when I walked into the house, I did just what Scott told me and headed straight for the bathroom. Usually when I went home, I stopped and talked with the old folks, but I needed to check myself out first.

"Hi, everyone!" I said when I walked in the door in a big rush. "Gotta go before I wet my pants. Be right back," I announced as I raced to the john.

Things really didn't look too bad when I stood under the light. I dusted myself off, checked for blood seeping through my shirt, and didn't see any so I wandered out to greet the Rents.

"So what have you been up to?" Dad asked not really being nosy—just making conversation.

"I didn't see anyone out and about so I cruised out to Marty's house. I pulled into the driveway and went up and knocked on the door, but nobody answered. I think they must have gone someplace because their car wasn't there. I kind of wanted to see how he's doing." I only stretched the truth a little bit.

"I know," Dad said. "It sounds to me like there's a really bizarre situation going on out there. Not sure you should actually go out there all by yourself. I don't think I trust Bashore all that far."

Mom gave me that look that was reserved for just her and me, "I agree, Honey! If you go out there again, I think you should make sure somebody else goes with you."

Talk about bizarre, sometimes I thought she knew about me and Scott, and other times I just didn't know what to think. Just every once in a while, however, she'd drop these subtle hints. Of course, it might be all my imagination.

At almost close to ten o'clock, I decided to check my email, get my books around for school the next day, take my shower and head for bed. I lay on my bed and stared at the ceiling, Scott and Mooshy had already gone to sleep. I called out very softly, "Scottie! We need to talk."

He woke up instantly. Mooshy never budged. We rehashed everything that happened that afternoon including my discussion with dear, sweet Bruno, his leaving, and our futile search for Marty.

"Okay, here's what we're going to do," Scott started after I finished. "Tomorrow we go to the sporting goods store in the mall right after school and pick up some night vision goggles for you. I don't need them, but you obviously do. Then we start our investigation in earnest."

Chapter 21

 Final exams started on Tuesday so the week would automatically be hectic. After Monday we only had to go half days for the rest of the week until Thursday. Then they gave us Friday off while the teachers screwed up our lives as they waded through all those final exams, figured out grades, and then punched them into the computer for our final first semester reports. Joy! Joy! Could hardly wait!

Monday we pretty much spent reviewing in every class. Still no Marty. As soon as the final bell sounded, I headed out to my car. Scott and Mooshy sat there waiting. I jumped in and we essentially just harassed each other, joked, and laughed all the way to the mall. So far the plan seemed pretty simple. I'd buy night goggles, and then we'd sit out in the field and wait for Bashore to head out to parts unknown so we could do who-knows-what trying to find Marty. Our plan—super sophisticated? Not!

As we walked down the right side of the mall heading to the sporting goods store, Scott mumbled under his breath, "Oh, oh! Trouble."

I looked at him and wondered what he was talking about. He held his index finger up to his lips and said, "Shh! Shh!"

I looked up to see Bobby and his mom walking down the hall right at us and understood. Bobby had this huge grin on his face and started heading right at him. I spoke up quick trying to distract her from what Bobby was doing. "Hi!" I said. "Boy, it's been a long time since I've seen you two. You remember me?"

"I sure do. We had a real nice talk in my front yard about your friend and my husband both while you got a drink from the hose. So how have things been going with you? You know, I feel like I know you, but I don't even know your name."

We introduced ourselves, and then talked for maybe another five minutes or so as Scott led Bobby over to the retaining wall around the wishing well pond in the middle of the mall. While we talked, people walked by and threw money in the pond and made wishes as Scott and Bobby watched. The mall supposedly gave all the money to charity. Hummm! I wonder.

From all appearances Bobby just sat there by himself and watched people throw their money into the pond. In reality he and Scott spent the time jabbering at each other telepathically. While all this went on, I found out that her name was Ginny Mercer. She also told me her husband's name was Franklyn and reminded me that he had been killed in Iraq nine months after Bobby was born.

I listened in while Scott talked to Bobby, "When we see each other, it's got to be our secret. Your mom can't see me so I've got to be like a pretend friend."

"Why can't she see you?" Bobby asked.

"I don't really know. You and Jeremy are the only ones who can. Remember when we were at your house that day getting a drink? She didn't see me then just like she never sees me out at the cemetery when she visits your dad. If she thought that you could see me and she couldn't she'd feel really sad. You don't want that do you?"

"No! I don't want Mom to feel bad," Bobby answered.

"That a boy!" Scotty told him. "We don't want her thinking she's missing out on all the fun."

Apparently, Bobby was like me—able to tune into a frequency band greater than most. We both could see and talk to ghosts. I had no idea if he had any other 'powers.' At his age, he had no clue either.

"Speaking of the cemetery," Scott continued talking to Bobby, "Do you ever see your daddy when you guys are out there?"

"No, I don't think so," Bobby answered. "There's some man who hangs around daddy's grave, but I don't ever mention him 'cause Mommy never sees him either."

"Really!" Scott said. "Does the man ever say anything?"

"No, he just stands around and watches us and listens to Mommy," and then Bobby laughed. "He always holds his finger up to his mouth and says 'Shhhh!' just like you do when he sees us. I think he's a nice guy though 'cause he always waves, hugs me when I come, and smiles. I like him."

After we finished our conversations, we headed to the sporting goods store for our second major surprise of the day. Night vision goggles cost from eighty to five-thousand dollars. The eighty dollar goggles looked like something you'd find in a cereal box. So much for that idea! Just as well too because they made you look like a complete dork. Back to the drawing board we went.

"So what do we do now?" I asked as we headed out of the store and back to the parking lot.

"How about if I just play Leader Dog when we leave the old school house where you park? I can see fine so you could just hold on to the back of my jacket, and I'll lead the way. That way we can keep you from getting hurt. We could put a leash on Mooshy, and have him lead you, but if he saw a rabbit, well, you know. He never acted like the best trained mutt in the world," he said with a smile as we both thought back on Mooshy's training, or mostly lack of.

If he were off leash, he would "Come!" if there were absolutely no distractions and you had a treat to bribe him with. I could see it all then—Mooshy dragging me across the field and into that barbed wire fence. I would hold on to Scott's jacket. At least he couldn't run as fast as Mooshy.

We went out there every night during the week and nothing happened. We'd hang around for an hour or so and then leave. Couldn't stay too long because the Rents would get suspicious. Besides I had to study for finals. Bashore stayed home and never left. We saw no sign of Marty. Period!

Friday night Mom and Dad headed out for the weekend. They wanted to celebrate their twentieth anniversary on Saturday so they planned to go to the resort where they spent their honeymoon.

"So where you guys actually going?"

"None of your business," Dad said with a grin. "We're reliving our honeymoon and we don't want to be bothered. You weren't around the first time, and you aren't hanging around with us this time either."

"Yeah, but suppose I need to get a hold of you?"

"If the house burns down, we'll take the call. Otherwise, leave us alone," Mom said with her raised eyebrow look.

They wouldn't even tell me the name of the place they were going. I had their cell phone number on my speed dial, but that wouldn't to do me a whole lot of good. I had strict orders to not bother them. I couldn't even check up on them to see if they were having fun. What kind of a deal was that? It's not like I had no idea what they planned to do. I'd just like to be kept in the loop.

"Jim Dad and Mom Sara are in charge. They're going to feed you over the weekend—provided you behave yourself. No parties and no getting into trouble!"

"Hey! You guys aren't cutting me a whole lot of slack here," I pretended to grumble.

They knew better, but they had to play the role. "Harass the kid and make him behave!" Right! I'd be fine, and they knew it.

After dinner I warned Jim and Sara that I just might be a little late. They suspicioned that I might be up to something, but they didn't know what, and they didn't ask. They just told me to be sure to make enough noise when I came home so they would hear me. I promised that I would.

Scott and I arrived at our observation post just as it started to get dark. The sun sets pretty quickly in late January so it must have been right around five-thirty to a quarter of six. Scott and I settled in while Mooshy chased rabbits around the fields. We didn't have to worry about him because he never wandered too far. This was the earliest that we had camped out there all week so we didn't know if anything would be different or not. We'd sat there maybe fifteen minutes when the back door opened. Mr. Bashore walked out of the house, ambled across the circular drive, and down to that old beat up, vine covered, wooden looking utility shed. He carried what appeared to be some kind of dish in his hand. We tried to figure out what he had.

"Looks like a tin pie plate full of food," Scott said. His perfect night vision forced me to take his word for it. I had no idea what he had in his hands.

Bashore stayed in the building maybe one minute when he came back out empty handed and slid the bolt back locking the door. He never uttered a word. He just headed back for the house.

Scott and I looked at each other and both said, "Marty!" at the same time.

"We'd better wait until it's pitch dark before we check it out," Scott said.

"Yeah!" I told him."It's a perfect night! It's cloudy and dark and there's no moon or stars shining. He'll never spot us."

About a half hour later we slipped out of our hiding place and headed for the shed. I held on to Scott's jacket as he led the way. I literally saw nothing except Scott's back. Neither one of us made a sound.

After we slipped up to the old shed, I unbolted the door and slid it open trying to be as careful as possible that we didn't make any noise. My heart thumped against my chest so hard, I thought it would probably explode.

When we sneaked inside and closed the door, Scott said, "Oh my God!" as he looked across the room.

Fortunately he noticed a light switch on the wall so he flipped it on so I could see. There lay Marty sprawled out on the ground on top of an old, dirty blanket. The plate of food sat beside him untouched. Marty didn't move. "Is he dead?" I asked Scott as he stooped down on one knee trying to rouse him.

"No, but he's pretty bad off. Get out your cell phone and call that cop buddy of yours and find out what we should do. I'm going to see if I can wake him up."

I dug Sergeant O'Connor's card out of my wallet and called him. I could hear traffic noise and knew he was in his car when he answered, "Sean O'Connor."

"Sergeant O'Connor, this is Jeremy Wright. I don't know if you remember me or not, but I've talked to you a couple of times and you told me if I ever needed help to call, and I need help bad. I talked to you at the restaurant down town and I talked to you at the hospital when I got mugged..."

"Slow down! Slow down! Stop! Jeremy, I know who you are. What's going on?"

"Are you familiar with the old school house at the corner of Summerset and North Road?"

"Yes! What about it?"

"I'm at the first house to the west of the school on the opposite side of the road."

"Isn't that Bashore's house?"

"Yes!"

"What are you doing there? I've had several run-ins with that guy ever since he moved to the area. There's something about him I don't like. You shouldn't be there."

"We were looking for my friend Marty, his step son. We found him locked up in the shed behind the house. He's in really bad shape. He's alive, but I'm not sure how aware he is. He needs an ambulance."

"I'm probably five minutes away. Hang up! I'll call for an ambulance and a backup. Stay hidden. If you have a light on, turn it off."

"Oh, no!"

"What? Jeremy, what's going on?"

"Mr. Bashore just walked in."

Bashore stormed across the room and grabbed the cell phone out of my hand and then threw it against the wall, "What are you doing here?" He roared scaring the crap out of me.

"I came looking for Marty. He's been hurt. He needs help! You've got to take him to the hospital!"

"I'll show you what I've got to do. I'm going to finish you off like I would have out behind the school if that damned janitor hadn't come out of the back door snooping around right when he did," he continued to scream.

He reached up, grabbed me by the throat, and started to choke me. I could hear Sergeant O'Connor's siren weeping in the distance—way too far away to do me any good. I gagged and choked and started to lose consciousness.

Right at that moment a whole bunch of stuff all happened kind of at the same time. Mooshy grabbed him by the leg, and those powerful Boxer jaws of his closed down on themselves. Bashore screamed bloody murder. At the same time Scott smacked him across the back of the head with a two by four that he'd snatched off the floor. As he started to collapse, he fell backwards over Marty who had somehow crawled up behind him.

Bashore landed in a heap in a pile of glass as his head thudded against the frozen ground. Within a minute, Sergeant O'Connor's car slid to a stop right outside of the shed. He jumped out, took a quick look around, rolled Bashore over and cuffed him, and then took me in his arms and just held me for a few seconds.

"Are you ok?" he asked after I started breathing somewhat normally again.

"I think so," I wheezed in between coughs. My neck hurt and my voice didn't sound right.

"So, he's definitely the one who attacked you at the school," he said. "I thought so. I just couldn't prove it until now."

"How'd you know that?" I asked as my voice kind of cracked and croaked. That was the first I realized that not only did I sound funny, but I could barely talk. My throat felt half crushed.

"When he threw your cell phone it didn't break. It stayed activated, and I could hear his screaming in the back ground including the fact that he intended to kill you."

Then he kneeled down and talked to Marty, "So how you doing, Buddy? You don't look too hot."

"I thought I was gonna die," Marty said in a whisper unable to lift his own head off the floor. When he crawled over so I could "push" Bashore over him, it just about did him in. He had nothing left.

"Well, you aren't. You're going to be fine. I hear the ambulance and my back up coming now. They'll take you to the hospital right away and get you all checked out and fixed up."

By that time Mr. Bashore was awake and sat leaning against the wall. He swore at me and Marty nonstop for ruining his life. He said he should have killed us both when he had the chance.

It took a while after the ambulance crew arrived to get Marty loaded up. They wrapped him in warm blankets, did his vitals, slipped in an IV, talked to him for quite a while, and tried to find out who would be responsible for him. They assumed they needed to notify someone in his family. There wasn't anyone. His mom and Bruno Bashore were the full extent of any known family, and she had disappeared.

They also checked me over more than I figured they needed to. Someone decided that I should go to the hospital to get checked out as well. I thought that was a waste of time and said so, but nobody paid any attention. What did I know?

As they worked on Marty, Sergeant O'Connor came over and put his arm around my shoulders again and asked, "You doing okay?"

"Yeah, I'm fine except for my throat," I answered barely able to speak. I have one heck of a sore throat.

"So, who came out here with you?" he asked with an impish grin on his face.

"Why, nobody. Why do you ask that way?"

"When you talked to me over the phone, you said, 'We were looking for Marty, and we found him.' Well, we normally means at least two people, now doesn't it?"

"Probably, but I was all shook up and just mis-spoke myself."

"Right!" he said smiling. "Now let me run something else by you. I watched when the paramedics checked out Bashore. They pulled his pant leg up to check out where he landed in the glass to see if they needed to stop the bleeding. There were some little glass scratches, but there were also some deep cuts. They looked like fang punctures to me. Also on the back of his head was a big bump which both paramedics said was way too large for having fallen on the hard ground. And there was a two by four lying about three feet away." Then he looked me right in the eye and asked, "Are Scott and his dog here?"

"Like you told me at the hospital when you left the other day, someday we've got to talk, just not today."

"Okay, but this will happen sooner than later," he smiled at me as he ruffled up my hair. I hate it when people do that to me.

By the time the police finally finished their investigation of the incident a few days later, they figured that I pushed Bruno over the squatting Marty, and he landed in the glass gouging his right leg and knocking himself out when his head hit the ground. They patted Marty and me on the back with all kinds of "Great Job!' comments, and that took care of that.

However, before we left and as they moved Marty's stretcher out of the shed, what should happen? Mooshy ran around from behind the building with what looked like a sleeve off of a sweatshirt. The wind gusted pretty hard right then so it looked to everybody else like something blowing in the breeze.

Mooshy ran right up to me and dropped it at my feet. As I picked it up Marty opened his eyes and saw it. He choked out, "That's my mom's."

I handed it to Sean O'Connor who stood right beside me. "Did you hear Marty?" I asked under my breath.

"Yes, I did," he whispered back. "Did you see where it came from?"

"Looked like it blew around from back of the shed," I answered.

"Ok, get the boys loaded up and out of here," Sean suddenly ordered as he opened up the back of the ambulance and stated to take charge of the ambulance crew.

Scott disappeared again and my mind churned into overdrive. What was going on? How did Mooshy get a hold of a piece of a garment owned by Marty's mom? What did it mean? I had lots of questions and no answers as the paramedics loaded me into the ambulance.

Chapter 22

We arrived at the hospital and they put Marty and me in adjoining cubicles in the emergency room. They started working on Marty immediately. They added a couple more bottles to his IV the paramedics had put in and checked over his entire body. I didn't think I even needed to be there, but I had people checking me out too. It wasn't long before some lady walked in with a clipboard to talk to me.

"You have a slightly bruised larynx and a badly bruised neck. However, we need to get parental consent before we can do anything else. Somebody needs to okay the procedures we want to do and bring insurance information. Are your parents at home or someplace where they can be reached?"

"My parents are out of town and can't be contacted. I'll have to call my neighbors who have the power of medical attorney over me in their absence. They also have our insurance information. They will probably also wring my neck which is already sore."

"Okay," she laughed. "Give them a call and let me talk to them before you hang up. Do you want to use your own cell phone or do you want me to take you out in the hallway in a wheel chair so you can use one of ours? We don't have a phone in this room."

"I'll use mine," I sighed. "They'll recognize the number."

What was the last thing they told me when I walked out the door? "Be good! Drive carefully! And, don't get into any trouble!" I reached over and grabbed my jacket that hung on the chair, pulled my cell phone out of my pocket, and hit number two on the speed dial.

Jim Dad answered, and I croaked out a question in my scratchy, raspy voice, "One out of three isn't too bad, is it?"

"What are you talking about and what's the matter with your voice?"

"I drove carefully, but you've still got to come bail me out," I said using a poor choice of works kind of on purpose. "I guess I wasn't all that good, and maybe I ended up in a little trouble."

"What? Where are you? Are you in jail? What's going on?"

"It's ok, Jim Dad. I'm at the hospital emergency room. I kind of ended up hurt and you need to come with the insurance cards and get me out of here. Here, talk to this lady." I said as I handed her the phone.

"Hi! This is Mrs. Reed. I'm a nurse over here at the Mercy Hospital emergency room. Jeremy's been injured, not critically I might add, but we need a parent or guardian to authorize treatment and to provide insurance information. Are you his legal guardian?"

"My wife and I have legal power of medical attorney for when his parents are gone. I'll be there within fifteen minutes with the insurance information. In the meantime go ahead and start any treatment that is necessary."

When Mrs. Reed hung up the phone, she looked at me and smiled. "He didn't sound like the happiest person in the world. Will you be okay when he comes?"

"Oh, yeah! No problem. They've been a second set of parents to me since I was born. He loves me just like my dad does. He's just worried about what I managed to get myself into this time."

It wasn't even fifteen minutes before Jim Dad and Mom Sara bounded into my cubicle. She grabbed me and gave me a big hug with tears in her eyes. It brought back vivid memories of Scott's accident which hadn't happened that long ago.

"Hi, Jim Dad. Hi, Mom Sara," I croaked after the hug.

"What happened, Honey? Your throat is all black and blue and your voice is horribly raspy," she asked as she looked me over for more signs of injury.

Jim Dad gave me a hug and then said, "We can't trust you out of our sight for a minute, can we?" he laughed as he messed up my hair again. "So, what happened?"

The orderlies had wheeled Marty down to x-ray about five minutes before they arrived so I felt free to give them the quickie version before they brought him back.

"That guy must be crazy!" Jim Dad said. "Who could do that to a kid and then whine because he hadn't killed his own kid and his friend? So who's here with Marty?"

"Nobody! He doesn't have anyone. He told me at school that they have no family or friends. His mother walked out and left him a few months ago, and his dad died in a car accident when he was a baby. He doesn't remember him at all. He vaguely remembers grandparents on his mother's side, but they were very old the last time he saw them and might even be dead by now.

"There may have been some uncles and aunts someplace, but he has no clue what their actual names are or where they might be. He hasn't seen any of them in years. They've moved three times after his mom and Mr. Bashore married, and he insisted that she cut all ties with her family. She was supposed to give all of her attention to him. He didn't even like it when she paid attention to Marty. The only reason he didn't run away is because he hoped that someday she'd come back."

"Oh, that's so sad!" Mom Sara said. "He's here all by himself with no one to look after him except for a bunch of strangers. He must be suffering horribly inside."

Right then they wheeled Marty back to his cubicle from x-ray. He waved and said hi as he passed by our open area. He still had his IV hooked up. Mom Sara shot around the corner in a flash before they even had the brakes put on. "Hi, Mrs. Adams," he said as the aides were getting him settled.

"It's Sara, Marty, and I'm so sorry for what has happened to you. You have no idea."

About that time Sean walked in and went right over to Marty. "Hi, Marty, how are you doing?"

"Fine! I feel like crap, but I think I'm going to be okay now."

"Good! Because we have to talk."

"Maybe I should leave you two alone then," Mom Sarah said as she stood up to leave.

"Actually, if you don't mind, under the current circumstances, I'd prefer you stayed," Sean answered as he looked back at Marty.

Sara smiled and sat down. She suddenly felt protective over Marty and wanted to be there just in case he needed her.

"Your mom did not leave you," he said softly. After a couple of seconds of letting that register, he continued.

"After you guys left in the ambulance, Mr. Bashore admitted killing her and burying her out behind the shed that he had you in. He was jealous of you, Marty. He couldn't stand it that she loved you more than she did him. He told us that your mom planned to take you and leave him just because he abused the two of you. He couldn't handle it so he lost control and hit her. He didn't say what he hit her with, and it doesn't matter. The point is he admitted it in front of six police officers holding a camera and a recording device."

Everyone just stood there holding their breaths waiting for Marty to respond, "I knew it! I just knew she wouldn't leave me. That son-of-a-bitch killed her!"

Sean left shortly after, and that's when Mom Sara sat down beside Marty on the bed and took him in her arms and motioned for Jim Dad to close the curtain.

And then quiet set it except for muffled sobbing. Jim Dad and I looked at each other and didn't say a word. After a couple of minutes he stood up and peeked around the corner. He mimed to me that she was holding him and rocking back and forth. I hoped she was easing some of that pain.

The doctors and nurses ran in and out of both of our areas for the next hour. Somewhere along the line Mom Sara opened the curtain between us so we could all talk without yelling or looking around the curtain. It made things much easier.

And, of course, there were times that were not all that easy or comfortable. Such as when Jim Dad pulled out his cell phone and hit his speed dial and then just handed me the phone.

It was past ten in the evening so when Dad answered the phone, he had a concerned tone to his voice.

"Hi, Dad, everything is under control. I'm okay—kind of. I'm in the emergency room at Mercy Hospital. They should be sending me packing pretty quick so you don't have to come home. Jim Dad can fill you in on all the details. Maybe he needs your insurance card information or something else. Here!" I said talking about as fast as I could before handing the phone back to Jim Dad. I didn't really want to hear what he had to say right then.

Jim Dad took the phone and looked at me and called me a lily livered coward. What a horrible thing to say to someone who's been injured!

"Hey, Ted. Your kid's a wuss if I ever saw one. Won't even tell his own dad what he got himself into this time," he said as he stood up, messed up my hair again, and walked out of the cubicle and down the hall and out the door to the outside parking lot. I think he just didn't want to tell the whole story again in front of Marty. He stayed gone for about a half hour. When he came back into the room, he grinned.

"Well, they aren't coming home until Sunday night as planned. He just told me to take you home and beat your butt and that would save him the trouble," he said teasing.

The brutality of his own life must have been too fresh for Marty and he kind of panicked, "You can't do that! He saved my life! You can't beat him for something that Bruno did! Please don't hit him!"

"Whoa! Whoa! Marty. Slow down. I'm joking and Jeremy knows it. He's never been 'beaten' in his life. I just wanted to hassle him a little. He's fine. He's going to stay at our house for the rest of the weekend so we can spoil him rotten."

That seemed to embarrass Marty a little, but that was okay. At least he knew that I'd be fine. About that time one of the nurses entered my room with a bunch of papers and discharge directions. She told me to take it easy for the rest of the weekend and do nothing strenuous. If I had any trouble breathing or any sharp pains, get back to the emergency room pronto. Otherwise follow up with our family physician in a week. I was good to go.

I dumped the sexy hospital gown that they made me wear on the floor and dressed as quickly as I could. Jim Dad got my coat and checked around the cubical to make sure I didn't leave anything behind. Mom Sara just sat there talking to Marty. They drove separate cars because she had been visiting her mom with Emily when Jim Dad called her. She left the baby with them and headed to the hospital and met Jim Dad at the door before they came in.

"I'll see you two later at home," she said. "I'm staying here with Marty for a while until he's settled in his room. Apparently they still have to get it ready. I don't really understand why it isn't just automatically made ready for the next patient when a room is vacated, but apparently that's not the case. Maybe they're over worked and under staffed, or whatever," she grumbled.

I have no idea when she finally walked into the house. It had to have been late. I went to bed shortly after Jim Dad and I got to their house and fell asleep almost immediately. All I know is she stood there in the kitchen cooking breakfast the next morning when I finally crawled out of bed about ten. Most of the breakfast conversation related to Marty and Mr. Bashore.

"You know what's going to happen, don't you?" Jim Dad asked. "That jerk will plead insanity and end up in a mental institution for a couple of years, have a remarkable recovery, and then walk for murder, attempted murder, aggravated assault, child abuse, and all that good stuff."

"At least he'll be out of Marty's life," I replied. That seemed to me like the most important thing. He would be safe, and Mr. Bashore couldn't get him.

"In the meantime," Jim Dad said. "Since we have to go get your car, let's cruise past Bashore's place first just to see what's going on out there."

Yellow crime scene tape blocked the driveway when we slowly drove by. We saw numerous police type vehicles parked around the back of the house. There appeared to be all sorts of activity out behind the shed where Marty's mom had supposedly been buried. I felt pretty sad for Marty.

When we stopped at the old country school to get my car, Jim Dad said, "Meet me at the hospital and we'll check up on Marty this morning to see how things are going with him.

We walked into his room together and Mom Sara sat there beside his bed eating ice cream at noon with Marty. She had picked up a couple of ice cream sundaes on her way up, and they were both laughing about something when we walked in. Marty sat up in bed and looked a lot better than he did the night before.

"Oh, oh!" Marty said. "Caught in the act!" as he took another bite of his sundae. We all laughed. I never heard Marty laugh like that—hard and happy. It almost choked me up.

All of a sudden his laughter sounded almost hysterical like he couldn't stop. Then he convulsed into tears.

"I shouldn't be laughing," he cried out. "My mom is dead. He killed her!"

Mom Sara held him tight and told him he would go through all kinds of emotions before he could feel peace again and it was perfectly normal. I think we all cried with him at one point. I did manage to remind him that at least he knew his mom loved him and that she hadn't walked out and left him like Bruno had said. Marty's life was preparing to make a drastic change.

Chapter 23

After breakfast Sunday morning I went back home. Mom and Dad were due back that afternoon some time, and I really needed to check for any messes I just might have made before I left Friday night for Bashore's. If I remembered right, I just might have left all my clothes thrown on the floor when I changed after school. That didn't always set too well with Mom. I also needed to check my email. Good thing finals were last week so I didn't have any homework.

I straightened up my room and just hung out by myself for awhile. I read the sports section of the Journal, and then ran up to the hospital to check on Marty. When I walked into his room, I found him sitting up in bed playing with Emily. I stopped in the doorway for a few seconds and just watched and listened. He giggled and baby talked and played kissy face with her and having a ball. Now, that was a side of Marty I had never, ever seen.

"You babysitting?" I laughed as I wandered in when he finally looked up and saw me. "Where's Mom Sara and Jim Dad?"

"Jim's coming up later and Sara went down to get me a shake so I'm watching Emily while she's gone. She should be back in a minute. Isn't she adorable? I think she actually smiled at me once."

"Oh, brother! She probably has gas. Hey, Dude! Yesterday when I showed up, you were eating a sundae and today she's down getting you a shake? You're gonna get fat!"

"Would you believe that I lost twenty pounds after Bruno jerked me out of the gym when I lost in districts? I've been absolutely starved ever since I got to this damn hospital. I just can't get filled up. The meals are fine; they're just way too small."

"Marty, while we're alone can you tell me what happened, or would you prefer not to?"

He started rocking back and forth with Emily and it poured out. He told me things about his home life that I found completely unbelievable. I don't mean to say that I didn't believe him; I just found it hard to believe a person like Bruno could be so evil.

Marty started out by telling me about the time soon after his mom disappeared, his step-dad decided that he would have to toughen him up.

"One night when Bruno came home from work, I'd been crying because I missed my mom so much. The old bastard flipped out and told me I was nothing but a baby for crying and that he intended to turn me into a man. Then he took off his belt and hit me with it. When I screamed, he started yelling at me to shut up. He claimed that real men don't cry.

"He made me stand up and face the wall. Then he let me have it again with that belt. I had to stand there like forever and not move. After that he'd walk by every few minutes and smack me. Usually he'd use the belt, but sometimes he used his hand or fist. I couldn't even squirm or walk around in between swats. He kept doing it until I could take it without screaming or crying. Then he doubled it.

"Over the next few weeks he eventually worked it up to the point where he could hit me five times in a row with that belt, and I wouldn't react. I literally ached all over. It was terrible!

"One day when I felt particularly lonesome for my mom, the old man and I had a little 'disagreement.' Right out of the blue I hit him with the fact that Mom had disappeared and that he would never talk about it. I said I wanted to know what happened to her, and I wanted to know then."

"What'd he say?" I asked.

"He started screaming and swearing that he'd told me what happened once, and he wouldn't tell me again. Then he whipped off his belt, grabbed me by the arm, and hit me ten times on my butt, my back, and the back of my legs. I counted them out loud. I never flinched. I never cried or screamed. I just stood there and took it. When he finished, he yelled at me to go to my room and stay there. So I did."

"Marty, that's terrible," I said. "Did you tell the police all of this?" I couldn't believe someone could be so evil. Not one of my four rents ever smacked me with anything but an open hand on the seat, and never when I didn't deserve it. Nobody ever swatted me

236

hard enough to really hurt anything to speak of other than my feelings.

"No, Jeremy, not yet. I know I need to tell someone, I just don't know who all I can open up to, maybe Sergeant O'Connor. I want to tell Sara and Jim too. They've been so good to me, I feel like I owe it to them. I didn't do anything before because he wasn't that bad all the time, plus I didn't know if anyone would really believe me. He would go in streaks. Most of the time he just pretty much ignored me."

"That truly sucks! How could you stand it? Why didn't you split?" I asked.

"The way I looked at it, at least I had a roof over my head, and that's more than what I'd have if I reported him. Like I told you before, I don't think I have any relatives out there anymore, and if I do, I wouldn't have a clue as how to locate them. Besides, I thought that if Mom decided to come back, at least she would know where to find me. I guess that's the main reason I stayed. I hoped and prayed she'd come back someday. I kept thinking that maybe she'd discover a safe place for just the two of us where we could go and he'd never find us."

"Tell me this. How could you stand there and let him hit you with a belt ten times and not scream, cry, and jump all over the place?" I asked him.

"I taught myself how to zone out. I would bring up an ugly image of his face into my mind and just keep repeating to myself, 'I hate you! I hate you! I hate you, you son-of-a-bitch!' I would do that every time he hit me so I could make it through the nightmare whether he used a belt or his fists."

"Marty, you have to report all of that to somebody," I told him.

"Right now I'm more afraid of living in the foster care system bouncing from place to place or being totally homeless living out of a box than I am about what he did to me. Only one more year after this and I'll be out of school and out of everyone's hair. I'll probably join the army as soon as I graduate. I talked to one recruiter once at school, and he said that I could take college classes while I served my time in the service and then get financial aid when I get out and go to college. I'll be ok."

Marty talked fast. I think he wanted to get it all out before Mom Sara returned with his shake. Fortunately Emily fell asleep in his arms while he rocked her back and forth.

Next Marty told me what happened when Bruno yanked him out of the districts.

"He beat the devil out of me with that belt of his and threw me into that shed where you found me. No 'loser' was going to live in his house. I could leave once a day to use the bathroom and clean up. For the in between times he put a bucket out there that I used. The past couple of days before you found me, I was so weak I couldn't even go to the house to use the bathroom or clean up. You probably noticed I was a mess. Bruno emptied my bucket by just throwing it out into the yard behind the shed. He brought out one metal pie plate full of undecipherable slop a day. I could either eat it or not. That's all he gave me."

Right then Mom Sara walked in with the shake, "Am I interrupting something? Sounds awfully serious in here."

Actually I let out a sigh of relief that she showed up. My head screamed 'information overload,' "Hey! What kind of a deal is this? Marty slurps down a shake, and I just sit here and watch? He didn't even leave an old package of crackers lying around from lunch. What a hog!"

"That's what happens when you show up late. Suffer!" Mom Sara laughed at me.

We sat around for some time laughing and joking. Our carrying on woke Emily up and she started to fuss so Mom Sara took her. After a minute she plopped her down at the foot of the bed where there was room. "Okay, you two. Pay attention! This is what's called a wet diaper, and wet diapers have to be changed or the baby gets all red and sore," she said as she stripped Emily right there in front of us. It embarrassed me, and I wanted to look away. Marty rubbed his finger across her cheek and exclaimed how beautiful she was. He also paid attention.

After Mom Sara powdered her up and had the new diaper in place, Marty said, "That's a no-brainer. I could do that."

"But would you?" I asked figuring I had him.

"Yeah! Why not? What's the big deal?"

"Suppose it's all poopy?" I asked not believing everything I heard.

"HELLO! Jeremy, I don't want to burst your bubble or anything, but somebody changed your poopy diapers when you were a

239

baby too," he said shaking his head not believing I'd be such a baby about something like that.

"Yes, and I can think of one person right off the top of my head who changed a bunch of them, if you want to get right down to the nitty-gritties," Mom Sara said giving me that wide-eyed look she was so famous for.

"I know, but it's so gross and yucky," I said conjuring up the worst images in my mind possible.

"What a wuss!" Marty said shaking his head. "That's what soap and water is all about."

We were still laughing when Sergeant O'Connor walked it. "Sounds like everyone is in pretty good spirits this afternoon," he said.

"Sergeant O'Connor, did you ever change a poopy diaper?" I asked betting that a big macho guy like him wouldn't be caught dead doing such a thing.

He looked me right straight in the eye and said, "Jeremy, You'll get no sympathy from me. I was raised in a good Irish Catholic family. I just happened to be an only child until I was nine years old. Then, out of the blue, I had a baby brother. One year after that I had a baby sister. One year later Mom and Dad had twins— one of each. Then I guess somebody must've finally figured out what caused it all because they were the last of the brood. I'll bet you my last bottom dollar that I changed more diapers, cleaned up more vomit, fed and bathed more babies, and took care of more spit up over my shoulder than my mother did. Just don't ask her."

So much for the sympathy vote as everyone laughed at my queasiness over the diaper routine.

"So are you married now and have kids of your own?" I asked smiling to myself visualizing this big cop playing nurse maid to a bunch of rug rats.

"No and no! I guess that's where it gets muddled. I married my high school sweetheart right after I graduated from college. We wanted to wait until we established ourselves and were maybe a little more mature before we had children. I guess we waited too long because five years later she died very suddenly from a brain aneurism. It's only been the past year or so that I've had any interest in dating again, but that's been pretty rare."

Sergeant O'Connor made it clear that on that particular day he was Sean. He had dropped in completely unofficially just wanting to say hi and to check up on Marty.

After a bit of small talk, Sean said, "Jeremy, before you salivate all over your shirt or in Marty's shake, how about if you and I mosey down to the cafeteria and scarf down a piece of pie along with a soda? I'm buying."

That sounded like a deal to me—especially the fact that he offered to buy. As usual, I was broke. I also had a sneaky suspicion that maybe Sean wanted to talk. Before we left, he asked if either Marty or Mom Sara wanted him to bring back anything for them. Surprise! Surprise! Marty wanted pie too.

...

The cafeteria wasn't that busy at that time of day so Sean and I found a booth over in the corner of the cafeteria and sat down.

"How do you think Marty's doing?" Sean asked once we settled in.

"Fine, I think. I also think he's ready to talk about Mr. Bashore and his home life. You wouldn't believe what he went through. He told me a bunch of stuff earlier this afternoon before Mom Sara and you showed up. Has he told you anything?"

"Not yet. I thought I'd hang around this afternoon until you and Mrs. Adams left and then see if Marty wanted to talk," he said.

"Speaking of talking," I said smiling, "Why do I get the feeling that maybe we're down here because you want to?"

"I do. Something happened out at Bashore's house that made me even more determined to talk and spend some time with you. You ready to hear the story of my life?" he asked sounding a little sarcastic as he said it.

"Shoot!" I said.

"Not always the brightest thing to say to a cop, Jeremy! Just kidding! Anyway as far back as I can remember, I've had these little flashes in my mind that are totally unpredictable and unexplainable as to what they mean or why I have them. I remember when I was just a little kid and one of them would happen, my parents would tell me it was all my imagination. I knew better.

"One day when I was maybe twelve, my dad sat me down for a very serious talk. He told me that there had been some mental illness on my mom's side of the family where certain other members all thought they saw things. They claimed to see ghosts, have the ability to talk to dead people, and a lot of other strange things. He told me that my great grandmother used to sit on the porch in the summer and talk to my great grandfather who had been killed in WW I. Apparently some of the family members wanted to institutionalize her, but most felt. 'Why bother? She's just a harmless, crazy, old lady.'

"Anyway, Dad told me to bottle up those images. It would be a bad thing for all my younger siblings to be exposed to. When I had one, I had to immediately think of something else. Whatever it happened to be, I had to erase it out of my mind. He said I needed to train myself not to have them. You can imagine how successful that turned out. So all the time growing up I thought there was something wrong with me. In recent years I've read a whole bunch of stuff on the paranormal and convinced myself that maybe I'm not totally crazy. So, what do you think? You think that maybe I fell out of the crib and landed on my head?"

"Not at all. As a matter of fact, I find it pretty interesting. Tell me more," I told him.

"There's not a whole lot more to tell except that ever since I first met you at the restaurant, I've suspected that there was something going on with you along those lines. At first I figured you were pulling a magic trick on me of some kind. I know my coffee cup moved all over the place along with my doughnut when I sat it down."

"You almost lost that doughnut!" I laughed. "So what else have you noticed?"

"At the hospital when you or whoever tipped my hat upside down and put my water bottle in the middle of it, and then switched it back, I knew I'd been had. I also knew it had to be more than just magic."

"You said something happened at Bashore's house that kind of clinched things for you. What was that?"

"When the wind blew that piece of material that belonged to Marty's mom around the corner of that shed, I got a flash of an animal, like maybe a big dog. Then I heard the words, 'Drop it!' and it landed at your feet."

"That was Scott's dog, Mooshy!" I answered looking him in the eye. That's the first time I had ever admitted anything to anyone except Scott. I didn't know for sure how I felt about it coming out that way, but I needed to be able to talk to someone about it too, and the Rents were not the ones. I had no clue how Sean would react to it either. I kind of held my breath to see if he'd freak out or what.

Sean looked right back as seriously as I had him and asked, "I take it that Scott was there as well? I'm assuming he's the one who yelled, 'Drop it!' "

"Yes, Scott yelled at Mooshy to drop the cloth. What do you think, Sean? Does that make both of us basket cases?"

"Not in my mind. I think I'm thrilled to death to find someone I can actually talk to about this. What more can you tell me?"

"There's a lot I want to tell you, but I can't do it all right now. First off, it would take too long and Marty would never get his pie. Secondly, I need to develop a trust factor with you that I've never considered having with another living person. Can you understand that?"

"Hell, yes! I'm thirty-two years old, and you are the first person I've ever actually told about this other than my parents, and they were worried about my mental health. I'm more than willing to take things slowly so we can develop the mutual trust that we both need. Can we meet every once in a while and share experiences? Nobody needs to know what we're talking about. We can use Marty's nut case father as an excuse for a long time."

"Sure, but before we go back up stairs to Marty's room just a couple of things. First off, it was Scott who screwed around with your food at the restaurant. And you know, wherever Scott is, Mooshy is. He came this close to giving him a bite of your doughnut." I said holding my thumb and index finger about two inches apart. "If you had actually looked down you would have seen dog saliva dripping on your shined shoes. Mooshy never was the best trained, especially where food is concerned. That would have really freaked you out. Needless to say, it freaked me out enough as it was. All I wanted to do was get out of there before Scott did something really stupid. His goofy sense of humor gets the best of him at times."

Sean laughed that big hearty Irish laugh of his. "I think I would have really liked Scott. I'm sorry I never met him. Was that also Scott messing with my hat and water bottle too?"

"Yep! Let's go give Marty his pie before he shows up in a wheel chair looking for it."

Marty had been recuperating well and would soon be out of the hospital. Then what? He surely couldn't go home and live by himself.

Chapter 24

On the way down to the parking lot my mind churned a mile a minute. Marty acted so happy. He smiled all the time and Mom Sara, Jim Dad, and Emily all seemed to be a huge part of it. It just seemed like their personalities clicked. Every time I saw them together they were smiling and laughing. Hadn't seen that since Scott died. Had never seen that part of Marty's personality. My mind drifted a million miles away as I climbed into my car. As soon as I sat down, I got a big sloppy Mooshy kiss behind the ear. Then I looked over and saw Scott sitting in the passenger seat.

"Hey, dude! We need to talk."

"Hi, Scottie! Hi Mooshy! Haven't seen you two for a couple of days. Sounds serious. What's on your feeble mind?"

"Mom, Dad, and Marty belong together. They should take him in. I think the hospital plans to release him tomorrow, and I don't think anyone in my family has even thought about what's going to happen to him. I know some lady from child protective services went up there late yesterday afternoon and talked to Marty. She gabbed about putting him in some foster care facility unless they find someone to take him. Most people don't want to take in a seventeen year old. If they can't find a home for him, they won't have a choice. They'll have to ship him off to that state institution in the capitol city where they dump all the unwanted kids until he graduates from high school. That's not right. Marty doesn't deserve that."

"Wouldn't you feel like they were trying to replace you or something?"

"Hell no! He wouldn't replace me any more than they would replace his mom. It would just be a good move for everyone involved."

"You're sure you wouldn't be upset then?" I asked thinking that would really be great for everyone if Scott could accept it.

"No sweat! I think you should mention it to them this afternoon before that old bag from protective services decides to put him in that kiddy jail. After O'Connor kicked you out so he could give him the third degree, did you notice Mom go over and say something to him?"

"I thought she just told him goodbye."

"You wish! She said she was going to stop at the store and get some chocolate chips. She's going to make him cookies this afternoon just to soothe his feelings after O'Connor gets through grilling him."

"Excuse me? She's going to have him so fat he'll waddle out on the mat next year as a heavy weight. I guess I'm going to have to make sure he doesn't get them all."

We drove around for a few minutes, and then I headed home. As I pulled into the drive way I noticed that Mom and Dad were both gone and Mom Sara had just pulled into her drive ahead of me. Guess I timed that one just about right. As she climbed out of her car, I noticed the little bag in her hands. Aha! Just the right size for chocolate chips. Scott had told the truth.

"What'd ya get at the store, Mom Sara?"

"Chocolate chips and walnuts, why?"

"You gonna make cookies?"

"Yeah! I thought I'd bake Marty some."

"He's not gonna get them all, is he?"

"No! Dad and I will have some of them too."

"Oh, okay," I said as I started for the house.

"Jeremy, get your butt over here. Now! You know I'm just messing with you. Besides, I need you to shell the walnuts."

"Aw! Why don't you buy the kind that is already shelled? You can't tell the difference."

"Force of habit. I always bought the shelled kind so you and Scott would have something that you could do to help. So, you're elected. Get in here and give me a hand," she said with a grin on her face.

So I did. I sat down with the nut cracker and cracked two cups of wall nuts just like we always did. While I did it, I had a chance to talk about Marty and his predicament.

"Has Marty said anything about child protective services to you," I asked. "He's probably going to be discharged from the hospital pretty soon. Wonder what's going to happen to him?"

"He told me all about it this morning. If they can't find a foster home for him, he'll end up in an institution for unadoptable kids in the capitol city."

"Mom Sara, I know I'm sticking my nose into something that I have no business in, but have you and Jim Dad even considered taking Marty in?"

"Really hadn't thought about it," she answered with kind of a wrinkled up forehead.

"I think I know Scott as well as anyone ever did, except for you and Jim Dad, and I think he would want you to do that. He wouldn't think you were trying to replace him any more than you would be replacing Marty's mom. It's simply a matter that he is a good kid who has no family or anything. He needs a home, love, and affection just like anyone else."

"You're right, but I just don't know what I think right now."

"Not only that, he'd make a great babysitter for Emily," I continued. "He absolutely worships her. And, you know what? I'm not so sure that you and Jim Dad don't have a need for some seventeen year old to be here chowing down on your spare groceries when I'm not here to help you out."

She laughed at that one. "Right! We've always 'needed' someone to take up the slack in the grocery department," she said. "I just don't know, Jeremy. I really hadn't thought about that possibility. I guess I really hadn't thought about what would happen to him. I've just been kind of going day to day. And you are right. He really is a nice boy and he does deserve more than being stuck in a state institution."

We changed the subject after that and just kind of rambled on from one topic to the next. What classes did I plan to take next semester, did I plan to go to the junior senior prom this spring, what kind of a load did I intend to take as a senior, had I considered going to the community college after that, or did I plan to head right to the State University just down the road? Everything we talked about seemed to be an avoidance of Marty.

The next day started the new semester at school. I was busy with my new classes when I got a text message from Mom Sara. "Meet me in Marty's hospital room this afternoon right after school."

That seemed strange. I wondered what that was all about. She hadn't done that before. When I showed up, Jim Dad, Mom Sara, and some strange lady were there talking to Marty. Marty was dressed in regular clothes and sitting on a chair beside the bed. It looked to be some kind of a formal meeting going on. When Mom Sara saw me standing by the door wondering if I should go in or not, she called me over to their group. "Jeremy, I want you to meet Mrs. Thomas from Child Protective Services for the county."

251

"Hi, pleased to meet you," I said full of questions in my mind.

She greeted me while I sat down on the edge of the bed since there weren't any more chairs.

Jim Dad spoke up first, "Jeremy, we wanted you to be part of this meeting because we consider you a part of our family. Just to bring you up to speed real quickly, Sara and I talked for a long time last night after I came home from work. You apparently told us what everyone knew and wanted and just hadn't mentioned out loud.

"We want to have Marty come live with us. We all know that there will be adjustments. We know we are not being replacements for the ones we have both lost because that could never happen. Marty is not going to replace Scott, and we are not going to replace his mother. We just think that it would be a really good thing for all of us.

"Marty has a year and a half of school left just like you do. He's already been in two different high schools besides this one. He doesn't need to have to start over. We're going to deal with the school and get him through his final exams, and then he'll start the new semester fresh. Then he has junior college and the university to deal with. Not only that, but we expect expert babysitting service cheaply. Have you heard what the high school girls charge? It's outrageous!"

Everybody laughed and Marty beamed from ear to ear. The meeting had been winding down apparently before I arrived on the scene. What Jim Dad told me had already been agreed to by everyone. In the eyes of the court they would immediately become Marty's foster parents, and he would go home with them that afternoon.

When we left the hospital, I went for a little ride and let them go their own merry way. Scott and Mooshy rode along.

"Super cool!" Scott exclaimed. "Marty even gets diaper duty."

"Yeah, he's more than welcome to that part," I laughed. We were both in a great mood.

Everyone in the new family group seemed extremely happy—even Emily who half acted like she knew what was going on. Marty carried her out to the car as both of them giggled at each other.

Next day in school Marty acted kind of nervous about the meeting that the principal had arranged for after school with all of his first semester teachers. We talked a long time in English class.

"I'm really nervous about finals," Marty told me. "So much has been going on I haven't studied or reviewed anything. Hope they give me a little time."

"They sure aren't going to make you take them this afternoon. They have to give you some leeway," I said trying to comfort him the best I could. I really had no inkling what they would do.

"Did you hear? Jim Dad and Mom Sara both plan to attend the meeting. That kind of blows me away. Bruno never went to a meeting about me ever. He thought it was a waste of time when Mom did. He always figured that the school would do whatever it wanted to anyway, so why bother?"

"Living with Bruno must have been a real picnic," I said shaking my head.

"While we're at it, I want to tell you what happened when you and Sara left the other day. I was really pretty scared and nervous about being left with that policeman all by myself. I had visions of him yelling at me and threatening me and maybe even hitting me trying to make me talk. The only experiences I've ever had with the police were when they came out to the house when Bruno was drunk and disorderly. The cops would chase him home and usually tackle him out in the yard before he could get into the house. Seemed like he never learned."

"So, how did O'Connor act with you? I'm pretty sure he's one of the policemen who had dealings with Mr. Bashore in the past."

"He couldn't have been nicer. He spoke very softly and put me at ease. He didn't try to threaten or terrorize me in the least bit. I think he really tried to be helpful. If I needed to take a minute before answering because I couldn't remember something right away or it hurt so bad thinking about something, he just told me to take my time. He also told me before he left that Bruno had hired a lawyer and that he would probably try to cop a temporary insanity plea."

About then the bell rang and we went our separate ways for the rest of the day. We did sit together at lunch, but there were so many kids within ear shot, we didn't talk about anything important. I told him I'd check in with him later.

That afternoon when I saw him come home from the meeting, I waited about a half hour and then slipped over there. Jim Dad and

Mom Sara headed back to work when they left school, so Marty stayed home by himself, I assumed. Actually he was babysitting Emily. When I walked in, Marty, grinned from ear to ear as he told me the big surprise.

"After all the introductions, our chemistry teacher, Mr. Oakes, started out the meeting with, 'I personally have no intention of giving Marty a final exam. After all he's been through he doesn't need that. He had a 3.5 going into finals, and that's going to be his grade in my class. I think he has enough on his plate right now with Chemistry 2 without worrying about a final exam in Chemistry 1—that is, unless he really wants to take it.'"

"I told him no, I really didn't want to. I'd be more than happy with the 3.5."

"Whoa! That's super!" I said. "What about the rest of them?"

"After that, every one of the teachers agreed. Whatever I had going into the finals would be my final grades," Marty said. "You have no idea what a relief that is. Believe it or not, teachers are human too."

I laughed, but right then Emily let an awful bubbly stinker. "Oh, yuck!" I gagged. "I think Emily just filled her pants.

"So, big deal," Marty said. "Throw me a diaper out of that bag, will you?" He asked as he started to strip her on the spot.

"Here!" I said as I tossed him one and headed for the door.

"Jeremy, you are the biggest pussy in the world," Marty laughed as I ducked out of the room without looking back. That was

Marty's job, and he could have it. My life could go on without smelly diapers. When I got to the door and opened it, Sean was just getting ready to knock. He asked if Marty was there, and I wrinkled up my nose and told him what he was doing. Then he asked if I would come back in while he talked to Marty for a few minutes. All I could think of was, "What now?"

We all sat down and Sean acted like he didn't know quite what or how he wanted to say what he had on his mind. Finally he blurted it out, "Marty, all the police officers in the surrounding communities know what happened to you and your mom. They all wanted to help but weren't sure what they could do. Finally someone suggested that all of us go in together and pay for the entire funeral package for her so that she can have a decent funeral and burial, and you will have a place to visit her any time you want."

Of course Marty lost it. Sean put his arms around Marty and held him until he finally could compose himself again. Right about then Mom Sara and Jim Dad walked in from work and found all three of us red-eyed. Naturally they wanted to know what happened. I guess when you come home and find your two boys and a policeman all broken up, you automatically think something terrible happened.

After Sean told them the news, the first thing she did was invite Sean and me for dinner so we could all kind of make plans. She had started a stew in the crock pot that morning so it wouldn't take long. All she had to do was make the dumplings.

While she was getting things around, she said, "You know, there isn't any reason why the funeral can't be held in our church. You and your mom weren't here long enough before it happened for you to get involved in a church community of any kind so maybe that would be an easy way to do it. What do you think, Marty? Want me to call our minister after dinner?"

"That would be great. You really think he'd do that for a complete stranger?"

"Sure! He's a really neat guy. You'll like him."

About then Sean piped up, "You know, Marty, Sara's right about your mom not being here long enough to make any friends and we're gonna need pall bearers. What would you think about me and five of my fellow police officers doing that honor for you?"

"Would you wear your uniforms? That would be special. Mom always like the police and military uniforms when we went to parades back when I was just a little kid. I just think she loved the formality of it," Marty said with a smile remembering back to happier days.

That settled it. The rest of dinner consisted of small talk and plans for the funeral and Marty's future.

They held the closed casket funeral on Saturday. A lot of people attended including all of the wrestlers and their families and most of our class who came to support Marty. After the service, we went to the cemetery. Her plot lay not all that far from Scott's. I looked over at his grave and there he and Mooshy stood leaning against a tree. Scott slipped up beside me and let me know that she was at peace.

After the graveside service we all went back to the church. The ladies' guild prepared a luncheon, so everyone ate and let down a little. I think every off duty police officer in the area attended. The whole thing choked Marty up, but he managed to go up to every officer there and thank them personally for what they had done. Marty finally managed to find the closure he needed for the loss of his mother. Next we had to deal with some kind of final outcome with Bruno.

Chapter 25

In March it finally happened. Bruno Bashore went to trial for the murder of Marty's mom. Marty had dreaded the event ever since leaving the hospital. We talked about it occasionally, but he really didn't want to deal with it. However, we both knew he had to. Neither one of us had a clue as to what would be happening legally. All we knew was the emotional effect on Marty.

"Mom," I asked Friday morning at the breakfast table. The powers that be had scheduled the trial for the following Monday, "Why isn't anything being said about the abuse that Marty lived with? I don't think that's fair. All the focus is being put on the murder. I know that's horribly important, but she's gone, and Marty is still here. What about a little revenge for him?"

"Is that how he feels?" Mom asked. "Is he looking for revenge?"

"I don't think so. At least he's never mentioned it. I guess that's just my thinking. That man almost killed Marty. If I hadn't showed up when I did, he probably would have died, Bruno would have buried him, moved away again, and nobody would have ever known the difference. Nothing is being said about that."

"Nothing is being said about how he tried to kill you as well," Mom mentioned, "at least publicly. We just don't know what's going on behind the scenes."

"I know, but apparently what happened to us isn't that important compared to the murder itself."

"It is to me," she said as her thoughts kind of wandered off into what might have been if the janitor hadn't shown up when he did to empty something into the dumpster.

"I know. It is to me too. So I wonder why they ignored all of the other stuff."

"I'm guessing that some of that is part of a backup plan that the authorities can use in case, by some technicality, Bashore gets out of this mess. You know that his planned defense is temporary insanity, don't you?"

"So how's that work?"

"I'm no lawyer, but from what I understand, if that defense works, and the jury declares him innocent because of temporary insanity, all he has to do is prove that he's currently sane and they have to release him."

"You mean he could go completely free of the murder of his wife if someone declared him to be currently sane?"

"That's my understanding of it," Mom said shaking her head. "I also think that's why nothing is being said about the child abuse, attempted murder, and threats of attempted murder regarding you and Marty. If the jury decides that he suffered from temporary insanity, and he gets out free, I think the authorities want to be able to arrest him again on these other charges and try him under the pretext that he was sane when he did those things. As I understand it, they definitely have to try the cases separately. If not, and he were declared innocent, he would be innocent of everything, and they couldn't bring up the other charges again."

"So will Marty have to testify at the murder trial?" I asked.

"I doubt it. I think the trial will be a parade of mental experts testifying one after the other trying to determine his sanity at the time of the murder and now. Bruno did admit to killing Marty's mom in front of a whole bunch of people, so the murder itself really isn't the issue. It's his sanity."

"Personally, I think the guy is completely loony," I said totally not believing that Bashore could ever be set free again.

"I know! I know! It's weird," Mom said as she picked up my breakfast dishes and shooed me out the door.

I started backing the car out of the drive and stopped by their back door and honked my horn. Marty charged out with his books and jumped in. Mom Sara and Jim Dad paid me ten dollars a week to take Marty back and forth to school. On the way home, we swung by the day care center to pick up Emily. Marty baby sat her until Mom Sara got home around five thirty from work.

"So are you going to talk to Mr. Bishop today about the trial next week, or what?" I asked as he climbed into the car. I knew he had been procrastinating. He wanted to go to the trial, but didn't know how it would affect his school work. Jim Dad and Mom Sara told him he had to work that out with the school himself. He had to show he had the maturity to do it the right way.

"I guess I've put it off for about as long as I possibly can," he said smiling. "I really don't know what I'm going to say to him. I'm sure he knows about the trial, but he might think that I shouldn't even be there. Will you go in with me when I talk to him?"

"Do you think that's a good idea?" I asked.

"It's a hell of a lot better than my going in by myself, especially since I don't even know what I want him to do for me," he said.

"Okay, but let's set up a game plan. We'll go find him right before school and ask for an appointment. I suppose we'll have to tell him what we want before we talk to him."

When we walked into the school, we found Mr. Bishop jaw-boning with a bunch of teachers in the commons area. We walked up to them and Marty spoke up, "Mr. Bishop, Jeremy and I would like to set up an appointment with you today some time. It's really important."

"What about, Marty?" he asked.

"Bruno's trail starts Monday, and I need to be there."

"Let's go into my office right now and leave the teachers to traffic control," he said with a smile.

We followed him into his office where he offered us chairs and closed the door. "So, boys, what did you want me to do?"

"I really want to go to that trial every day. The DA said it's supposed to last a week, and I think I should be there. He killed my mom, and I want to see him get his just due. I think …" Marty was talking as fast as he possibly could, trying to get it all out before he had a panic attack or something.

"Slow down! You're getting the cart ahead of the horse here. First off, there is no question at all about you going or not going to the trial as far as the school is concerned. You are totally excused for as long as it takes. I did talk to the assistant prosecuting attorney, and you are not going to be called to the stand so there is no reason why you cannot attend.

"The only thing that poses to be a problem is your classes and home work, and I think we've worked that out. When I talked to Mrs. Adams yesterday, she suggested that since the two of you were in all the same classes this semester, that Jeremy just pick up all your assignments and kind of act as a tutor for you until you get back. Every one of your teachers said that they will do whatever it takes to get you through this."

"You already talked to Sara yesterday about this?"

"Yes! Why? Didn't she tell you?"

"No! She and Jim both told me that I was on my own with this and that I would have to be man enough to come in and make my own deal with the school. You mean she already had this all worked out for me? Why didn't she tell me so I didn't practically have a nervous breakdown by coming in to talk to you?"

We couldn't help it. Mr. Bishop and I both laughed at him. The Rents had come through again. They just wanted him to grow up a little and do some of the work himself, and he damned near panicked in the process.

"I didn't know I came across all that scary. Oh well, I guess that since I spilled the beans, I must as well tell you the rest. I talked to your mom too, Jeremy. That's when we decided that you were going to be responsible for Marty's education for next week. You have to come to school every day, take notes, get all the assignments, and then tutor Marty after dinner every night until the trial ends. It will be good for both of you."

The Rents and principal developed the game plan, and Marty and I had to execute it. Marty would go to the trial; and I would go to school, take notes, and pick up extra copies of all the handouts. Then I would tutor him that night. Wondered how that would work out. Never tried to actually teach anyone anything before. Might prove interesting.

Not a whole lot happened over the weekend. Marty acted pretty antsy and nerved up as could be expected. I kind of wondered how he planned to get back and forth to the trial and what about Emily? Probably she would just stay at day care until Mom Sara got out of work. So much for my easy gas money that week.

Monday morning I headed out to school without Marty. The trial didn't start until nine a.m. so he could sleep in an extra hour or so. He'd probably need it. If it'd been me, I know I'd have trouble getting to sleep Sunday night.

The kids at school practically drove me nuts with their questions. How's Marty holding up? What's he thinking? How does he think the trial will go? What'll he do if Mr. Bashore gets acquitted? At least they cared. A lot of them were questions that I really couldn't answer. He still kept a lot of his personal feelings pretty much bottled up inside. That part was getting better, but I still didn't always know what was going on in that head of his. Not like it had been with Scott. I always knew exactly what rattled around in his brain.

The day progressed pretty slowly as my mind didn't exactly connect with subordinate clauses, the periodic tables, or looking for X in some stupid algebra 2 problem. However, since they put me in charge of making sure Marty learned this crap too, I had to pay as much attention as possible. The three o'clock bell finally rang, and I bolted out of there. When I arrived at the courthouse, I was in for a bit of a surprise. First off there was a recess going on so everyone in the court room just sat around talking. I spotted Marty right off because he was hanging with Mom and Mom Sara. Both of the moms were there. I hadn't even realized that they were going.

"Hi, Honey!" both moms said practically in unison like always. "How was school today?" one of them asked.

"Horrible! All I did was think about this place all day. What's going on?"

"I think they just might have the jury pretty much figured out. That's about what the whole day has been about since this morning," Mom said.

"I thought they just kind of drew twelve names out of a hat and called it good," I said.

"Not quite. They have this big pool of people, and they give them all questionnaires. Some are excused because of what they put down for answers. Others are dismissed from what the lawyers ask them personally. They keep going through the list one person at a time until they find enough people who are acceptable to both sides. From the sounds of things, they may have finally wrapped up jury selection," Sara told me.

"So what happens then?" I asked.

"I'm guessing they will adjourn until tomorrow and actually start the trial then," Sara said.

All this time Marty sat pretty quietly. Wasn't sure what was going on in his head. He probably just wanted for it to be all over. I know that I would have if it'd been me. Shortly afterwards the lawyers came out of their conference and somebody announced that a jury had been selected and that opening arguments would start the next morning at precisely nine a.m.

By four p.m., the proceedings were done for that day. We headed out going our own separate ways. Mom and Mom Sara rode together after giving explicit instructions, "Meet us at the restaurant at five-thirty and don't be late."

Marty and I rode together to go get Emily from daycare. After we picked her up, I asked, "So what do you want to do now?"

"Let's go to the mall and hope we don't run into anyone who's gonna ask a bunch of questions, Marty answered. "I just want to play with Emily and have some fun before dinner if that's ok with you."

"Fine with me," I said turning right at the next intersection as I headed for the mall.

I think Marty wanted to get away from his problems and think about something totally different from the trial thing. He really didn't want to talk about it so we didn't. We wandered down to the food court to see who was around. Fortunately, there wasn't anyone we knew. That was a rarity. So we just walked around and talked about nothing in particular—took turns carrying Emile, and literally just killed a bunch of time. About five-fifteen we headed to the restaurant so we wouldn't be late for dinner.

That night I started my roll of playing 'Joe Teacher.' Marty's a pretty bright kid so it wasn't too tough a task. I showed him my notes and explained what we did in each class and what he needed to do. He did it, asked a couple of questions, and that took care of our homework for the night. I did mine at the same time he did his so it was a piece of cake.

"Now what?" he asked sounding tired and somewhat frustrated after we'd compared answers and made the necessary changes.

"Get on the computer. I'm going home and get on mine and spend the next hour whipping your butt at a hot and heavy game of Mad Demons. You get first move."

"You're on!" he grinned as I headed out the door. For the first time in a week he acted a little fired up.

Two hours later I logged off and went to bed. The turd! He beat me six straight games, and I was trying too. Good for him.

I arrived at the courthouse the next afternoon, and things were pretty intense. "What's going on?" I asked.

"They've spent all day explaining trying to determine what exactly he's being tried for," Marty answered.

"What do you mean? That doesn't' make sense," I whispered back.

"Bruno's already admitted killing Mom, so that part's a no-brainer. All they've talked about all day is his mental condition—then and now."

"Everyone knows he's totally nuts!" I protested.

"Yeah, but they have to prove that beyond any reasonable doubt to the jury." He said.

"And after they do that?" I asked.

"What I'm hearing, if I've got this right, is that the jury's going to have to determine if he were sane or insane at the time of the murder, and if he is currently sane or insane. It doesn't seem to me that should be too hard," Marty continued.

I guess it really wasn't all that simple after all. As the days progressed it became pretty clear that it kind of depended on which expert was talking at the time as to how you considered Bruno's mental condition.

Marty told me, "When you listen to one person, you're convinced that he was completely insane then and now. Then the next person makes you believe that he was insane then and completely sane now. Another expert made an excellent case that he was completely sane both then and now, and that he's been faking the insanity thing. That view indicated that he should be convicted of first degree murder and sent away for life. I liked that idea."

"I thought this whole thing would be completely cut and dried—declare him nuts and throw his ass in the slammer," I answered.

"Yeah, me too. I'm glad I'm not on that jury."

On Wednesday, Sergeant O'Connor testified about what had happened out at Marty's house when he arrested Mr. Bashore. He told of the telephone call that I had made to him and all that entailed. He told of hearing Bashore coming into the shed and grabbing my cell phone and throwing it against the wall and not breaking it like he'd obviously intended. He told of all the things that Bashore had screamed at me while he tried to choke me. He told it all just exactly the way it happened. He told of the arrest and the confession right there in front of a whole room full of police officers with a tape recorder running which included the reading of his Miranda rights. He also told of the threats he made against Marty and Me. The whole thing was kind of surreal listening to them talk about me. I half wanted to yell out, "Hey! I'm right here!" Of course, I didn't.

However, fortunately for my sanity, there were some things that he didn't tell. He said nothing about how deep the gashes were in Bashore's leg, and that the glass he had fallen in couldn't have caused them. He also said nothing about the knot on the back of his head that couldn't have been caused by falling on the frozen ground. He didn't say anything about Mooshy running around the corner of the shed with the shard of cloth in his mouth. I guess maybe he didn't tell about as much as he did, fortunately for my sanity anyway.

The trial finally ended up all of its deliberations, summations, and all that crap and sent to the jury early Friday for them to decide on a verdict. When I showed up at three thirty, the jury still hadn't returned a decision. Marty acted extremely nervous about the outcome as I am sure I would have been.

"What happens if he walks?" he asked. "Is there any way I would I be sent back to live with him?"

"Over my dead body!" Mom Sara said. "You're mine now. There's no way I would ever permit you to return to that rat hole way of life."

Everyone just kind of smiled. I don't know when I had ever seen Mom Sara as fired up. She normally stayed pretty calm. You could tell as much by the intensity of her voice as the actual words. She had a lot of feelings for Marty, and she didn't care who knew it.

Jim Dad put his arm around her and gave her a little hug. "I don't think we even have to worry about that one," he said. "Marty is seventeen. I think he would have some say as to where he wanted to live. What do you think, Marty? Would we have to worry about losing you?"

Marty walked over, nudged his way in between them, and put his arms around both of them. "What do you think?" he asked with a smile on his face. "I'm very happy right where I am. Besides what would Emily do without me?"

At that point everyone was all smiles and hugs. Then all we had to do was wait for the jury to come in and tell us what they'd decided.

Not long after that the bailiff called the court to order. They escorted the jury and Bruno back in, and the moment we'd been waiting for had arrived. The judge asked the foreman if they had a verdict, and he answered, "We do, your honor."

The verdict was short and simple. "We, the jury, declare Bruno Bashore insane at the time of the crime and still insane."

That was it—short and sweet! Probably the best we could possibly hope for. The state would institutionalize him until whatever time the doctors decreed him sane enough to function in society. Hopefully that would never happen. I didn't totally understand it, but somebody said that if the doctors ever declared him sane, they could put him on trial again. I had no idea how that worked, and I didn't care.

Bruno blew our minds away when they led him out. He suddenly stopped in his tracks and looked over at Marty and me. He glared at us with hatred and then snarled loudly enough to be heard by all, "I will get both of you if it's the last thing I ever do." Right then he didn't sound crazy to me. He sounded downright evil.

That certainly put a chill on our festive moods after the jury's decision. He detested both of us and actually threatened us right there in court. A couple of reporters raced over wanting a story. Dad and Jim Dad both jumped between us and told them to buzz off. No interviews—end of discussion.

After dinner that evening, Mom Sara called and asked if we could all come over for desert, milk, and coffee. Mom asked her what was going on, and she said that Marty asked for a meeting with all of us. She said that she didn't really know what he wanted.

When we showed up, they sat around the table as Marty held Emily. We sat down at the kitchen table making small talk for a while until Mom Sara asked Marty what he had on his mind.

Marty got this strange look on his face and just sat there. Jim Dad said, "You aren't in trouble are you?"

"Of course not!" Marty said. "I'm just not used to pouring out my feelings."

Mom Sara got tears in her eyes and said, "You aren't threatening to leave us again are you?"

"No way! What I really want is to be a bona fide member of this big extended family."

Mom Sara said, "But, Marty, you are a big part of our family. We all love you."

"What I want is to be able to call all four of you Mom and Dad and not feel funny about it. I'm not trying to horn in, but I want to feel like I really belong. Besides, have you ever thought about when Emily starts to talk? She might think she's supposed to call you by your first names too. Listen, I'll understand if you say no, but I am not trying to take Scott's place. I just want to be me because I love all of you."

He buried his face in Emily's hair, but we could see he was fighting the tears. We looked at each other and smiled. Mom Sara got up and hugged him and told him that nothing would make her happier. Mom joined in and said she would be honored. Then the dads got in the act.

Marty looked over at me, and I said, "Don't expect me to hug you, but I think it's a good idea too. Now, can we have desert?"

Little did Marty or any of us realize, Emily would not end up as his only babysitting duty. There'd be more to come.

Chapter 26

With spring lurking right around the corner, the weather started to break, and the days grew longer. Our lives moved into a regular routine. I started working part time at the golf course mostly on weekends. After school we typically picked up Emily and headed to the mall. By then we had our own group at the food court that met there almost every afternoon. We'd buy our after school snacks and just hang out acting, as Dad always said, like a bunch of goofy teenagers. There were a couple of girls who always liked to play "Mommy" with Emily. That was handy because they also took care of the diapers. Needless to say, we encouraged that wholeheartedly.

"What do you weigh now?" Marty asked one day as we sat in the mall.

"Roughly 135. Why?" I responded.

"I've gained back the twenty pounds I lost plus another ten. I'm close to 140 now," he grinned.

"You fat hog!" I laughed. I knew you'd gain a ton the way Mom Sara feeds you. You actually outweigh me now!"

I have no idea how much of that's related to normal growth spurt, and how much is making up for the starvation mode that Bruno put him into.

"Doesn't matter," he laughed. "I feel the best I can ever remember feeling."

Marty turned into a pretty happy kid. He absolutely worshipped the ground that Jim, Sara, and Emily walked on. Of course, Emily didn't walk yet, but you get the idea. Life treated him well.

One afternoon when we headed for the parking lot after our after school snack, who should come down the mall from the opposite direction but Bobby and his mom. "Hi, Mrs. Mercer. Hi Bobby! I called out to them when I saw them.

"Hi, Jeremy!" both Ginny and Bobby called out. "Who are your friends?" she asked looking at Marty and Emily.

"This is my friend, Marty and his charge, Emily," I said laughing to myself about the 'Marty and his charge' comment. "He baby sits her every day after school. We pick her up from day care, and then he takes care of her until everyone gets home from work. Can you believe that he actually gets paid for doing this? The girls down at the food court do all the work," I said sticking it to Marty just a little.

"Not true! I take care of her all the time that we aren't down at the food court," he said defending himself trying to feel a little put out. He still wasn't a hundred percent used to being picked on in fun. Things were getting better, but he wasn't totally there yet.

"So do either one of you do any other babysitting other than Emily?" she asked.

"No, but that doesn't mean I couldn't on occasion," Marty piped up. "I'm always in dire need of extra money."

"What do you charge?" she asked pushing the point for information just a little.

"I have no idea. All I know is that I would charge less than the girls do just to get the job."

"The reason I'm asking is because the hospital asked me to start working half days on Saturday for the next few weeks. Bobby's day care doesn't do Saturday so I need to find someone I can trust to take care of him for about five hours every Saturday for the next month or so. Would either of you be interested?" she asked.

"I would," Marty spoke up immediately.

"I don't want you to take this wrong, either one of you. However, I barely know Jeremy, and I don't know you at all. Before I could agree to an arrangement, I would really need to meet your parents. I've never even considered using boy babysitters for Bobby. I don't know why not, though, especially since there aren't any girls in our neighborhood who could do the job."

We took her telephone number, and promised that I would set up a meeting with all the Rents within the next couple of days. When

I told the plan to Mom and Dad at the dinner table, Mom had a suggestion.

"Jeremy, knowing you, I doubt if you're real interested in babysitting. It sounds like Marty wants to. What would you think about both of you going the first two weeks just so everyone can kind of have an adjustment period and really get to know one another? It's just in the morning so it won't interfere with your golf course duties in the afternoon and evening. Marty can be the official sitter and get paid for it. It's not fair for her to have to pay both of you, and you don't need the money. You can just kind of hang out and help him when and if he needs it. I seriously doubt that he would, but he'd probably feel more comfortable too."

The following night all of us loaded up in Dad's van and headed for Ginny and Bobby Mercer's house for our meeting. Everything went well. Mom Sara explained Marty's situation in enough detail so she had the basic history. They decided that the following Saturday Marty, Emily, and I would all show up at the Mercer's at eight thirty in the morning. Mom Sara suggested taking Emily along because it would give Bobby someone to play with besides the older boys who took the authoritative role as official baby sitters. That worked for us.

When I went to bed that night one major problem nagged at me big time. "Scott, we need to talk!"

"Yeah, Bro! What's up?" he answered immediately with Mooshy curled up rubbing against my leg looking for attention. It always amazed me the way they could just show up that way.

"You know about the babysitting situation with the Mercer's?" I asked.

"Yeah, I've been tuning in on that one. Great idea, if you ask me. Bobby is such a neat little guy, and he needs some males in his life—notice I didn't say men? You and Marty don't quite qualify," he said sticking it to me as usual with that weird sense of humor of his.

"Yeah, yeah, and the horse you rode in on. Anyway, I can't get the fact out of my head that she's the one who killed you in that damned hit-and-run accident," I just don't know about getting involved with her in any way.

"Hey! We've already hashed that one out. It's over and done with. Forget it!"

"I can't!" I said. "You've always been my best friend. I feel guilty about knowing what happened and not telling anyone."

"Okay, let's make a deal. Let's face it, she'll never be prosecuted. It was an accident pure and simple, and she doesn't even know she did it. I see no reason for her or anyone else ever finding out. However, if the time ever comes that it's bugging you too badly, and a situation arises where you can let the cat out of the bag sneakily, and it isn't going to jeopardize our situation, go ahead. I'll understand."

"Deal! I just wish I could get it out of my head."

Saturday morning turned out to be a ball. The only thing that would resemble a hitch was when Bobby asked about Scott.

"Don't know where he is, little buddy!" I told him. "I haven't seen him for a while." I lied.

I tried to be as nonchalant as possible with Marty standing right there listening. He pretended not to even notice, but I did see his ears pick up on the comment. He never said a word.

After the second week I drove Marty and Emily to the Mercer's, and then went home. Mrs. Mercer took him home when she came home from work. I had better things to do like play 'Mad Demons' for example. Besides the weather was getting nice enough so there were a lot more golfers out there on the course. Coach wanted me to start coming in earlier and earlier all the time. Marty did his thing, and I did mine. Fortunately we both got along real well so we just accepted what the other did and didn't make a big deal out of it.

I guess it must have been the second or third weekend in May when I heard the news. It was a Sunday night and we had finished our mid terms the week previously so it was a slow homework weekend. Marty baby sat both Saturday and Sunday and felt flush with money. I had a number of suggestions as to how I could help him spend it, but he didn't bite. I think he wanted to start saving enough money for a car. At least, that's the impression I had. He sure didn't spend any that he didn't have to.

I had just climbed out of the shower and hit the rack. I'd been reading a novel that didn't particularly interest me, but it gave me something to do until I fell asleep which usually didn't take too long. I was almost out when I felt pressure against my foot. I looked down and there lay Mooshy curled up at the foot of the bed. Beside him sat Scott Indian style staring at me.

"Hi, guys! Hadn't noticed you before just now. When did you show up?"

"Few minutes ago. Been trying to figure out how to break the news to you,"

"What news is that?" I asked. Scott usually didn't try to be all that mysterious. Normally he just blurted out any old thing that happened to be on his mind.

"Bruno Bashore escaped from the state mental hospital about an hour ago."

The End

Coming Soon

Life Moves On

by

LARRY WEBB

Chapter 1

Tied to our chairs, we watched Bruno slowly meander over to the work bench and snatch that large butcher knife sticking out of its top. He cackled this God awful sick, eerie laugh under his breath, and then he started singing some hideous song I'd never heard before. It terrified me. He wasn't just trying to scare us, he actually planned to slit our throats and throw us into that barrel of acid. He roughly grabbed the front of my shirt with his left hand while clutching the knife in his right. The sneer on his face... I screamed!

...

I woke up wringing wet with cold, clammy sweat drenching my entire body. I've had other strange psychic like visions during the day about Marty's stepdad, Bruno Bashore, ever since the judge sent that lunatic to the nut house for killing his mom. I'm sure they're somehow related to the fact that he threatened to kill both of us when the officers led him out of the courthouse after his trial. However, this is the first time I dreamed the vision. I don't suppose that Scott's ghost showing up last night just before I went to sleep telling me that Bruno had escaped would have anything to do with the dream I just had either, would it? Yeah, right! Thanks, Scott!

Fortunately, my screaming didn't wake up the Rents. Maybe it only happened in my dream. I hope so. They don't know about my psychic like visions, or, in this case, nightmares about that asshole. Oh well, I can't dwell on that. I've got to get my butt out of bed. It's Monday morning, and I need to get ready for school. Only a couple of weeks left before vacation—can't wait!

After breakfast I met up with Marty in the driveway, and we headed out. I didn't say anything to him about the dream. He still suffers from the actions of his deranged stepdad so he doesn't need to hear about my problems. We pulled into the student parking lot to quite a surprise. Cop cars were parked all over the place including the one driven by our old buddy Detective Sergeant Sean O'Connor. When we walked up to the gym door, where we normally entered the school, an officer stood there directing foot traffic away from the locker room.

"What's going on?" I asked trying to see around him.

"Have to use one of the other doors this morning, boys. Nobody's allowed in here until the area gets cleared by the investigating officers," he told us.

"So what happened?" I asked again wondering why they were there and if he would actually tell us. Marty didn't say anything, but he tried to gawk through the door to see if he could see anything going on. He couldn't. That fat cop blocked our view.

"Just some vandalism over the weekend. Can't say that much about it. You'll hear all the details as soon as you get in the building," he replied laughing. He knew how fast gossip flew inside a high school. "You'll just have to use one of the other doors this morning."

Marty and I bitched all the way to the front door. "Typical cop!" Marty grumbled. "Nothing like blowing us off. Jerk!"

"I know," I complained. "No reason he couldn't tell us. It's not like it would hurt anything."

"Yeah, I know. Too bad O'Connor isn't at the door. He'd tell us," Marty answered.

"We saw his car out back so he's gotta be inside someplace checking out whatever happened," I said. "That's better yet. We'll get all the inside dirt that way," I laughed as we made our way around the building to the front door.

Looked like they'd herded the entire school into the commons area just inside the door to wait for whatever was going on to clear up. Kids and teachers alike all clustered themselves around into little groups—some at the lunch tables, and some just standing around. Conversations and speculation ran rampant. However, nobody seemed to have a real good handle on what had happened. If the teachers did, they weren't telling us.

Maybe fifteen minutes after the first hour bell rang, Mr. Bishop, the principal, came out and shouted at us, "Everyone go ahead and head to first hour class now."

Naturally, he didn't give us any details either—just go to class and clear the halls. The teachers all started shooing us towards the hallways like we were a herd of cattle or something. As Marty and I started walking towards our wing, the principal flagged us down.

"Jeremy, Marty, I'd like a word with you. Would you come with me, please?" he asked as he turned around and headed for his office. He didn't even look back to see if we followed.

"Have a seat, guys," he said pointing to a couple of chairs. "I need to get this note to the secretary before she reads the morning announcements. Be right back."

"What the hell does he want?" I asked Marty under my breath as soon as he walked out of the door.

"Beats me! Have to admit, though, it makes me a bit on the nervous side. It's not like we're regular guests to the inner sanctum."

Not more than a minute or two later Mr. Bishop returned, sat down, folded his hands, and just looked at us for a few seconds before saying anything. "Good morning, boys. I have something to ask you, and I'd like a straight forward answer. I think I know what you're going to say, but I need to ask you anyway. Did either one of you come back to the school over the weekend?"

"No! I spent the whole weekend at home working on that huge English project for Mr. Andrews," I said wondering why he'd singled out us to ask out of 600 or so kids. Obviously, whatever had happened had something to do with all the cops being in the gym.

"Mrs. Mercer had to work overtime at the hospital so I stayed at her house almost all weekend having absolutely no life of my own. Between babysitting for Bobby, Emily, and working on the project, I did nothing else. Period! So why are you asking us about our weekends?" Marty asked in a tone hinting of just a little bit of a chip on the shoulder. That didn't sound like him at all.

"Somebody broke in and vandalized the gym over the weekend," he answered ignoring Marty's obvious irritation. "I'm sure that the police will want to talk to you this morning so I might as well tell you what I know. Someone took a knife or something sharp and carved up all three wrestling mats and completely destroyed the main one. Then they spray painted an ominous note on the side of the mat stating, 'Marty and Jeremy—you gonna die!'"

"Bruno!" Marty and I both gasped at the same time as we looked at each other. It had to be him. Who else?

"So, who've you guys been fighting with that'd be mad enough to trash the mats and write a stupid threatening note on the thing for evidence," Mr. Bishop asked ignoring our Bruno declarations. "Sounds to me like somebody either really hates the two of you, or somebody's got a pretty warped sense of humor. Or, of course, it could be just plain old malicious destruction, and they put your names on the mat to throw everybody off. Any ideas?"

"It sounds like something Bruno, my so-called step dad, would do except for the fact that he's in the state mental hospital. We all know he's crazier than a loon; but, he shouldn't be out yet. He's only been in there two months," Marty said.

"I seriously doubt that your dad or any other adult would ever do anything like that even if he did suffer from mental issues. The whole thing looks too much like kid's work," he said. "Besides, like you said, there's no way Mr. Bashore could have been released all ready. Let's face it, Marty; he did murder your mother. He's not going anywhere for a long, long time if ever. So let's brainstorm here a little. Have you two been bullying or picking on anybody lately? Is there anyone out there that you know is mad at you?"

"No, we haven't done a thing like that. We don't bully people. I still think it had to be Bruno. You just don't know him like I do," Marty said very softly as he withdrew into his own little world no

286

longer showing any if that little flash of anger he'd showed previously, just sadness.

Just the mention of Bruno cranked up the depression in Marty, and he would look and sound so sad. I always tried very hard not to even mention the creep if I could help it. Besides, he considered Jim Dad and Mom Sara as his parents now anyway so why bother?

"Oh well! I did want to kind of warn you about what happened since it does sound like somebody might be out to try to get you into trouble or something. Why don't you go on to class and not say anything to anyone about the threat? I'm sure that the news will spread fast enough without your help. The police will probably talk to you when they finish down in the gym so stay in class and don't be sneaking out of school or anything," he said smiling only half picking on us.

He knew we wouldn't do that now, especially with all the police and excitement at school. No way we wanted to miss anything. However, I suppose he thought he needed to get his point across and make sure we stayed available. It wouldn't look too cool if the police decided to talk to us, and we were at the soda shop down on the avenue or at the food court in the mall. It wouldn't be the first time we'd done it during school hours, but today wouldn't be one of them.

As soon as we walked out the door, I turned to Marty and said, "Before we go to class, we need to talk. Let's find an empty room."

"Ok, the computer lab behind the library is usually empty first hour. Let's check it out."

We were in luck. Nobody was in there, and the lights were out so we slipped in and went to the back of the room, sat down, and turned on a couple of the computers to make it look like we were working in case anyone came in.

"Marty, what I'm gonna tell you sounds really freaky and you're probably gonna think I'm nuts."

"So, try me. Probably won't think you're any freakier than normal," Marty grinned.

"A week after Scott was killed I went to the cemetery for the first time, and saw him his dog Mooshy sitting on his burial mound."

"Whoa!" Marty exclaimed. "How did that happen? What do you mean?"

"I can see and talk to Scott and Mooshy's ghosts."

"Cool! Tell me all about it," Marty said wide eyed and engrossed.

"I can't tell you everything, at least not all at once. And for God's sake, Marty, promise me you'll keep everything I tell you a secret? I've never told anyone else except for a couple of people who also can see things. My parents don't even know."

"No problem on this end. After all you've done to help me, there's no way I'd screw you up. So, what's going on? Why are you telling me now?"

"Bruno escaped yesterday. Scott slipped in and told me within a couple hours or so after it happened. Typically, when he needs to get me information or contact me about something, he does it at night after I go to bed. He and Mooshy just show up," I told him.

"No kidding?" Marty exclaimed.

"Yeah, I'm sorry I didn't tell you about it earlier. I just wanted to wait until the police or the media said something. Then with the mat damage and the threat, I had to tell you." What I didn't do was tell him about the dream that woke me up. Had to hold off on that for a while.

"Man! That just about blows my mind. You said there are a couple of other people who can see Scott. Anyone I know?"

"You're sworn to secrecy, right?"

"Promise!"

"Nobody else knows about Scott and me except for Bobby and Sergeant O'Connor."

"Bobby? The kid I babysit for?"

"Yes. He's fully sensitive to Scott's spirit. He talks to him out at the cemetery when his mom goes to visit his dad's grave. But he knows it's a big secret so they communicate telepathically all the time just like Scott and I do. It's happened a couple of other times too like at the mall and at his house."

"He's never mentioned anything at all," Marty said.

"I know. He's really smart and knows that he has to keep the whole thing hush-hush. Scott convinced him that it's a big secret, and that they don't want to make his mom or anyone else feel bad so they can't tell anyone. That's why he hasn't said anything."

"What about O'Connor?"

"He knows all about Scott but can't see or hear him. He has a slight sensitivity to the spirit world so the phenomenon really intrigues him. After meeting him sometime back when Scott and I were trying to figure out what had happened with his accident, we've talked fairly regularly."

"What kind of stuff does he want to talk about?" Marty asked.

"He acts like he's half jealous of my sensitivity and his lack of," I laughed. "He's always asking about what he can do to make himself more accessible to his own powers. He wants to be able to see and talk to Scott so bad he can practically taste it. I've no clue what to tell him other than to relax and not fight it like Grandma told me to do after she died."

"Your grandmother talked to you after she died?"

"Yeah, I spoke to her ghost a few days after she died, and she also sent me a message through Scott later on."

"Awesome! Anyone else?"

"My mom has something going on too, but neither one of us has ever mentioned it to the other. My sensitivity comes down from her side of the family."

"How do you know?"

"That's what Grandma told me after she died. Her family thinks their sensitivities started wearing out with each new generation. Mom has a very slight sensitivity. According to Grandma, sometimes Mom will get a flash of something, and then she tries to block it out. Grandpa thought that Mom and Grandma had emotional issues and urged both of them to fight off the flashes of intuition when they had them. Apparently I'm the exception to the rule. Since I've never tried to block them, the sensitivity or whatever you call it seems to be growing stronger—maybe because of my relationship with Scott? Who knows?"

"So do you think Bruno did the mat stuff? Sure sounds like a possibility," Marty asked looking off into space again.

"I really don't know. However, if anyone says anything about it, we've got to play dumb.

By the time we made it to English class third hour, the room literally buzzed. Mr. Andrews had disappeared someplace. Not real surprising. As wrestling coach, he practically considered the mats and equipment his own private property. It turned into a free hour for us because no sub showed up either. By then everyone knew about the threat written on the mat so a crowd gathered around our table wanting all the details. At that point we really didn't know anymore than they did. We sure weren't going to tell anyone what we thought.

We sat there talking to our friends for maybe fifteen minutes when a girl from the office showed up at the door with a note from the principal telling Marty and me that he wanted us in the conference room. I'm sure that gave the class something to really chatter about after we left. They probably figured we were suspects or something.

"Now what?" Marty grumbled as we headed down the hall.

"Has to be more about those darn mats. Probably the cops want to grill us now," I said hoping it would be Sean O'Connor doing the inquisition.

"Wonder if they found out anything," he said. "Just don't understand why anyone other than Bruno would do something like that. It had to be him. But why? He just trying to scare us?"

"Yeah, I know what you're saying especially since he did escape last night. Remember, we gotta play dumb on that one. Anyway, I can't imagine why he'd come back here though when all the cops in town know him. If it was me, I'd head out for parts unknown as fast as possible," I said trying to downplay the possibility of it being Bruno even though I thought that it probably was. If that little mess in the gym was an attempt to scare us, it worked.

When we showed up at the office, the secretary told us to head right straight back to the conference room. Much to our surprise Mom and Mom Sara, both sat there along with Sergeant O'Connor, the principal, and a couple other people we didn't know. During the introductions we learned that one was a detective and the other was from the state hospital for the criminally insane.

Anytime Detective Sergeant Sean O'Connor had ever talked to me about official police business—like after Scott's death, I called him Officer O'Connor. When he tried to pump me about my sensitivity to Scott's ghost, he wanted me to call him Sean. This time we kept everything pretty formal.

As soon as Marty and I sat down after the introductions, O'Connor looked around at everyone and started speaking, "I asked that a parent or guardian for both boys attend this meeting because of the nature of the situation. I think that by now everyone knows about the vandalism over the weekend to the wrestling mats and the graffiti that someone painted on one of them which constituted a threat on Marty and Jeremy's lives. What you don't know is that Mr. Bashore escaped from the state mental hospital last night.

From what they've been able to determine at the hospital, he hid in the bottom of a laundry cart that was full of sheets."

Both moms gasped as Marty and I faked surprise as well. "How'd it happen?" Marty asked really wanting to know since we didn't know how he'd managed to do it.

"They transport filled laundry carts out of the facility every Sunday evening to an offsite laundry where they wash the bedding on Monday and then return it later in the day. Normally they search the carts very carefully. In fact the driver and one of the guards both claimed that they'd checked the carts. However, after the search, they left them unattended for maybe two or three minutes when the driver made a quick trip to the men's room before he headed out.

"Now, that doesn't guarantee that Mr. Bashore had anything to do with this, but we can't rule him either. Anyone have any questions or anything to say before I continue?" O'Connor asked.

"My biggest concern's for the safety of the boys," Mom stated. "Has there been any sign that he's actually in the area?"

Mom Sara, Scott's mom and Marty's foster mom all rolled into one, nodded in agreement. "Do we need to take the boys out of school until the authorities capture him or what?"

"We don't really know where he is, but I don't think we need to be overly concerned about their well being," O'Connor said. "They should be fine here at school and at home. What I would like to see, though, just to be on the safe side, is that neither one of them goes anywhere alone at any time until this thing resolves itself. Marty, are you still babysitting every day after school?"

"Yes. Jeremy drives me to day care where I pick up Emily and Bobby, and then he drops me off at Bobby's house where I stay with the kids until Mrs. Mercer comes home from work. Then she gives Emily and me a ride home." Emily is Scott's baby sister who was born six months after he died.

"So, Jeremy, would you be willing to stay with Marty at the Mercer's after school until Bruno is recaptured?" O'Connor asked. "I don't want you home alone either. I'll call Mrs. Mercer before this meeting's over and make she's ok with the idea. She might not want to take any chances either by putting Bobby in any danger, even though I don't think that'd be the case."

"Sure! That's no big deal for me. I can always do my home work or help Marty with the kids if he needs it." I answered.

"Do you think either boy is in more danger than the other," Sara asked.

"I really don't know, to be perfectly honest with you. I just don't want either one of them anywhere alone right now until Mr. Bashore is either captured or we can confirm that he has left the area."

O'Connor made his call to Mrs. Mercer, and she agreed with the plan after Sean answered some of her questions and concerns apparently to her satisfaction. Everyone also settled on the fact that Marty and I would stick together like glue until the dads came home from work in the evening. That worked well with the two of us. We got along fine, and neither wanted to take the chance of running into Bashore while we were all alone. The guy was huge, scary, and crazy as a freaking banshee.

As we walked out of the conference room, Sean slipped up beside me and whispered, "Did you know about Bashore escaping last night before I told you?"

I just glanced at him and nodded slightly.

"I figured as much," he said as he ambled away. "We need to talk later."

9326673R0

Made in the USA
Lexington, KY
17 April 2011